COLLIDE

MELANIE STANFORD

INTRODUCTION

When their worlds collide, neither will be left unscarred

Suffocated by her small-town life, Maggie Hale runs away to Las Vegas to pursue her dream as a contemporary dancer. But Vegas doesn't turn out like she imagined. She doesn't make it into Essence Dance Theater and the only job she can find is working in a greasy diner—again.

Jay Thornton wants to quit enforcing and own his own boxing gym one day. But his loan shark boss saved him from the streets as a kid and he owes the man everything. Cutting ties isn't so simple.

When Maggie pledges to pay back a friend's loan, she becomes Jay's next mark. Sparks fly between them, but choosing each other could mean the end of both their dreams.

Inspired by Elizabeth Gaskell's *North & South*

Cover by Gabrielle Prendergast
Digital ISBN: 978-0-9959153-5-0
Print ISBN: 978-0-9959153-4-3

ALSO BY MELANIE STANFORD

Sway

Clash

Becoming Fanny
featured in *Then Comes Winter*

The Beast of Pemberley
featured in *The Darcy Monologues*

To Jeff,
For being more understanding
than I deserve

CHAPTER 1

MAGGIE

THE SKY WAS A RICH BLUE, the kind that belonged over a Van Gogh wheat field, not the lawn in front of Hank's family ranch. The bright sun warmed the bare skin of my arms and legs while a breeze blew into my hair, twirling the ends like silk. But I couldn't breathe.

All this cloying perfection suffocated me, right down to the plaid blanket I sat on, the wicker basket full of wine and roses, and Hank. Especially Hank, and the four words he had just spoken. Four little words that sucked the air right from my lungs.

It really was a sweet proposal, and I knew Hank thought he was going all out with the picnic and the perfect day, as if he had ordered it all especially. It would've been easy to say yes. In fact, I felt the word at my lips, so close, so ready to slip out, before I swallowed it back down.

Hank knelt across from me, the cowboy hat I used to think was so sexy perched against his knees. He'd ruffled his hair as soon as he took it off to avoid hat head, but all it did was give him a look of wispy childlike innocence. The kind of look that was hard to erase. And yet, all too easy.

"I can't."

1

His smile froze before it fell altogether. He leaned back on his heels. "What?"

"I'm really sorry," I said, not taking my eyes from his, "but I can't."

"Maggie..." He reached for me, then dropped his hand. "Why?"

I couldn't answer because I didn't know. I'd loved Hank since I was a freshman in high school. Everything about him, from his worn jeans to the dirt under his fingernails and how he masked the smell of horses with Calvin Klein cologne. How he called all women "ma'am," how he could tame the wildest horse and yet every touch on my skin was gentle.

I loved Hank. But I couldn't say yes. It was the "yes" that made it so hard to breathe.

"I'm not ready."

I should have seen this proposal coming. We'd talked about the future lots of times, of being together and living on Hank's family ranch and having kids one day. But it seemed so far off. Unreal. We were only nineteen, after all. It was an adult's life we talked of, and I didn't feel like an adult.

"Then I'll wait. We'll wait." Hank scooted closer, his knees pressed into my thighs. "You can finish community college, and by then Dad will let me run the ranch on my own and—"

"No." I couldn't let this go on. This was *his* dream. For a long time it had been my dream too, but I knew in that moment I'd only been borrowing it until I could find my own.

Hank gaped. Then, jamming his hat on his head, he stood and walked away, his shoulders hunched.

"Hank." I followed. I couldn't leave things like this. "I'm sorry. I really am."

He whirled around, brushing my forehead with the brim of his hat. I was taller than Hank without it. The hat gave him height, which is why he wore it all the time, even in church. My dad thought it was sacrilegious, but he never made Hank stop.

2

"You're *sorry*?" His sunburned face turned a deeper shade of red. "Maggie, we've been dating for *four* years."

The pain he was trying so hard to hide brought tears to my eyes. "I know."

"This is what comes next." He tipped my chin up with his finger. Hank loved to touch my face, always marveling at my smooth, pale skin compared to his year-round sunburn. "I want it, your parents expect it—"

My eyes narrowed at that, and he quickly changed tack.

"I love you. Don't you love me?"

I swallowed. "I'm sorry." I couldn't explain, couldn't say *I love you* like I had so many times before. There was nothing I could do but escape.

Hank followed. He pleaded. He even cried. I cried. He didn't touch me.

"Please don't do this," I said.

The swish of his footsteps behind me died out. He'd finally given up.

"Maggie!" he shouted. "At least let me give you a ride home!"

But I couldn't do that either. I needed to get away from him. Away from myself.

Hank called out again but I ignored him. I didn't stop until I reached the gravel road leading off Hank's family property.

I half expected Hank's pickup to come by, with him hanging out of the window telling me to get in. But he never showed and I was grateful. It was a long walk back into town, but it gave me time. Time to cry, to hate myself, and to think.

A year ago, I'd graduated high school with a mediocre GPA and a diner job I'd had since I was fourteen. My grades weren't good enough for a top university, so I'd enrolled in the local community college, kept the job where everyone knew my name and gave me crappy tips, and stayed with Hank.

But the whole time I'd had this dream. An alternate life I imagined living when I went to bed at night, or while zoning out at the diner.

In this alternate life, I left Hank and Hillstone behind and moved far away—to Las Vegas. I had fabulous friends, a big studio apartment, a job at a trendy boutique, and best of all I danced with Essence Dance Theater, a renowned contemporary dance company I'd seen perform once.

Maybe this alternate life was straight out of a TV show, but I couldn't help wanting something different from what I knew. It's not that I didn't have great friends, because I did. But Drina was at Brown, Stace and her boyfriend were backpacking in Europe, and Melissa had changed her name to Misty and moved to California to be closer to the Mother Ocean, as she called it.

Only I was left, and Hank. Me and Hank. Hank and I. And my parents. Me and Hank and my parents. And his parents and his horses. Me and Hank and my parents and his parents and his horses.

It wasn't enough, yet it was all too much.

My pinkie toes began to sting, the beginnings of blisters. Hillstone was still a mile off. I passed the Williams farm and their pasture of Jersey cows. The same pasture where I'd watched Stace and Melissa/Misty get wasted at Fox Williams' annual New Year's party while I drank a hot chocolate, because my dad would have murdered me if I had one sip of alcohol. I trudged by the old, rotting barn that everyone said was haunted by headless chickens. I slipped off my sandals as I entered Hillstone, the gravel turning to chipped pavement, hot under my bare feet.

Hillstone was all I knew. It was familiar and safe. Like Hank. But if I couldn't say yes to Hank, I couldn't say yes to Hillstone either.

Maybe it was time to make my daydream a reality.

By the time I got home, the perfect sun was setting in perfect rays of pink and orange. It turned the white siding of my house into the color of Pepto Bismol. I sat on the porch, wrapping my skirt under my legs, unwilling to go inside.

"Maggie?" Mom's voice called through the screen door. "How was your date?"

She knew about the proposal. I could hear it in her voice—the hope, the barely contained excitement.

"We broke up," I said, quick and painless. Like how I'd refused Hank. Except that hadn't been painless at all. And neither was this.

My mom was by my side in seconds—one of those superhero Mom tricks I figured I'd inherit one day if I ever had kids. I didn't even hear the screen door slam like it always did.

"Honey, why?" Mom put her arm around my shoulders. "What happened?"

I couldn't meet her eyes. "I said no."

Her silence said everything.

I gave her the side eye. "You knew he was going to propose, didn't you?"

"I might have known a thing or two." She pulled my head against her shoulder. "Are you okay?"

"Not really." I'd given up something. I'd given up a life, a future that was certain once, a future I'd set for myself whether I'd wanted it or not. I couldn't keep living in Hillstone, going to community college, working at the same diner. I wanted to be a different Maggie Hale. I *needed* to be.

It was time for me to try.

CHAPTER 2

MAGGIE

To: Frasier Hale, frazedaze@mymail.com

From: Margaret Hale, maggie-hale@mymail.com

How did you run away? Hank proposed and I said no and now I have to get out of here. I'm thinking of going to Vegas. And no, NOT to be a showgirl. I've always wanted to audition for the contemporary dance company there. I saw them perform a couple of years ago and it was magical. What do you think? Am I crazy? I've got a little saved. I figured I can take a bus, stay in a hotel until I can find an apartment and a job. You've been to Vegas, do you know a good neighborhood? Preferably cheap?

Anyway, how are you? Are you still in Vancouver? Or have you moved on again? What about that girl you were seeing, Kimmi, wasn't it? You sounded pretty SERIOUS in your last email. Maybe you should bring her around. You know Mom and Dad would love to see you.

I hadn't seen my brother Frasier since I was sixteen. He'd come home to visit after being away a couple of years, although I was pretty sure he was just there begging for money. He hadn't been back since.

Frasier and my parents didn't exactly get along. He'd always been a "reprobate," as Dad liked to call him. Skipping school, hiding pot under his mattress, getting drunk at our church Nativity one year and "accidentally" letting the sheep loose through town. Where I was the dutiful preacher's daughter, attending church and Bible study and staying away from the demon alcohol (and the other demons my father preached about—there were a lot of them), Frasier was the typical black sheep, and he embraced the role, right down to the tattoo of a flaming skull he got on his back when he turned sixteen.

But he loved me, always had. Frasier was the one person I knew would be fully in my corner on this. The one person who wouldn't tell me how foolish I was to give up being the Maggie Hale that everyone knew.

To: Margaret Hale maggie-hale@mymail.com

From: Frasier Hale frazedaze@mymail.com

You said no to Hank?! Did he cry? Did he turn to his favorite stallion for comfort? I always thought that guy was a little too close to his horses, if you know what I mean.

So as soon as I got your email, I called my old friend Bronwyn. You remember her? The girl who looks like an Amazon goddess? (We may or may not have hooked up in a snowdrift at the annual Williams party when we were fourteen.) ANYWAY, she lives in Vegas now and after some begging and pleading (and coercing and blackmailing), I convinced her to take on a roommate. YOU, in case you were wondering. She said she's barely at her apartment anyway, she spends a lot of time with her boyfriend, blah blah blah, but you can move in with her for decent rent. You'll still have to get a job though and I can't help you with the dance company. Good luck on your audition. Maybe if I come to Vegas I can seduce the owner or head dance lady or whoever and get you in.

Have fun running away. It's about frickin' time. And don't sweat Mom and Dad. Mom will understand and Dad loves his gospel more than us anyway, so he'll get over it. Just remember to bring earphones to the argument because it'll be a doozy.

Maybe I'll see you in Vegas soon. ;)

I was actually doing it. Leaving Hillstone. I'd booked a bus ticket, emailed Bronwyn about the details, and packed my stuff.

Next step: break it to my parents.

Mom cooked shepherd's pie for dinner, my favorite. It felt like a farewell meal. Beside my plate, cucumbers floated in vinegar and pepper, almost translucent from swimming there so long. I took a swig of milk to wet my throat, the words I'd practiced earlier jumbling in my head.

Dad looked at me. "Is everything okay, pumpkin?"

I choked on the milk. "Went down the wrong tube, is all."

Dad wiped his mouth with a napkin. "Are you sure? You seem a little anxious."

"Honey," Mom said to Dad.

"No, I'm fine. I—"

"I'm sorry about what you went through with Hank." Dad reached his hand out to me. I took it, the coldness of his palm sharp against my sweaty one. "It must have been very hard for you both."

I nodded.

"But I think you did the right thing," Dad continued. "If you really feel like you don't love him, then saying yes would have been a mistake. It could have led to unhappiness, divorce, perhaps even sin of a worse kind."

Mom shot Dad a look. She probably thought this sermon of his wasn't helping. Truth was, it made no difference. For one, I knew I'd made the right choice, nothing my dad would say could change that. For another, I was used to Dad and the way he handled problems—both his own and everyone else's. I loved my parents. I'd never understood Frasier's constant need to battle them. My parents were good people, if a little strict and stifling at times.

That was how I felt now. Stifled.

"I'm moving to Las Vegas."

Dad let go of my hand and leaned back in his chair. He stared at Mom as if she had spoken, or this was her fault somehow.

"I've bought a bus ticket," I said. "For Friday. I've got an apartment set up with one of Fraze's old friends. I'll look for a job right away but I plan to audition for Essence Dance Theater at the end of August."

"Oh, honey," Mom said through a sigh.

Dad spoke right over her. "Absolutely not."

"To which part, exactly?" I asked.

Dad's chair scraped against the wood floor as he rose. My announcement had officially ended dinner. "Contemporary dance is not only a waste of time, it's inappropriate."

My jaw tightened. Dad had never objected to me taking dance classes here in Hillstone. "So if it was ballet, you'd be fine with it?"

"Dance was a perfectly acceptable after-school activity. But it is not a future."

"Maybe we should discuss this," Mom said.

I rose from my chair so I was on the same level as Dad. "There's nothing to discuss. I've made up my mind." I went for the door.

"Margaret," Dad called. "Please."

I turned around. Mom looked at me with sad eyes, already accepting that I was gone. Dad's face was firm, however. He wouldn't change his mind. I'd always admired his strength. I still did. But I had strength too. I squared my shoulders.

"I don't want to leave with bad feelings between us. But I'm going. There's no future for me here."

Dad circled the table. "There's no future in Las Vegas, either. It's an awful place. They call it the city of sin for a reason." He lowered his voice. "I'm afraid of what might happen to you there."

I tried not to roll my eyes. Dad's Bible was showing. "It's not Sodom or Gomorrah." I placed my hand on his arm. "I'll be fine."

He shook his head. "I can't approve."

I'd won. He wouldn't stop me. "I'm sorry." I was getting good at disappointing people lately, and apologizing.

Mom followed me from the dining room. Dad stayed behind, probably considering his next move. "Are you really sure about this?"

"One hundred percent." I walked up the stairs to my bedroom, ignoring the creaks under my feet from the old hardwood. Mom leaned against my doorframe.

"And you're sure this isn't about Hank?" She watched me pull out the suitcase I'd hidden in my closet.

"It's not about him," I said, "but it's sort of *because* of him."

She sat down on the edge of my bed. Her hands refolded my yellow and white baby quilt, still on my bed after all these years. "What do you mean?"

"I might not have done this if he hadn't proposed. I mean, I've always wanted to, but…"

She nodded as if she understood. "I don't know if your father will ever approve of this. But he's only thinking about your future. Is that really contemporary dance?"

"I know it won't last forever. It's not an ideal career, if I even make it into the company. But I love it. And I'm good."

"You are," she said with a small smile. "Very good. But make sure you have something to fall back on, just in case."

It was the responsible thing to have back-up plans or five-year plans or some kind of long-term future goals. But I was sick of the future, I wanted the now. The now that would start on Friday.

CHAPTER 3

JAY

RAFAEL'S bloody face stared up at me.

"Please, amigo," he pleaded. "Stop. I get your money. I get it. Please stop."

I smashed my fist into his nose, blood gushed under my knuckles. "You don't owe me the money. I'm just here to collect."

Rafael held his hands up, blocking his face. "Please, Jay. *Please.*"

I dropped him. I hated when they begged. *Please, don't hurt me, I need more time, I have a family, I have bills, I need to eat, I'll do anything…* I'd heard it all before. But the rules were simple: you borrow, you pay it back. End of story. They never seemed to get that.

Rafael groaned and rolled over, trying to stop the blood pouring from his nose.

"You have one more day," I said, "then I start visiting your friends."

His pleas followed me out of the apartment, but I ignored them. Rafael Antonio was a dealer who couldn't stay away from his own product. He'd borrowed from Simon, and barely paid back a cent, and so it was up to me to get the money, plus interest. That was my job, and I was good at it.

Especially with Rafael. It was almost fun, letting out my frustrations on someone who should've been locked up years ago. The same kind of scum who'd tormented me as a kid on the streets. It would be a pleasure to "visit" his friends tomorrow when he didn't cough up.

Sweat dripped from my hairline, thanks to the cursed Vegas heat. I'd lived here my whole life and still hated how hot it got every summer. I climbed into my truck and reached for the AC. Blood stained my knuckles and I cleaned it off before driving downtown.

I pulled around the back of Pearl of China, parking beside Simon's charcoal gray Lexus, being careful not to ding his door when I got out of my truck. I'd seen him lose it over one tiny scratch.

The kitchen door was propped open and one of Simon's girls was smoking a cigarette, chopsticks sticking out of her wispy blonde hair. She gave me an inviting smile as I went by but I ignored it, pushing past her into the restaurant.

The kitchen was all spices and steam and a babble of voices shouting in Chinese and English and Spanish. I grabbed an egg roll, winking at Mingyu as I passed. She tried to whack me with her fork but I jumped out of the way.

Alfonso stood in front of Simon's office door, the designated bodyguard for the day. A handgun poked out of the top of his pants.

"Aguda's here," Alfonso said.

"Rance Aguda?" It was unnecessary of me to ask. There were no other Agudas in Vegas worth mentioning. What he was doing in Simon's office was the money question.

"Careful," Alfonso said.

I didn't need the warning. I chewed the last bite of egg roll, and Alfonso opened the door. No one else would be allowed into one of Simon's meetings, but I could go anywhere. I slipped inside.

Rance Aguda stopped talking but didn't look at me. His fingers twitched, like he wanted to reach for his concealed weapon.

"Continue," Simon said.

Aguda frowned, pulling the scar that stretched from his temple to his jaw like a rope. Rumors said it was a memento of his time as a child soldier in Africa. "I prefer to speak in private without your Joe-boy listening in."

"He is my son. You can speak freely in front of him." There was force behind Simon's words, but I didn't take pride in them like I used to.

Aguda glanced at me. It was as obvious to him as anyone that Simon and I weren't related. Simon's Chinese, I'm not. The only similarity we shared was the color of our hair.

"Very well. Your proposal is interesting, but I'm afraid I'm going to have to decline."

Simon's mouth thinned, though the change was almost indiscernible unless you knew him. "I would think, after the favor I did you, my proposal would receive more consideration."

I hid my surprise. Rance Aguda was one of the most notorious criminals in Vegas and Simon was a cop. These two things didn't go together. Even though Simon had his little side-business, he put people like Aguda behind bars. I helped him do it. He made nice with the petty crooks to get rid of the bosses. This meeting made my knuckles itch.

"I appreciate what you did in the Arthur case, but I'm afraid I cannot change my mind." Aguda didn't sound too choked up about it. In fact, he almost sounded smug. "You're still welcome to invest."

"I'll consider it." Simon got to his feet and held out a hand. Aguda took his time rising from his chair—a show of power—and returned the handshake. He didn't so much as glance at me as he left. After all, to him I was nothing more than a hired thug.

When we were alone, I took the empty seat across from Simon's desk. "What was that about?"

Simon answered me in Chinese. I'd known him for eleven years and still didn't understand a word, not for lack of trying, either. I didn't need a translator to get the gist of it, though. Simon Ting rarely showed emotion, but when he did it usually manifested as Chinese curses.

He pressed a thumb just below his wrist until he calmed down. "It's difficult to get close to that man."

But why would you want to? Even as a kid, I'd heard Aguda's name whispered on the streets, warning the weak and enticing the power-hungry.

"He mentioned the Arthur case."

Simon applied pressure to his other wrist. "I did him a favor. It didn't pay off."

My stomach clenched. Andrew Arthur was one of Aguda's cronies. He'd been convicted of multiple counts of rape and assault but the only thing that had stuck was a minor charge, hardly any prison time. If Simon had something to do with that... Worse, if I had helped without knowing it...

I was one of Simon's enforcers, collecting loans for the lending company he ran off the books. I was good in a fight and people were intimidated by me. Plus, I enjoyed it. But I also ran errands for his legit job as a police officer. I made deliveries, transported people, made things disappear from crime scenes, that kind of stuff. I'd never had a problem tampering with evidence, or planting a gun, or helping someone change their identity and disappear. Simon used dirty methods to put even dirtier people away, and I was that dirty method. I got that. I didn't question it.

But things were changing. The lower Simon sunk—like doing deals with Aguda—the more I wanted out.

Simon straightened the pens on his desk until they were in an ordered line. "How was your meeting with Rafael?"

I rubbed at my sore knuckles.

Simon handed me a wet wipe. "How many times have I told you to use gloves?" He hated blood. Leftover blood, the kind that didn't get mopped up after the deed was done. He didn't mind it during. But I'd never liked using gloves, unless I had to avoid prints. Skin on skin contact was raw, and real, the way it should be.

"It went as expected," I replied. "He asked for more time."

"What's your next move?"

"He's got a gang of dealers and clients I'll meet with tomorrow. See if I can't make any headway there."

Earlier, I'd been looking forward to "meeting" Rafael's friends. Now, I was just tired. The adrenaline was gone, leaving me empty and dissatisfied.

"If that doesn't work, you know what's next."

I used to get a rush from the snapping sound a bone would make when you applied just the right amount of pressure. I was master over the body, and I could destroy it with my bare hands. But that was back when I had all the recklessness of a eighteen-year-old and no conscience. Or, at least, a conscience I could easily drown out with rage. That rage had ebbed into disappointment, and that conscience had started pricking at me ever since I realized I could do something else with my life. Ever since I started questioning.

"Arrest him. I'm sure there's a boatload of crank in his apartment."

"Not yet." Simon leaned forward. "He owes me money. I won't get it if I put him away."

Simon needed to stop lending to scum like Rafael. Then again, it was the petty criminals and the truly desperate who borrowed from a loan shark in the first place.

"I know I don't have to tell you what to do."

I looked him straight in the eye, this man who was like my own father. "I know my job."

"Good."

The threat was implied. He didn't need to say it. I owed Simon everything, and because of that, I would never break free of him.

CHAPTER 4

MAGGIE

To: Frasier Hale, frazedaze@mymail.com

From: Margaret Hale, maggie-hale@mymail.com

Mom and Dad took it surprisingly well. They even drove me to the bus station. Of course, I had to promise weekly church attendance and Sunday night phone calls.

I talked to Bronwyn (she emphatically denied ever making out with you), and she seems...great? Not all that enthused to have me living there. What exactly did you bribe her with? I'll be taking my first ever cab ride from the bus station. Wait, do I sit in the front, or the back? I'll have to figure it out. It'll probably depend on the driver and if he/she is scary/smelly or not.

BTW, I highly recommend NOT trying to seduce the director of Essence Dance Theater. She's in her late fifties and although she's still fit, she looks sort of like Miss Brooke from Anne of Green Gables. Google it. Not your type, even if she happened to be into twenty-four-year-old tattooed hobos.

Hope to see you in Vegas soon. But not until I have a fabulous life that I can show off to you, 'mkay?

———————————————————————————

———————

THE BUS PULLED up to the station in Las Vegas. My heart pounded double time as I stepped off and into my new home. Unfortunately, the bus station wasn't much to look at and the noise of car honks and people itched inside my skull. Once I got my suitcase, I wheeled it onto the street where I was supposed to catch a taxi.

They were lined up in a long yellow row like a giant banana. The ads on top displayed girls barely covered with sequins and pink feathers. I could imagine what my mom would say about their lady parts being on display. I picked a cab advertising a magic show. The cab driver was nice enough, but I decided to sit in the back. I didn't want to give him the wrong idea.

"North Nellis Boulevard, please," I said.

The bus station quickly vanished from sight, replaced with old, run-down casinos. I wanted to see palm trees and the sun but instead all I got was parking lots and gray sky. My eyes caught on the Vegas strip in the distance.

Air conditioning blasted through the taxi, cooling my neck. It was the thick of summer, but not the alive kind I was used to. Everything was brown and dusty except for the odd tree here and there, probably planted to brighten up the place. There was no green grass, no forests of tall lush trees, no wildflowers. This was a dry, dead kind of summer.

The cab finally pulled off the highway. We passed shopping malls and apartments, run-down hotels and liquor stores. And casinos, more than I thought one city could hold. Everywhere advertised slot machines and gambling. People walked the streets, proof that despite the grunginess, it was still safe to live here. Maybe. I'd never worried about safety before. The worst things we'd had in Hillstone were petty thefts and bar fights. The occasional graffiti from drunk kids who had nothing better to do than splash Van+Regan=Forever on the sides of old barns. But suddenly I was worried about real crime, the kind that only existed on TV in my world yesterday.

"Traffic, as usual," my driver drawled.

A thumping bass resounded from a car nearby and I shrank into my seat.

My eyes drifted from the liquor store advertising five-dollar wine, to the pawn shop with neon lights in the windows saying "cash for gold," to a Chinese restaurant whose name was actually in Chinese instead of being called Empire Garden or Garden Empire. Two women leaned against the window, both wearing knee-high boots and skirts so short I was surprised I couldn't see their undies. They might've been prostitutes, or maybe that was just the way the staff dressed. I averted my eyes so they wouldn't catch me staring.

My new apartment, the Crampton Oasis, looked like an old motel from the fifties. It was two stories, with faded pink stucco and a metal staircase. The building was shaped like an L, the apartment doors all on the outside. A pool rested in the middle, the sparkling water inviting in the stifling heat.

I went up the narrow staircase, lugging my suitcase behind me. I held onto the metal railing until my fingers found something sticky, and then quickly let go.

Bronwyn's apartment was on the second floor, number fifteen. I stood at the door, staring at the tarnished gold numbers. I didn't have a key. How idiotic. It was the one thing I'd overlooked in my rush to get out of Hillstone. I rang the doorbell and knocked, but there was no answer.

I didn't want to lug my suitcase back down the stairs or leave it unattended, so I parked it in front of the door and took a seat. I rested my head against the door. My stomach growled. Sweat trickled down my neck into my t-shirt. Hopefully Bronwyn would be back soon. Even if she wasn't, I needed a bit of a rest before I braved the streets of Vegas with a big suitcase and my purse in tow. That was a theft just waiting to happen.

It was four in the afternoon. I played solitaire on my phone (how appropriate), checked the time again, played some more, social networked, checked again. Thought seriously about jumping in the pool. The heat was making me sleepy. My butt hurt. I was starving. An apartment down the hall was blasting rap music, making my headache worse. The smell of feet and cooked onions wafted from next door. At least that killed my appetite.

My eyes slid closed, I could picture Hillstone in my mind. The wildflowers at Hank's ranch. The huge cypress tree in my front lawn. The sun turning my house pink and gold.

"Hey, you!"

My eyes popped open and I lifted my head from the door with a groan. I must have fallen asleep because I had an awful crick in my neck.

A tall black woman stood over me, a street bike dangling from her shoulder. "You must be Maggie," she said. "If you're not, you better get lost."

I stood up. "Yeah, sorry. I couldn't get inside. You're Bronwyn, right?"

"No, I just mugged her and stole her bike. What do you think?" She stared at me. I stared back. "Well?"

"Well, what?" Was I supposed to hug her or something?

"Get your crap out of the way!"

"Oh, right. Sorry." I moved my suitcase while Bronwyn rolled her eyes. She lowered her bike to the ground, put a key in the door and opened it.

"I have an extra for you," she said, going inside. "I didn't want to leave it sitting around."

I assumed she meant key, not bike. I followed her into a narrow hallway, which opened into one big room. It was a kitchen and living room combined. The walls were papered to look like worn-out brick, peeling in the corners, the cupboards and floors faded wood. A small kitchen table and a couple of chairs filled the kitchen space, and a red couch faced a small flat-screen in the living room. Framed black-and-white photographs covered the walls. The whole place had a vintage feel to it.

"My room, your room, and the bathroom," she said, pointing to a series of doors. She leaned her bike against the back of the couch and then popped open a bottle of water.

I headed to my room. Bronwyn followed.

"After I shower, I'm heading to Nico's. My boyfriend."

I turned the knob and pushed the door open.

"The room's been empty for a while, since my last roommate moved out," Bronwyn said. "Anyway, you probably won't see much of me, I'm a bike courier during the day and then I usually hang out at Nico's place. But I like it clean. I hope you're not a slob."

My room had a double mattress on a metal frame, no bedding, and a wood dresser shoved against one wall. That was it. With only one tiny window and a dome light lighting up the room, the first word that popped into my head was, *hellhole*.

"I'm not messy," I said, my voice weak.

She uncrossed her arms. "Good. I'll see you later."

"Wait," I called. "The key?" I wasn't sure when Bronwyn would return and I didn't want to be stuck here. I had bedding to buy and a job to get.

"Top left drawer in the kitchen." She disappeared into the bathroom.

The noise of the shower was like a dull roar. I sat on the edge of the mattress. There were no pillows, no sheets, and I cringed at what substances might decorate the mattress under a black light. The whole day hadn't gone the way I expected. I just wanted it to end.

Thinking about home felt like defeat, like I shouldn't already be missing a place I'd wanted so badly to get away from. But my mind was full of grays and browns, of bad smells and harsh words. I wanted to turn off the ugly channel and I did it the only way I knew. By picturing the home I had left behind.

CHAPTER 5

MAGGIE

TURNED out I left my diner job at Hillstone only to get a diner job in Las Vegas, because it was the only job I could get. I had no qualifications, no experience outside of waitressing, and nothing past a high school diploma. Pathetic.

But I didn't let that deter me. I didn't let my absentee roommate deter me, or the constant wailing sirens through the night, or the dude who spit on the street right by my shoes, or the near-crippling loneliness. I was undeterrable.

It took me three days to find my new job, waitressing at a place called *Holy Diner!* It was nothing to get excited about, that exclamation mark was part of the name. It smelled like grease and sour milk, and an alarming gray fuzz covered the bathroom floor, but my dad would appreciate the name at least.

When I wasn't searching for a job, I bought some home essentials: bedding for my mattress—a cheery yellow that reminded me of the wildflowers behind my house—and some groceries. Bronwyn didn't keep much in the fridge or pantry.

My bank account was getting scary low. Luckily, I was saved by my new job at *Holy Diner!* and my years of waitressing experience. Never thought I'd be grateful for *that*.

"Hi, my name is Maggie and I'll be your server," I said, smiling wide to a twenty-something couple who slid into one of my booths. "What can I get you to drink?"

The man scowled.

"Can you give us a minute?" the woman asked. "I mean geez, we just sat down."

My smile wavered. "Of course."

"Why do we always get the peppy ones?" she asked as I walked away. "So annoying."

That's what I got for smiling.

"Are you ready to order?" I asked five minutes later. I knew it was only five minutes because I'd been watching the clock.

The woman blew her breath out so loud, her bangs fluttered. "Finally. We've been waiting forever."

A vein in my forehead throbbed. "What can I get you?"

"I'll have the Ja-cobb Salad," she said, "with no bacon, no cheese, no olives, and with the dressing on the side."

The man chimed in before I'd even finished writing. "The Romans burger, extra cheese, extra mayo, no lettuce, with your Bible fries."

I jotted it all down while the woman reamed out the man for getting extra mayo. I grabbed their menus and hurried away. They were one of *those* tables, the kind a waitress will surrender her tips to avoid. Not only did they have to special order their meal, but I could tell right away the woman would never be satisfied.

First, she thought the lettuce looked wilted. Then she wanted her ham cut into smaller pieces, like she couldn't pick up a fork and do it herself. Then she asked for a different dressing because she didn't like the vinaigrette. We were a crummy theme diner with cracked leather seats and old bible art on the walls. What did she expect, a Michelin-star experience?

"Waitress, oh waitress," a young boy yelled, flicking his hand at me.

I plastered my smile back on and headed over to his table. I'd been there just a few minutes earlier. Four boys and one girl crammed into a booth, practically sitting on one another's laps. Their faces shone with acne and sweat, they cursed too much, and I swear I smelled angst and hormones on their breath.

Man alive, I felt old. Three hours at *Holy Diner!* and I'd already aged ten years.

"Waitress, what's the special for today?" the boy asked. He was reclined near the window with his elbow propped on the sill, his other hand braced against the back of the seat.

"I already told you the specials." I said, trying to sound polite.

"I can't remember. Could you be a sweetheart and repeat them for me?"

I sighed. "We have the Red Sea Chowder, Shekel pancakes topped with fruit, and our famous Gomorrah pie, made with pecans and butterscotch."

The boy smirked. "Red Sea Chowder, as in Moses, parting of?"

"I would imagine so."

"Not that then, I never did like Moses." The boy perused the menu like he was picking a pricey wine. "I'll need a few more minutes."

I walked away.

"Dude, I'm hungry," one of the boys said. "Pick something."

"Whatever, she wants me," I heard as I rounded the corner. "Don't mess with my game."

I snorted. Dream on.

My first shift at *Holy Diner!* lasted seven hours and by the end, I wanted to cry. I'd had a few nice customers and some okay tips, but all around it had been a rotten day. People were rude, annoyed, angry, cocky, bored, disinterested, and basically jerks. Jerks who gave lousy tips. At least in Hillstone people were friendly as they handed me their leftover pennies.

I undid my apron, which was a reprint of a page of scripture (Dad wouldn't like that so much), and slipped it into my bag. I was *so* ready to go home.

"Margaret?" It was my new boss, Craig, a late-forty-ish man with a bald spot, hairy arms, and a skinny tie. He seemed like a nice enough guy. "Could you clean the bathrooms before you leave?"

Nice? Sorry, I meant he was a sadistic gorilla with unresolved priest issues.

I scrubbed the sinks and the toilets, mopped the gray fuzz (which didn't disappear at all from the floor), and emptied the trash cans. I wiped the mirrors clean, my reflection going from murky, to soapy, to clear. But I didn't want to see myself, or the gold button-up shirt I'd spilled coffee on, or the black mini that was too short for my long legs. I didn't even want to marvel at my power bathroom cleaning skills. I just wanted out of there.

This wasn't the fabulous life I'd had in mind at all.

At least I had an audition to look forward to.

To: Margaret Hale, maggie-hale@mymail.com

From: Frasier Hale, frazedaze@mymail.com

Bronwyn and I DID make out. I distinctly remember snow up my back and our combined snotty noses while the horrifying sounds of Nickelback serenaded us. Remind her. Remind her of "How You Remind Me." And then punch her in the face for not being nice.

You know what, never mind. When I get there, I'll punch her in the face for both of us. I can take her and I'm pretty sure you can't. Don't try either, because she'll probably kick you out and then where would you go? And how could I visit? And seduce my new girlfriend? Miss Brooke is *totally* my type. I love that whole pale, buttoned-up, stern matron kind of thing. The things Miss Brooke could do with her ruler! Hot. I'm bored with Kimmi anyway. Too clingy. Too *why can't you get a job?* Isn't one job enough for both of us? I left Vancouver and I'm in Seattle now. Home of the plaid flannel shirt and grunge. I have found my people.

P.S. Sit in the back of the cab, it's more sophisticated.

Three weeks I'd been in Las Vegas. Three weeks working at *Holy Diner!* and coming home to an empty apartment with a ghost of a roommate. Three weeks I'd spent my off-hours stretching on the scratched-up hardwood floor, trying to maintain my flexibility. Three weeks choreographing a short routine in the living room, pushing the big wooden chest out of the way and dancing around the couch. The space wasn't big enough so I could only mark it, but I'd done it so many times that performing it full-out wouldn't be a problem.

Essence Dance Theater was a weirdly shaped building, kind of swirly and round, with a balcony on the roof. It was special—I could tell before I walked in the front door.

I waited inside a hallway full of girls who looked exactly like me: wearing dark leotards and light tights, buns slicking back their hair. Some wore ballet shoes, others had on foot gloves or Undeez —shoes that barely covered the balls of the feet and were flesh-toned so you wouldn't see them off stage. Mine were ones I'd made myself, cutting up an old pair of ballet slippers and patching them together with nude-colored elastic. A few girls saw them and smirked but I didn't care. So I couldn't afford Capezio. I would out-dance every one of them.

Probably.

Maybe.

Hopefully.

Truth was, my confidence drained as the minutes ticked by and we waited to get called into the studio. I was a good dancer, I knew I was...for Hillstone. But what if I wasn't good enough for Las Vegas?

Pictures covered the walls of dancers in beautiful costumes and stunning poses, their bodies rippling with muscle and showing off perfect technique. They were inspiring and somehow mocking at the same time.

Nine a.m. hit and we filed into the studio. The wood floors were polished and smooth, the mirrors spotless. They only made me more self-conscious. I was a giant next to most of these girls. Too tall for ballet, an examiner had once told me. Too tall for partnering. At least I was skinny enough that I'd never had to barf my way through my dance years. I glanced at the girls around me. Not as skinny as most.

The head of the company, Mallory Hugo, sat at a desk in front of the mirrors. She looked exactly like her pictures—an older version of Miss Brooke, complete with bun and down-turned mouth, the kind that never smiled. Two people flanked her on either side, one of their choreographers and EDT's principal male dancer. Another woman stood in front, tiny and Asian, appraising us as we stood there trying not to twitch with nerves.

"Three rows, please," she said. Girls shuffled to get places in the front. I went to the back—seeing over their shorty heads wouldn't be a problem.

"I'm Miss Aiko, and I run the dance school here," she said. "If you get accepted into the Company through open auditions, you will take Master classes with me three times a week."

Miss Aiko paced in front of the table. Some of the girls hunched their shoulders under her scrutiny. "You should know that it is *very* difficult to be accepted into the Company when you have not attended the school. We might take one or two of you. Maybe.

Even our students have to work hard to get accepted into the Company."

I felt myself shrinking and put a stop to it right away. I wouldn't get in if I showed weakness. The runts would be the first to go, and I was no runt.

"I will run through the combination twice, you will have five minutes to practice on your own, and then you will perform in groups of three." Miss Aiko turned and faced the mirror. "Let us begin."

The combination was extremely difficult. The steps were strange and a little off the music, and the piece wasn't pleasant to listen to—screechy, jumpy violins and pounding drums. Everything about it was weird. I think Miss Aiko did that on purpose, to see if we could handle it. My body felt awkward in the movements, but I caught on to the choreography with no problem.

When it was my turn to perform, I didn't miss a step. My mind took my body through the choreography, but that was the problem. It didn't feel natural. I was thinking too hard about the steps and I didn't *perform.*

"Girls to the middle of the room, please," Miss Aiko called when we'd all performed the routine. "If I call your name, you will stay and show us your solo. If not, you may leave."

A couple of girls in front of me grabbed hands. I took a breath. Mallory Hugo handed a paper to Miss Aiko. "Can we please see Shonda Jefferson, Nita Santiago, Katherine McDougall, and Margaret Hale. The rest of you can go. Thank you for coming."

I let out the breath I'd been holding. My cheeks threatened to stretch into a grin. I'd made it into the next round!

The rest of the girls filed from the room while the four of us left stood in a row in the center of the studio.

"You will perform your prepared pieces in the order which I called your names," Miss Aiko said. "Wait outside until it is your turn. Shonda Jefferson, you may take the floor."

I waited in the hallway, my sweaty hands leaving streaks on

my phone as I tapped and swiped. I hoped I'd picked the right song. A piece of music could make or break a dance number, and I didn't want to blow it because of that. I went through the choreography in my mind while I stretched my calf muscles. The other girls came and went, and I couldn't tell if they'd made it in or not. Maybe they wouldn't tell us today.

When it was my turn, I handed Miss Aiko my phone, prepped on the right song. The three teachers had their eyes on me as I settled into my opening pose.

I performed my choreography flawlessly, made every leap, mastered my quadruple pirouette, and only wobbled a little as I came out of my fouetté. The music ran through my veins, my body responding to every shift in tempo. I didn't have to think the steps, I just did them. When I finished, I held my head high, my cheeks flushed, my chest heaving.

The four of them bent their heads together. They whispered for a long time while my feet shifted. Finally, Mallory Hugo looked at me, her eyes narrowed into rulers.

"You're not good enough."

I stood there, frozen. It wasn't that I hadn't understood her, I had. Oh, I really had. But the words themselves had molded my feet to the floor, had paralyzed me against walking away from this humiliation.

"You have raw talent, and great musicality," Mallory said, her voice clipped and harsh, "but your technique is horrendous. You're not ready for this company. Or any company."

She turned her head to the papers in front of her, swiping her pen in a giant X across the page. It was like I'd been released from my paralysis. All I wanted to do was run away and cry.

"Thank you for the opportunity," I said, my voice thick. And then I retrieved my phone and my bag and left the studio.

"Margaret!" Miss Aiko had followed me out. I didn't want to face her. Didn't want to hear more of how I wasn't good enough.

Didn't know how long I'd be able to keep the tears at bay. But I gathered my courage and turned back.

"You came close, Margaret," Miss Aiko said. She had to lift her chin high to look at me, she barely came up to my chest. "James, he's a principal dancer, and I, we both fought for you."

I swallowed. "Thank you."

"You have great musicality, like Mallory said, and she rarely gives compliments. But your technique does need work. Maybe if you took some classes?"

My eyes dropped. "I can't afford this school."

She placed her hand on my arm, a gesture that said I shouldn't be ashamed to be poor. "There's a studio near the strip. Fluidity. They have drop-in classes for a decent rate and their teachers are excellent. I know because I taught there before I came here." I met her eyes. "Take some classes, train, and come back in the spring."

I blinked rapidly. Those tears didn't want to stay away. "I appreciate the advice."

"You'll come back?"

I shouldered my bag. Right now I didn't want to step one pointed toe back in EDT. But for some reason I said, "Yes. Yes, I will."

CHAPTER 6

JAY

A SIREN WAILED. Flashing lights lit up my rearview mirror, coming from a tinted SUV right on my tail. I glanced at the speedometer—barely five over the limit.

I pulled over, cursing, my body tense. Part of my job was staying off the radar. I didn't visit Simon at the LVMPD, and I always made myself scarce at crime scenes.

A badge appeared at my window. I rolled it down.

The cop peered inside. "License and registration, please."

"Is something wrong?" I asked, handing over what he wanted. He didn't answer, just took my info back to the car parked behind me.

I clenched the steering wheel, then told myself to take a breath. He'd have nothing on me. My record was clean, as far as his database was concerned. The boy I used to be didn't exist anymore, Simon had made sure of that.

I glanced at the unmarked SUV behind me. Not a regular officer. A detective maybe, or a CAT. But there was no reason for the Criminal Apprehension Team to come after me.

He came back, leaning against the window frame, my license

and registration dangling from his hand. "This truck is registered to a Simon Ting. You know him?"

"The registration is under my name." I took the paper and opened it up, pointing to my name so obviously there.

"Records say otherwise." He squinted at me. "You steal this car?"

I almost laughed. If I was the kind of guy to steal a car, it wouldn't be a Ford. "Of course not. I've had the truck for four years. Something must be wrong with your computer."

His lips pressed into a thin line. "So, this Ting. You know him or not?"

This guy was wearing a uniform, he had a badge, but no name tag. The SUV behind me was unmarked. Adrenaline flooded my body, my knuckles itched. A quick jab to the chin and he'd be flat on his back. He'd never see it coming.

"Nope. Never heard of him."

He stared at me for a long moment. My right hand was curling into a fist on my thigh and I loosened it.

He scratched his chin. "I'll double-check the records. Maybe it was a glitch. Sorry for the inconvenience." He sauntered back to his car.

My muscles wouldn't uncoil, even after he drove off. Suspicious. The whole thing didn't make sense. Simon's name shouldn't have been anywhere near my truck registration. He'd given me the cash to buy it, but there wouldn't be a record of that anywhere. There should be no paper trail that linked Simon and me at all. Whether this guy was a cop, a CAT, or something else entirely, it wasn't a coincidence that he'd stopped and asked me specifically about Simon.

I headed to the gym. Time alone with the bags would help clear my mind, but I had a class to teach first.

Eastside Boxing was in an old part of Vegas, near the Arts District. The building was a massive square on a street corner, dwarfing everything around it. A faded painting of a shirtless boxer covered one side of the brick, something Conall McCrary, the owner, had painted himself when he bought the building forty-two years ago.

"Barely on time, Thornton," McCrary said when I pushed through the front door, gym bag over one shoulder. I glanced at the clock. Five minutes before three. The first class of the day came straight from school, arriving between three thirty and four. But to Conall McCrary, on time meant an hour early.

"I got pulled over."

"What for?"

"No clue."

McCrary raised an eyebrow. "Bergin cancelled again so you'll be on your own for the afternoon." He shuffled through some papers on the front desk and then rammed them in a drawer. I'd tried to convince him to go paperless, but the old man wouldn't even consider a computer. He was so disorganized, papers shoved here and there, I didn't know how he could keep track of class payments or tournament dates, or even the names of the kids. But he never missed my salary so I didn't push it.

"I swear I should can that kid," he muttered.

Bergin was older than me but smaller, prompting McCrary to call him 'kid' all the time. It drove Bergin crazy, but he deserved it. The slacker rarely showed up for work.

"And the toilets need cleaning. Let that janitor know, would you?"

I patted the top of the desk on my way by. "Got it."

"Thornton."

I stopped.

McCrary leaned forward, his nose wrinkling. "You smell like a baby's bum again."

I took a sniff at my knuckles without thinking, then shrugged. "You know Simon."

His face clouded over. "Yes, I do know Simon."

I'd met McCrary five years ago when his brother borrowed

from Simon and I had to pressure his family to collect. McCrary had seen my fighting potential then and agreed to train me. I paid him by cleaning the gym, then later, by assisting in his classes. Now, I was the head instructor at Eastside Boxing while he took care of the business side. And I'd become his only family after his moved back to Ireland.

I headed upstairs and banged on the door to Nico's apartment. "Open up, Higgins. I know you're in there." I pounded my fist a few more times for good measure.

Nico opened the door. His eyes were bloodshot but he gave me a sardonic grin. "Jay Thornton, how nice of you to drop by. What can I do for you?"

The thing I liked about Nico Higgins—he wasn't scared of me, and he didn't whine or beg. Unfortunately, it was only a matter of time.

Nico glanced at his watch. "You're not due for a check-in for another...week?"

"Five days." I leaned against the doorjamb. "That's not why I'm here. The toilets?"

Nico made a face. "I'd rather it was about the money. Kids do not know how to aim, I swear."

"Why, you got it?" I couldn't hold back my surprise. Nico was a janitor and a drunk, not exactly the poster-boy for paying back a large sum of money.

"You're not allowed to ask yet," he said.

I crossed my arms. "In five days, I won't be asking."

Nico paled, but he didn't argue.

"Kids will be here soon," I said. "Get those bathrooms done."

"What's the point?" he grumbled. "It'll be a sprinkler party before we close tonight."

I went back downstairs and changed into my boxing shorts. When I came out, Nico was already at work scrubbing the sink in the girls' bathroom. I still had about fifteen minutes before the kids showed up, so I strapped on my boxing gloves. It didn't take me long to work up a sweat pounding the heavy bag.

"Offer's still open."

I grabbed onto the swinging bag, then turned to McCrary. His skinny arms were folded over his chest, his old man's gut hanging out underneath.

"I know. I need more time." I cringed. I sounded like a mark.

"Time ain't exactly on my side."

McCrary's hair was snow white, a patch on top completely bald. His face was worn down, a testament to years of struggle and hard work. I knew McCrary was old, but I didn't want to *know* it.

"I can't take over until you let me in on the secrets of your filing system." I ripped off a glove with my teeth. "Otherwise I'll be sunk before I start."

McCrary tapped the side of his head. "It's all up here, son."

He was seventy and had a way better memory than me. "You know that won't work for me."

He turned away. "Uh-uh. Don't even try to convince me to buy a computer again. I'm old and set in my ways. Once you take over, you can do what you want, but until then I'll stick with good ol' pencil and paper."

He shuffled back to the front desk, a slight limp in his right leg from a boxing match gone wrong. I was afraid McCrary was right, that he didn't have much time left, but I wasn't ready. I had a little money saved, but no experience running a business.

Most of all, I didn't know how to tell Simon I wanted out. He wouldn't just say "have a nice life," and let me go. I owed him. Not money, but for who I was. With a guy like Simon, no matter what I did, I could never pay off that debt. The more I tried to pull away from him, the more he reined me in. With a guy like Simon, you didn't walk away, not even if he called you "son."

Especially not then.

McCrary would hold on a few more years, give me time to work it all out. He would've given me the gym right then if I let him, but I didn't want handouts. Both Simon and McCrary had worked hard for what they had, and I would do the same. My way.

A school bus pulled up to the curb out front, a load of noisy boys spilling out. They shoved their way inside; a bunch of them gave me high fives as they headed to the back of the gym to hang up their backpacks and change into their shorts and Eastside Boxing t-shirts.

"Alright, let's go." I started jogging around the gym, quickly followed by a trail of nine and ten-year-olds. "Hurry up, Moises," I said to a kid who was still fiddling with his backpack, "we're starting without you."

Containing a smile, I slapped the Eastside Boxing logo on the front wall as I jogged by. I'd never felt more at home.

CHAPTER 7

MAGGIE

I WAS NUMB. I couldn't even remember how I got home. The only thing going through my head was, *not good enough, not good enough, not good enough.*

Inside my apartment, I sank to the floor, sobbing. I'd left Hillstone behind, and Hank and my parents—my *whole life*—only to be not good enough. Not good enough for anything but working at a diner. I buried my face in my hands and cried snotty tears into them. I'd come to Vegas with no back-up plan. No other goal than getting into EDT. Right now, that goal seemed impossible.

Something touched my hair and I reared back, my head hitting the door. Bronwyn stood over me.

"What's wrong?" For once, her voice sounded kind. Not that she'd ever been mean. More brutally honest than anything.

I scrubbed my eyes, wincing at the black streaks mascara left on my fingers. "Nothing."

Bronwyn snorted. "Really? I'd hate to see you upset then."

I scrambled off the floor and walked away. "I'm fine." I didn't want to talk to Bronwyn about it, or anyone. Failure wasn't something I wanted to broadcast to the world.

She followed me into my bedroom. "Look, I know I barely know you, but Frasier is my friend and he'd kill me if he knew something happened to you and I did nothing."

"Thanks for your concern," I said without turning around. "But there's nothing you can do."

I face-planted on my bed. The tears were gone but the sense of defeat lingered. I didn't even want to think about what came next.

The bed rustled. Bronwyn was still there, another problem I couldn't get rid of.

"You don't have to tell me what happened," she said. "In fact, I really don't want to know." I rolled my eyes. Too bad she couldn't see. "Come out to dinner with me. It'll take your mind off whatever."

I didn't respond.

"I'll...pay."

Those words sounded like they were difficult for her to say, and that in itself made me want to take her up on the offer. But I didn't want to go out. I didn't want to reapply my makeup and pretend life was peachy. I wanted to wallow in my misery. Truth was, I hadn't had much of it so far. This whole misery feeling was new to me and I clung to it, though I had no idea why.

"Let's go, Hale," Bronwyn barked. I turned, trying to give her a dirty look. "Whoa, ugly. Go wash your face. You're scaring me."

My mouth dropped open.

"Move it, or I'll revoke my offer and you'll have to pay for your own dinner." She headed for my door. "And put on something sexy, it always helps."

A n hour later, Bronwyn and I were at a small but fancy restaurant. Or at least, fancy to me. The only nice place we had in Hillstone was the Garber B & B, and the only thing that made it nice was their overpriced steak, red wine, and the candles they lit at night.

Bronwyn raised her wine glass to me. She had on a very short purple dress, tight around her hips, and stiletto heels. Her lips were colored purple to match her dress and a light dusting of glitter made her dark skin glow under the dim lights. And here I'd figured her for a tomboy. Her muscles, spandex outfits, and racing bike were very misleading. I was tall, but she had an inch or so on me. She would have been extremely intimidating if I hadn't known she'd made out with my brother once.

Who was I kidding? She was still intimidating as heck.

"I asked Nico to come," she said, "but he's not feeling great." I nodded like it meant something to me. "You'll have to meet him another time."

"Have you been dating long?"

"Over a year." She skimmed the menu. "Nothing over twenty bucks, got it? I'm not made of money."

I stared at the menu. The prices were decent, and I settled on a seventeen-dollar chicken and vegetables meal.

"How is Fraze, anyway?" she asked after we'd ordered.

"He's good," I replied, adjusting my top. I didn't have a whole lot of sexy to wear—my dad wouldn't allow it—so I'd settled on skinny jeans, heels, and a dark blouse. Bronwyn had been vocally disappointed. I refrained from snapping that I'd get a new wardrobe when I got a new life.

"I haven't seen him in a few years," I said. "But he's good. Traveling all over, you know, being Fraze."

She laughed like she knew exactly what I meant.

"Did you two make out, or not?" I asked. "It's hard to believe everything Fraze says. Gotta set the record straight here."

Her lips twitched. "If I told you the truth, it would ruin my reputation."

"What reputation is that?"

She waved at herself. "Fraze isn't exactly my type."

"But you're his?" I asked with a raised eyebrow.

"*Every* girl is Frasier Hale's type."

It was true, he wasn't picky. He liked them tall, short, dark, light, big, small, mean, nice, smart, dumb, and every weird combination in between. Frasier couldn't settle on a type any more than he could settle on a job or a place to live.

I stared Bronwyn down, waiting for a confession. After a few long minutes, not that she was intimidated by me I'm sure, she finally gave it up. "Fine, yes. We made out. I was fourteen and stupid."

"You could do worse." She could do better too, but I would never speak out against my brother. Even in my head it sounded like treason.

She swirled her wine around in her glass. "We've been friends ever since. That's what's really great about it, you know? Not the kissing. The friendship that came after. He still sends me these random postcards from whatever city he's in, with lipstick kisses pressed into them. I can totally imagine him putting on sample lipstick in the drugstore, just so he can kiss the stupid things."

I smiled.

"Are you going to tell me what happened now?"

I looked down at my plate. "I thought you didn't want to know."

"I don't. But I have a feeling you need to spit it out."

So I did. I told her about running away from Hank and his proposal, then my dream of dancing with Essence Dance Theater being crushed.

"Seriously?" she said. "That's what you were all sobby about?"

I glared.

"So you didn't get in this time. You're what, eighteen?"

"Nineteen."

"Whatever." She leaned toward me. "You don't give up after one try. How pathetic would that be? Take classes like that chick said. Practice. Get better. Audition again. And again and again if you have to."

"I know, but—"

"Shut up," she said, but there was no sting. "Do you really want to dance there? Or do you want to pretend like you do and whine about it while working at a diner for the rest of your life? Maybe you wanna go back and marry that hick after all because you have nothing better to do?" She leaned back, resting one arm beside her plate. "Yeah, you should do that. Forget all this. Vegas isn't for you anyway. Go back and marry your cowboy and have a million babies."

I bristled. "Just because I told you a little bit about myself, doesn't mean you know me."

"Run back home and you'll be doing exactly what I expect."

I hated that she was right. It would be easy to go back to the life I knew. To give up. I'd failed the first time, I didn't know if I could handle it again. But I'd never get the life I was looking for if I slunk back home.

Bronwyn drummed her fingers on the table but didn't say anything.

"Are you being a jerk to get me fired up?" I asked.

"If that's what you want to think."

"I hate you." The words surprised me, I'd never said them to anyone before. But she laughed.

"I know. But stick around, you'll grow to love me."

To: Frasier Hale, frazedaze@mymail.com

From: Margaret Hale, maggie-hale@mymail.com

I've got good news and bad news, which do you want to hear first?

I guess you have no choice since it's my email and I'm God here, so there. (Don't tell Dad I said that.)

The good news: Bronwyn and I are friends. Sort of. She took me out to dinner and reamed me out and was generally nice in a mean sort of way. I'm starting to see it—why you like her. We've hung out a few more times since and she wants me to meet her boyfriend, Nico, which I'll be doing on Thursday because I finally get a night off from the diner.

Did I tell you I got a diner job? That's not good or bad news, just a reality and I don't really want to talk about it.

The bad news: I auditioned for EDT (Essence Dance Theater but that's a pain to spell out all the time) but I didn't get in. Miss Hugo, AKA Miss Brooke, told me I wasn't good enough. Yep, those were her exact words and yep, they hurt like a you-know-what. But I've decided to take some classes and try again in the spring. A teacher at the audition told me I should, she was rooting for me, so at least there's that.

Anyway, I've got a scripture apron to put on. (Don't ask.) Have fun in Seattle. Wasn't that whole grunge thing over in the nineties? Or do they still worship Kurt Cobain? Don't wear too much flannel—it's not a good look for anyone.

I took my first drop-in contemporary class at Fluidity after my shift at the diner on Thursday. I was exhausted from crabby customers and scripture-themed menu items, and my feet hurt something fierce, but I forced myself to go. I'd never improve my technique if I didn't practice.

The studio faced a busy street where anyone on the road could look in and see the dancers. I paid my twenty dollars and then stretched while waiting for class to start. The class was a mix of adults and kids in their late teens, both men and women. I hung back but the teacher—an African American woman named Robbie—quickly drew me out. She had that way with all the students, engaging them in the class, and free with both praise and correction. The pressure to be the best threatened to stress me out, but Robbie made the class fun and I couldn't wait to go back for another.

Afterward, I bussed back to the diner, grateful that I didn't have to work the late shift. I was on my way to meet Bronwyn and her boyfriend at his place, which was supposedly nearby. Almost kitty corner to the diner, if I had the address right.

I glanced at the address in my phone and then at the building in front of me. It was a gym, large and square with a giant shirtless man wearing boxing gloves painted on one side, a sign proclaiming it Eastside Boxing. I must've typed in the wrong address, Bronwyn's boyfriend couldn't live here.

Movement down the road drew my attention. A tall man had ducked into a big SUV. He started the car, but didn't drive away. From a distance, it seemed like he was looking at me. He probably wasn't, but my heartbeat quickened and I darted inside the gym.

Inside, Eastside Boxing appeared empty. Lights shone over the front desk and down one side of the gym, but it was dark over the boxing ring. Punching bags hung from the ceiling, and there were mats on the floor. The faint hum of voices reached my ears so I planted myself in front of the desk, looking for a bell to announce myself. There wasn't one.

I texted Bronwyn, asking if I was at the right place.

That's the place. He lives upstairs. Running late. Be there soon. Just yell for him.

Shoving my phone in my purse, I peered around the gym. There was an upstairs landing at the back of the gym. I headed toward the voices, skirting the ring, my flats noiseless on the mats.

At the back of the gym, a light dangled over two guys fighting on the floor, one clearly winning. Two men stood on either side watching the fight, one tall and brown-skinned, the other short, stocky, and white. Both were wearing gray sweatsuits. I stopped, not wanting to interrupt a class. There was a cry. Blood flew.

I rushed forward. "Stop! What are you doing?"

Three big men all turned their ugly stares to me.

CHAPTER 8

JAY

I'D REACHED the point where I actually wanted my marks to have the money they owed Simon. He wouldn't like that very much. It wasn't that he didn't like to get paid, but the longer it took them to pay up, the more interest they owed. At a twenty percent rate per week, that was a lot of extra cash Simon raked in. Plus, the longer he owned them, the more info he could squeeze out of them in the process, which was good for his day job.

Nico Higgins was different than most of my marks. He wasn't a dealer or some crook that couldn't get a proper loan because of their record. Nico just couldn't catch a break. Simon was ticked that the only damage I'd done to Rafael was a broken arm, and then some bruises and broken bones to his gang. My heart hadn't been in it. It rarely was anymore, but my mind had been occupied with that cop who'd pulled me over, and what he wanted. I hadn't told Simon about it. After my shoddy smackdown, if he found out I was keeping something from him, I'd be screwed. So, even though Nico was almost a friend, I had to do things properly, with witnesses.

I didn't expect one of them to be a girl.

"Stop! What are you doing?"

I looked up without letting go of Nico. She was probably around twenty, with hair that tumbled past her shoulders and legs that didn't quit.

"Okay," I said to Alfonso and Alonso. "Which one of you geniuses forgot to lock the front door?" They started toward her.

"Hold it," I said, and they froze. They answered to me on this one, though Simon had only sent them to make sure things were done right.

"Who are you?" I asked the girl.

Her wide eyes didn't leave Nico's face, her mouth hung open.

"You know this girl?" I asked Nico.

He shook his head and coughed, blood spraying from his mouth.

"You've hurt him," the girl said.

With a short laugh, I let go of Nico and stood up. I wiped my hands on my pants. "Keep your eyes on him," I ordered Alfonso and Alonso.

I walked toward her and she didn't back away. Impressive. My gaze slid from her bare ankles, over the thin tights covering her legs that showed every curve and muscle, to the short skirt. Then higher, to her loose shirt which hung off one shoulder, showing a hint of smooth, pale collarbone. "What are you doing here?"

I brushed a knuckle under my nose. Her eyes met mine and she let out a squeak. I'd probably smeared Nico's blood on my face.

This girl was beautiful, her dark eyes holding me in place.

She was also terrified. Whatever guts she'd had were used up. She wouldn't be a problem.

"Get out of here," I said, then turned back to Nico, who was hunched and trembling on the floor, pressing one hand to his ribs. Beside him, Alfonso and Alonso were having an argument over who was better in the *Rush Hour* movies, Jackie Chan or Chris Tucker.

I grabbed Nico and hauled him to his feet. He moaned. "You know I have to."

"Please, Jay." One of Nico's eyes had swollen shut and he gasped for breath as if I'd done some internal damage to his lungs. I hadn't. "I'll get it, I swear, I just need more time."

What a disappointment—the begging had begun. And Nico had seemed so promising. I'd almost respected him. I hit him again and he doubled over, wheezing. "You know how this works." I put my foot on his chest, holding him down.

There was a click, and I turned around.

The girl hadn't left. She was holding up a cell phone. "Stop now or I'll call the police. I've already taken a picture."

One girl against three men, and she hadn't run away. Her voice didn't even waver. Her threats were cute, but I had to admire her spunk.

"Want me to take care of her?" Alonso asked. He sounded bored, as if he were asking to take out the trash. The girl blanched.

"I'll do it, I swear I will," she warned, her finger poised over the screen.

Trouble, that's what she was. I couldn't let her call the cops. I motioned to Alfonso and Alonso and they went for her. She backed away, fingers frantically tapping the screen. Then she broke into a run.

Alonso grabbed her before she made it past the boxing ring. Her phone went flying across the mats.

"Let me go," she yelled, struggling to get away. Alonso dragged her back to me, his hand over her mouth, while Alfonso picked up her phone.

"No, we're good," he said, probably talking to a 911 operator. "My little sister. She likes to prank. Yeah. Sorry."

Nico had started to crawl away and I grabbed onto his chin, forcing him to look at me. "Two more weeks. And that means interest." I let go and he rolled over, clutching himself.

Alonso pinned the girl's arms behind her body. She was still struggling. She stopped when I grabbed a towel sitting on a shelf then walked toward her, wiping my hands.

"Wait for me outside," I said. Alfonso handed me her phone, which I pocketed. Alonso let her go and they both left the gym without looking back.

As soon as they were gone, she bolted. I grabbed her, pulling her against my chest. "I just want to talk."

Her eyes narrowed as if she didn't believe me. I loosened my grip but didn't let go of her arms. Her bare skin felt cool under my fingers.

I stared at her, this girl who'd interrupted my business. She shivered under my gaze. I would've liked to see her body move that way for different reasons.

"Wrong place, wrong time," I said. "I get it."

"I don't think I'm the one in the wrong here," she replied.

"What about trespassing?"

"The door was open."

I laughed. The girl was gutsy. It was sexy as hell.

I tilted my head. "Haven't you heard that saying about curiosity?"

Her eyes were dark brown, framed by impossibly long lashes. Her lips lush and inviting. She was tall, barely shorter than me, and it seemed to give her a certain power, the way she looked at me without flinching.

But I knew who I was. This wasn't a prelude to something great. She had courage, but this kind of girl would never go for a guy like me. Not after what she'd seen. Not based on the way she was looking at me now, her chin high and her mouth tight, as if she knew she was better than me.

My hands tightened on her skin. "Next time, things might not go so easy for you."

"Is that a threat?"

"A warning. To be careful." I let her go. "Not everyone in my line of work is as nice as me."

She let out a snort of laughter. It was unexpected, and I smiled before I could wipe it away.

"Maggie?"

I blinked at the voice. It was Bronwyn, Nico's girlfriend, still in her biking spandex. I'd met her on my first visit to Nico. She was the kind of girl I was used to, tough and hard. Jaded.

"*You*," Bronwyn said to me, an accusation. Her eyes widened. She rushed past me and the girl. "Nico, baby, talk to me." She placed her hand gently on his face, turning it to hers. "Where does it hurt?"

I glanced at the girl—Maggie. She was staring open-mouthed at Bronwyn and Nico and the little show they were putting on. She didn't see me slip past her. I'd become beneath her notice. I quickly scrolled through her phone, deleting the picture she'd taken of me with my foot on Nico's chest. I put the phone on the front desk and left.

CHAPTER 9

MAGGIE

BRONWYN PRESSED a baggie of ice to Nico's face. He winced, cracking open a cut on his lip which began to bleed again. She tsked.

We were in Nico's "apartment," which was one big room above the gym floor. He had a dresser with a fat TV on top, the kind I hadn't seen since I was a kid at my grandma's house. There was also a small fridge and a rusty sink. Shelves covered the empty wall space, full of books, baskets, clothes, shoes, dishes, as if he had a whole houseful of stuff crammed into one room. Bronwyn and Nico were sitting on a low bed, and I perched on the corner of a wooden rocking chair. Sitting in these always made me think I should be knitting something, not that I knew how.

"Shouldn't you go to the hospital?" I asked, grimacing at Nico's beat-up face, the red cuts marring his light brown skin. It was a mess now but it would look even worse tomorrow.

"No!" they said at the same time.

"No hospitals," Bronwyn added.

"Can't afford them." Nico rubbed his chest. I hoped he didn't have any broken ribs. Bruises would heal on their own but broken bones could lead to internal bleeding, couldn't they? Nico needed professional help, not ice and a tensor bandage.

"You should've seen your girl here," Nico said to Bronwyn. They sat close, legs pressed into legs. His hand rested on her knee as she took care of him. It seemed an unconscious thing, as if he didn't know which parts were him and which were her. I'd been like that with Hank, once.

Bronwyn shot me a look. "What did you do?"

"She stormed right in," he said. "Told Jay where to go and how to get there."

"Fat lot of good it did." I couldn't believe this was Bronwyn's boyfriend. He was slightly shorter than her and a bit on the pudgy side, with a round face and an easygoing smile. He wasn't what I'd pictured at all.

"I especially liked it when you threatened to call the cops." He laughed. "Classic."

I frowned. Wasn't that what you were supposed to do when you encountered bad guys? Too bad it hadn't worked. I should've called before taking the picture.

Bronwyn shook her head. "Don't get on the wrong side of Jay Thornton. Seriously." She leaned back and inspected Nico's face.

Like I needed a warning. I'd already seen what this Jay guy could do with his bare hands.

"He's not that bad," Nico said.

Bronwyn gave him a withering look. "You're an idiot."

There'd been a moment when Jay held me, his touch like fire, his eyes searing into me, and I didn't know whether to run or stay and be consumed. Maybe I was just as much of an idiot as Nico.

"He just kicked the crap out of you and 'he's not that bad?'" I asked.

Nico shrugged. "Okay, he's bad. But there are worse out there, believe me. And it's not like I didn't know this was coming."

I leaned back in the chair and began to rock. I felt like Mrs. Win, a lady back in Hillstone who I swear had always been old. No matter what time of day it was, you could find her on her porch in a rocking chair, rocking and watching. That's what I was doing now, rocking and watching a world I wasn't a part of. I wondered if Mrs. Win felt like a spectator too.

"I don't understand," I said. "Why the beatdown?"

"Money," Nico replied.

Bronwyn sighed. She left Nico clutching the ice pack and took the stained cloth to the sink. She rinsed it out, blood tinting the stream of water red.

"Nico borrowed some money from a loan shark," Bronwyn said, her back to us. "Jay's job is to make sure Nico pays him back."

I stared at Nico's purpling face. "By *beating you up*?"

"A reminder," Nico said, "of my deadline. Well, missed deadline."

Yeesh. And Jay had called himself *nice*. "Is this normal?"

"Borrowing from a loan shark or getting beat up by his enforcer?" Nico asked. He eyed me. "The butt kicking, yes, the borrowing... I don't know. Not for someone like you."

I didn't take offense to that. "Why did you do it?"

Bronwyn returned to Nico, taking up the task of holding the ice baggie. "He needed the money, *duh*." She seemed annoyed and I didn't know if it was with me, with Nico, with Jay Thornton, or the universe in general.

"I'm sorry, it's none of my business."

"It's not a big deal," Nico said. Bronwyn's lips tightened. "I lost my job. It was a little over a year ago now. Haven't found a decent one since. I already had a loan with the bank that I couldn't pay off. Lost my apartment. I needed the money and this was the only way I knew how."

"How are you going to pay him back if you can't pay back the bank?" I asked.

Bronwyn snorted. "Good question."

Nico put his head in his hands and Bronwyn rubbed his back.

"I don't get it," I said. "You can't pay so they, what, take the cost out of your flesh?" It seemed almost Biblical. "How will that help?"

"Motivation," Nico replied through his hands. "A warning when I miss a payment. A reminder that the interest has gone up."

"Can't they just tell you...with words...?" Borrowing money from a loan shark in the first place seemed like a dumb idea, but what did I know? I'd never been in dire financial straits before— who knew what I'd do if it came to that. But hurting someone to get the money back, how would that help? It was bad business in my opinion.

Not that anyone cared about my opinion.

"That Jay guy is a piece of work." I got up from the rocking chair and went to the window that looked down on the gym. It was dark; I could barely make out the ring, but it was easy to remember Jay Thornton's intense gaze holding me in place. How he'd laughed and the warmth of it had caught me completely off guard. I bristled. It annoyed me that I'd been afraid of such a low-class jerk.

"Jay is the one who set me up with the loan in the first place," Nico said. "He works downstairs."

I turned back to him. "I don't get it."

"I needed the money, I knew he worked for a loan shark, so I asked him to arrange a meeting with his boss. He didn't want to. He warned me not to do it but I was desperate. I knew what I was getting into before I signed the contract. I knew Jay would be the one. If you get on the wrong side of a loan shark, trust me, Jay is the guy you *want* to come knocking. The others aren't so nice."

I looked at Bronwyn but her face remained impassive.

"Those other guys with him?" Nico said. "Tweedledee and Tweedledum? They would have put me in a coma."

"So this loan shark sends Jay because he's...nicer?" I asked, incredulous.

Nico laughed. "He sends Jay because Jay gets the job done. Tweedledee and Tweedledum don't get the same results."

"I feel like I'm in the middle of a noir movie," I said. "Or something by Quentin Tarantino..." Fraze and I had been caught watching Pulp Fiction once and Dad had grounded us both for a month.

Bronwyn growled. "I hate to break it to you, but this is real life. And getting in the middle of Jay Thornton's business could have gotten you worse off than Nico."

An apology rose to my lips but I stopped. I'd been there to meet Nico like we planned. And I was only trying to stop him from getting hurt. Why should I apologize for that?

Nico lay back on the bed, groaning. "Sorry we didn't show you a better night."

I grabbed my bag. Clearly they wanted to be alone. "Don't apologize. It's not your fault." It was Jay Thornton and his crazy sweatsuit goons who had ruined this night, and my view of the whole world while they were at it. "It was nice to finally meet you, Nico."

Sort of. I mean, it was. Nico seemed like a good guy, and Bronwyn was clearly crazy about him. But if the whole meeting had gone down a little different, I wouldn't have complained.

I headed for the door. "I'll see you later," I said, though it didn't matter because Bronwyn had lain beside Nico on the bed and they were talking to each other in low voices.

Outside Nico's room was a giant open space. The wood floors were worn and lighter in big square spots, as if mats used to lay there. It must have been part of the gym once but the room was empty now. Such a waste of space.

I circled the floor, tiptoeing so I wouldn't bother Bronwyn and Nico. The space wasn't big, but it had plenty of room. If they put mirrors up on the far wall, the gym could have classes in there—

aerobics or kickboxing or something. Maybe they already used it for that.

As I headed down the stairs to the door, I noticed my phone sitting on the front desk. Jay hadn't kept it. I scrolled through the photos but the picture of him was gone, like it never happened.

If only I could forget so easily.

CHAPTER 10

MAGGIE

THE NEXT TIME I went to Nico's over at Eastside Boxing, I had backup, aka: Bronwyn. I didn't want to tackle that place alone— who knew what I'd find. Jay Thornton beating up another helpless person, or maybe him and his minions having a Battle Royale in the middle of the ring, a big melee of women and children getting pummeled because they couldn't afford bread.

My imagination had been getting the better of me ever since I'd witnessed Nico's beatdown, but now it was just getting silly. And given where I worked, it wouldn't be long before Christians and lions got thrown into the mix.

We pushed through the door and there he was, standing in the ring just like I remembered. Except instead of women and children and a giant brawl, there were two teenage boys wearing boxing shorts and gloves. They circled each other, and Jay circled with them. He towered over them, broad shoulders hunching and muscles bulging as he showed them how to jab.

"You're staring," Bronwyn said.

I followed her, skirting a group of students stretching on a black mat. "Am not."

Jay's eyes met mine. I *was* staring. And now, so was he. I

57

wrenched my gaze away but I could still feel his eyes on my back as I took to the stairs.

Bronwyn burst into Nico's apartment without bothering to knock. They greeted each other with a sloppy kiss that I tried to ignore. The room smelled of garlic and basil, despite the lack of a stove.

"I made lasagna," Nico said, cutting into a foil pan. It had been over a week since I'd seen him and his bruises had faded a little.

"Meaning he called Ricardo's down the road and *ordered* some," Bronwyn said. Nico handed me a plate with a small piece of lasagna oozing on it, a fork sticking out of the top.

"You can have seconds," he said. "I just don't like wasters."

"Yes, sir." I sat in the wooden rocking chair so Bronwyn and Nico could share the bed.

I took a bite, the sauce almost burning my tongue. The flavor was good, but it didn't lessen the sting of my third-wheel status. Bronwyn had invited me, and it didn't *seem* like they cared. Then again, maybe she felt sorry for me.

She'd biked past me as I was walking home after a drop-in class at Fluidity, my shoes leaving wet footprints behind because they'd somehow ended up outside in the sprinklers. I hadn't seen her until she circled back, screeching her bike to a halt inches in front of me.

"What now?" she'd asked.

"It was Mean Girls Day at dance class," I'd replied.

She offered to take me home on her bike but I doubted it could carry both of us. When I finally got home, she practically forced me to come to Nico's for dinner, after throwing my soaked flats in the trash.

Bronwyn was busy telling Nico the story while I ate the rest of my lasagna. "What was with the vendetta, anyway?" she asked.

"I accidentally bumped into one of them," I said.

They both stared at me. "That's it?" Nico asked.

"Well, they said some stuff, I said some stuff. Names were

called. It wasn't pretty." Not that I'd stop taking classes at Fluidity. Robbie was an incredible teacher—one of the best I'd ever had. I'd spend every day there if I could afford it. I thought about taking fewer shifts at the diner, but I needed the money. And after hearing about Nico and the loan shark, I didn't ever want to be without some kind of cash flow.

"Point me to this dance studio," Bronwyn said. "I'll wait outside with my bike and run over their feet when they come out."

I laughed. "You don't know what they look like."

She shrugged as she took a second helping from the pan. "I'll just do it to every female who goes there. I'm sure I'll nail the right ones eventually."

"Sounds like a full-time job," Nico said. He stood over the lasagna, as if debating on seconds. He sighed and took his plate to the sink. "If you got paid running over ballerina's toes, I'd be all for it."

"Ask Jay Thornton's boss," I said. "He might be in the market for that kind of thing."

Nico washed our plates then tossed us some sodas from the mini-fridge. "You don't want to work for that guy, trust me." He sank back on the bed, putting his head in Bronwyn's lap, forcing her to lift her plate. "If he was a bit nicer, I probably *would* ask him for a job."

"What do you do now?" I asked.

Nico groaned.

"Sore subject," Bronwyn muttered.

"Sorry," I said.

"I hold the very dignified position of decontaminating this fine establishment and maintaining its level of hygiene to state industry standards."

"Like a janitor?"

Bronwyn shot me a look.

"Not *like* a janitor. A janitor," Nico said.

It could've been worse. At least he had a job. Cleaning the bathrooms at the diner wasn't much better.

"Nico's tried to get other managing jobs, but he can't," Bronwyn said.

I frowned. "Can't?"

"No one will hire me," Nico replied.

Bronwyn stroked his hair. "I'm pretty sure the loan shark had something to do with that."

Now that *really* made no sense. How did he expect to get the money back off a janitor's salary? Maybe he liked having people afraid of him?

Nico's face had gone red.

"If only you could—"

Nico spoke over Bronwyn. "I've just had a streak of bad luck for the past, oh, two years. Not counting you." He looked up at her, tickling underneath her chin. She slapped his fingers away. "Next time you bring home a stray, pick a rich one."

He was talking about me. I pulled my feet up on the chair. I wished I was rich, someone with a family inheritance, or maybe a lottery winner. Then I could help Nico out. And Frasier, and my parents...

"She wasn't a stray," Bronwyn said, as if I wasn't in the room. "She was a favor."

"Nice." I was getting used to Bronwyn's blunt way of saying, well, everything.

Nico swiveled his head to look at me. "Then I guess you're owed one in return, right?"

"Next time I see Frasier Hale," Bronwyn said, "I'll be sure to mention it."

"Next time you see Frasier Hale," I said, "be sure to mention it fast, or it'll be too late." If he did come around, he wouldn't stay long. He never did.

Nico pushed himself off the bed. "Forget all this nonsense. Let's do something where I can actually have a chance of improving my situation."

Bronwyn rubbed her hands together. "Ooh, yes. I'm sick of getting whooped by you every time. Maybe with Maggie, I'll actually have a chance."

"In what world could you ever beat me?" Nico said, going to one of his many shelves. I had no clue what they were talking about.

It became clear when Nico turned to me with two game boxes in his hand. It went from clear back to unclear in a matter of moments as Nico and Bronwyn tried to explain *Settlers of Catan* to me. The instructions sounded like a foreign language, and I was still the third wheel, but I was glad to be there. I started having fun, and for a while I forgot to be lonely.

CHAPTER 11

JAY

EVERYONE HAD GONE home for the night, but Maggie was still upstairs. When she'd walked in, I'd felt her judgmental stare burning into me. I'd stared back, first to make her keep her distance, and then because I just couldn't help it.

The gym was quiet. I straightened the mats, picked up items left behind by forgetful kids and tossed them into the lost and found. The sound of laughter echoed above me, and I suppressed a flash of jealousy. Those weren't my friends, and I didn't want them to be. Maggie was just some girl, like any other girl. Except I couldn't get this one out of my head. Nobody had ever stood up to me before. Well, not without some kind of weapon anyway.

I flicked off the lights and headed out, locking up behind me.

My apartment was even emptier than the gym. There was no ghost of laughter, no Maggie, close but not close enough. The memory of her that night, looking at me, haughty and unafraid, was like an itch I couldn't scratch.

I jumped straight into the shower. The water pounded on my body, the heat easing the tension that always lingered after a workout.

When I got out, I made myself a sandwich, then cleaned up

the mess. The apartment was spotless. Bare. I didn't know how to decorate and I didn't have photographs. It was home, but it never felt like home. Probably because it didn't belong to me. It was just a place. The apartment and everything in it belonged to Simon. Only the clothes were mine, my endless pairs of sneakers that I couldn't throw away even when they wore out, my first pair of boxing gloves, and one faded photograph of my old foster family, tucked inside a drawer. Those were the only things that belonged to me and the only things that made this place feel human.

I grabbed my keys and left, hoping a drive would clear my head. But I got no satisfaction out of my truck. That belonged to Simon, too. Even the money he gave me was more like a father doling out allowance rather than an employer paying his employee. This was why I couldn't get free of him. Because you can't be free of family.

Bass pumped from a nearby car. The lights of the strip glowed bright, enticing people to come closer, but all I could think about was Simon and Maggie. If I ever wanted a girl like that in my life, I had to live right. I doubt she'd understand doing dirty work for a cop, no matter the results. She definitely didn't understand lending. Maybe I could ask Simon. Ask him to quit. It's not like he'd be cut out of my life completely, just no more enforcing. No more tampering. No more errand boy.

I snorted. I'd ask, but I knew what the answer would be. Simon hated my job at the gym, he'd never understand my desire to own it. But I'd ask anyway. There was always a possibility that he valued our relationship more than my ability to get things done.

Maggie's face flashed through my head again. I made a left and headed to The Wall, a bar near Pearl of China. I needed a drink.

"Jay, baby," Annie said as soon as I came in. "It's good to see you." She leaned over the bar and I gave her a peck on the lips. "The usual?"

I nodded and she handed me a shot of whiskey which I

downed in one gulp. The burn going down my throat didn't relax me. If anything, I felt even more antsy.

With her hands braced on the bar, Annie stared at me. Her tank top was tight, drawing eyes to the roundness of her chest. Her mascara had started to run from the heat, black pooling under her eyes, but she probably didn't know. "My shift is over in an hour if you want to hang around?"

The thing I had always liked about Annie was that she didn't ask questions. She didn't pester me with, *are you okay*, or, *tell me what you're thinking*. She just *was*, and I just *was* when we were together. She was a distraction, but tonight I didn't want it. Didn't want her.

When I didn't answer, she turned away, but not before I saw the hurt flash over her face. She ignored me for a while, flirting with a guy a few stools away. I didn't even care. That's how I knew Maggie had gotten to me, more than I wanted to admit.

Annie let out a throaty laugh. The guy she was talking to, he looked familiar. I couldn't place him, but tension rolled down my back. Something felt wrong...

"Want another?" Annie asked. I blinked. I hadn't noticed her return. Her fingers trailed over her neck and into the hollow of her throat. She bit her lip.

"I'd better not." The antsiness hadn't gone away. If anything, it was worse. There was something about that guy. Something...

He was looking at me. "You okay?" he asked.

I'd been staring like a creep. "Yeah, fine."

Annie's eyes flicked from me back to him.

"Can I buy you another?"

This guy had gotten the wrong impression. I turned to tell him no, when it hit me. It was the cop who'd pulled me over, asked about Simon. It couldn't be a coincidence. I tensed for a fight. "What do you want?"

Simon would tell me to get up and leave, stay under the radar, don't cause a scene. But right then I didn't care what Simon wanted.

"Excuse me?" the guy said.

I wasn't in the mood for games. "You pulled me over last week. Now you're here. What do you want from me?"

He left his seat and took the one next to me. "A little privacy, ma'am, if that's okay."

Annie's tongue pushed against her lips. She hated being called ma'am. But she turned away without a word.

The guy gave me a shrewd look. He was old, his hair greying, deep lines etching his face. Probably around Simon's age, maybe older.

"You don't waste time," he said. "I appreciate that." I waited. "Fine. I'll give it to you straight. My name is Hopkins. Internal Affairs. I'm looking into something that Simon Ting may be involved with. I know you two are close."

"And how do you know that?"

"What exactly is your relationship with Officer Ting?"

"Go ask him."

"Don't play games with me."

He didn't answer my question, so I sure as hell wasn't going to answer any of his. He took one last pull from his glass, the ice tinkling as he set it down.

"I can help you, you know. You do something for me, I do something for you."

"Who says I need anything?"

He studied me. "Here's my card, in case you change your mind." He put it on the counter and tapped it twice, but I didn't pick it up and he finally left me alone.

I pushed away from the stool. The bar had lost its appeal. I didn't want to go home to my bare apartment. Usually I'd go back to the gym and let it out on a punching bag, but with Maggie there, the place felt tainted. I could've gone to Pearl of China but I didn't want to see Simon either. Like he'd somehow know a cop had cornered me, asking questions.

I had nowhere to go and no one to see and I was getting on my own nerves. If I couldn't fight it out, I had to find another way. I drove back home.

Hopkins, Simon, Maggie—they were all problems for another day. I had a stack of books on my end table: *The Small Business Bible, 50 Tips for Marketing Your Business, Accounting for Dummies...* I hated them all but I needed the knowledge they held in their pages of tiny, cramped words. I couldn't buy the gym from Conall McCrary until I knew what I was doing.

I sat in bed and grabbed the top book in the pile, opening to the folded-down page. My fists would only get me so far in life. It would be easy to keep relying on them, but I had to start using my brains, too, or I'd never be anything more than a hired thug.

CHAPTER 12

MAGGIE

My feet ached in my brand-new shoes. Bronwyn had thrown out my wet pair, which had been literally falling apart. I couldn't afford anything expensive so I'd had to settle for ten-dollar flats from Walmart.

Stupid cheap shoes. Blisters had formed on both heels and the bottoms of my feet were on fire from standing all day. My shift at the diner began at eleven in the morning. It was now almost six and I still had two hours left to go.

After dropping off an all-day breakfast order to a table of women in their thirties who were too old to be giggling the way they were, I leaned on the counter and raised a foot. The pressure eased a little but only increased on the other. I switched them out, wishing I could take off my shoes and rub, but I wouldn't touch my feet in the middle of a shift. Gross.

"You've got another table," Emme, another waitress, said as she passed by with a tray of stew and hot buns.

One thing I'd learned about *Holy Diner!*: despite the blasphemous menu names, the cook who sang Bollywood songs, and my boss Craig's wife who came to yell at him every Tuesday at 4:45, the food was actually not that bad.

My mouth watered. I hadn't eaten since breakfast. But food, and my feet, would have to wait. I turned to my new table and froze.

Jay Thornton had his hands folded over the table, his eyes on me.

I grabbed Emme's sleeve as she walked by. "Is that my table?" I hissed.

"The one with that hot dark-haired guy?" she asked with a grin. "Yep, he's all yours, you lucky girl."

"Are you being for real?" I asked but she only winked and walked away. I grabbed a menu, then paused when a uniformed policeman took a seat across from Jay. They started talking, and I wasn't sure if I should interrupt. It seemed friendly enough—not like Jay was getting arrested for assault or battery or anything like that. With a deep breath, I grabbed another menu and headed over.

"Welcome to *Holy Diner!*" I said, placing the menus on the table and avoiding Jay's eyes. "I'm Maggie, and I'll be your server. Can I start you off with anything to drink?"

I pulled my little notebook and pencil from my pocket and stared hard at it.

"Coffee, black," the policeman said, sounding bored. He had Asian features, but barely a trace of an accent.

It was silent. I waited, my eyes boring into the tiny blue lines of my notebook. Jay made no sound.

I couldn't take it any longer. I looked at him.

The corners of Jay's mouth curled. "Maggie." He said my name like he'd won something. My lips tightened. "I'll have a Corona."

I jotted it down.

"No," the policeman said.

I paused.

"No alcohol."

I glanced at Jay. He seemed unfazed that a policeman was telling him what to drink. "Make it a Coke," he said.

"I'll be back in a moment to take your order."

When I returned, Jay and the policeman were deep in conversation. Or rather, the cop was talking, Jay was listening.

"—unacceptable. I won't allow him to run free, doing whatever he likes, especially when he hasn't held up his end. Handle it. I know you can be persuasive."

My hands shook a little as I set the cup of coffee down. Some of it sloshed over the side.

"Sorry." I grabbed a napkin from my pocket to wipe up the mess, but my hand hit the coffee mug and it went flying off the table, showering the floor with black coffee. The mug shattered on the tile.

"Hail, Mary!" the entire staff shouted.

My face was on fire. When I'd learned about *Holy Diner!*'s dish-breaking ritual, I swore I would never be clumsy. But this man, this *policeman*, had just told Jay to *"handle it."* To be persuasive.

He couldn't be his boss, the loan shark, could he? Maybe Jay owed him something. Like an informant—trading information for freedom from jail.

"I'm so sorry," I mumbled. "I'll get you another one right away." I cleaned up the mess on the floor, carefully picking up the broken shards before Sanjay came with his mop. Jay watched me.

I returned with a fresh cup, making sure to keep my hands as still as possible. My eyes trained on the uniform. Officer Ting, the name badge said.

"I'm sorry about the delay. Can I take your order?"

Officer Ting perused the menu. He looked to be in his late fifties, with age spots on his hands and wrinkles around his eyes. Aside from his dark hair, he was the total opposite of Jay. His face was soft, his nose round, his lips fuller than a man's should be. Jay was all angles—sharp nose and wide forehead and jaw carved from granite.

"I'll have the ten-ounce Adam's Ribeye, medium rare."

It took him another minute to pick a couple of sides and then it was Jay's turn.

"I'll have the Three Wise Men platter," he said. He handed me both menus, and his fingers brushed mine.

I turned to leave when I felt a yank on my skirt. Officer Ting had grabbed the hem, pulling me toward him. "*Medium* rare. Don't make a mistake."

My heart pounded. His knuckles dug into my thigh. Words wouldn't form in my mouth. Finally, he let me go, giving my butt a shove as he did.

I seriously considered spitting on Officer Ting's *medium* rare steak, policeman or not. No one in Hillstone had ever touched me on the bum before, not even the rednecks who'd come every summer for the rodeo. Did he think because he was a cop, that he could get away with it?

I pasted on a fake smile each time I returned to their table—first to deliver the food, then to top off drinks, ask if they wanted dessert, bring their dessert, bring the bill, and finally to bring the machine so Officer Ting could pay. Somehow, I managed to be polite.

Thankful when they'd finally finished, and wishing they'd never return, I gathered up my tip. There was a pile of change— pennies and nickels and dimes, not even a quarter in the bunch, strewn over the middle of the table. It came out to seventy-two cents. It figured. I picked up their used napkins.

Hiding under Jay's was two twenty-dollar bills.

I stared at it. Forty bucks was way too big a tip for their meal. I didn't want to owe Jay Thornton anything. Maybe he was showing off. Or maybe he actually felt bad for Officer Ting's behavior. I snorted.

I didn't trust the money, but I couldn't say no to forty bucks, either—that was two classes at Fluidity. I tucked the twenties into my scripture apron then gathered up Ting's plate of half-eaten Eden's apple pie and Jay's ice cream bowl. Leftover chocolate fudge sauce pooled in the bottom; it looked good enough to lick off.

"Maggie."

I groaned inwardly. Couldn't Jay just leave me alone? I was tired. Tired of working, of being at the diner, of making nice with Jay Thornton and his slimy policeman friend.

I turned but didn't stop cleaning off his table. Maybe he wanted change for his tip. He'd have to speak up because I sure wasn't going to offer it.

"I want to apologize." Jay stuffed his hands in his pockets. He looked genuinely sorry. I didn't buy it.

"For Si—my friend. He can be...abrupt sometimes."

I balanced the tray of dishes on one shoulder. "I've seen worse." Though not from a lawman.

I headed for the kitchen to unload my dirty dishes for Sanjay, the seventeen-year-old dishwasher.

"Thanks, Maggie," Sanjay said, then his eyes widened.

Even without looking, I knew. Jay Thornton had followed me into the kitchen. I sighed and turned around. "Do you need something else?"

"No."

I started past him but he grabbed my arm. Gently, but I gave his hand a pointed look and he let go.

"Are you okay?" he asked.

I wanted to laugh. Behind Jay, Badri—Sanjay's father—launched into another Bollywood song. Emme passed us, almost bumping Jay with her tray. Another cook had his head bent to his work, chopping onions. The kitchen was hot and noisy and Jay was making it fifty times more unbearable.

I planted my hands on my hips and looked Jay full in the face like a dare. "Perfectly fine."

He smiled and it transformed his entire face. Heat rose up my neck. "Good. I just wanted to make sure—"

"Las Vegas may be a disgusting, dirty place, but I can handle

71

myself." I stalked away. Jay probably regretted his forty-dollar tip now.

Or not, since he followed me out of the kitchen and stepped in front of me. "Vegas isn't so bad, you know."

"Really?" I peered over his shoulder at the couple who'd taken over Jay's table. "That's great. You should add that to the tourism brochures. Can I get back to work now?"

He made an exaggerated sweeping motion, allowing me to pass.

"I'll prove it to you," he said.

I didn't want to turn around. I really didn't.

I turned around. "Prove what?"

He stopped next to my shoulder. His lips lowered to my ear. "How great Vegas can be." His breath hit my skin and I shivered.

"Not interested," I said, my voice shaking for some reason.

He smirked. "We'll see."

CHAPTER 13

MAGGIE

I THOUGHT Las Vegas was one of the ugliest places I'd ever seen. Then I found Sunset Park. It had green grass and trees and even a lake with ducks. The colors were bright, popping out of the brown and gray like a rainbow. It reminded me of home and I was drawn to it like an artist to a beautiful painting, wanting and needing to suck the color from the scene into me.

Bronwyn didn't get how I could sit in Sunset Park for longer than five minutes. She was always moving, always biking, always going somewhere. She'd left Hillstone behind long ago. I hadn't quite managed yet.

"I've gotta get this package over to the medical district," Bronwyn said, getting up from the bench and tossing her coffee cup in the trash. She gave Nico a quick peck. "See you later, babe."

As Bronwyn pedaled away, I glanced at Nico. When I told them I'd found something amazing, they both agreed to meet me. They were less than impressed that my definition of amazing was green grass and no litter.

"Jay came into the diner yesterday," I said. "Him and a policeman. Officer Ting. I waited on them."

A wary expression crossed his still-healing face. "They were there together?"

"Yeah. Why?"

"No reason." Nico spoke slowly, avoiding eye contact.

I angled toward him. "I'm surprised Jay has such a law-upholding friend."

Nico scuffed at the grass under his feet.

"What with his line of work and all."

Nico stared straight ahead. "No comment."

Which said everything. I gaped. "But he's a—"

"Sure is."

I leaned back against the bench. Officer Ting *was* the loan shark. But how could that be? Did the other officers know? And why live that kind of double life—enforcing the law on one side, breaking it on the other?

"So you served them some food," Nico said. "Was it everything you dreamed it would be?"

As if I'd dream of Jay. "Officer Ting was...rude."

"I only met him the one time," Nico said. He swung an arm over the back of the bench. "Thought I was gonna wet myself."

"No kidding." A bird circled overhead and I prayed it wouldn't poop on me. I hadn't been afraid of Officer Ting at the diner—more like angry. But knowing who he was and what he could do scared me. "What if you don't pay him? What will he do? What will happen to you?" Would it be like the movies? Would Ting kill Nico? Dump him in the desert outside the city like on CSI? Or was I just being overdramatic?

He smiled, a thin thing. "I'll be fine. He won't get paid if I'm dead."

Would a police officer go that far? Who was I kidding—he was dirty. He'd already crossed that line. Morality wasn't a factor now, assuming he'd had any in the first place.

"I'm just..." I hesitated, knowing this would sound stupid. I barely knew Nico after all. "I'm scared for you."

Nico's smile went from thin to genuine. "Aw, that's sweet." He patted my head like I was twelve. "How about you loan me a few grand? Then you won't have to be scared anymore."

"If only I had that kind of money."

"Then I guess I'll have to go with plan B," Nico said.

"What's plan B?"

He shook his head. "No idea."

A fter Nico left the park, I grabbed a book from my purse and started reading. My phone dinged with an email. I assumed it was from Fraze, I hadn't heard from him in a while, though that wasn't unusual. Looking at my phone, I was surprised to find an email from Hank.

To: Margaret Hale, maggie-hale@mymail.com

From: Hank Markham, hlmcowboy@mymail.com

It's been over a month since you walked away from me. I can't stop thinking about it. Where we went wrong. Where I went wrong.

I shouldn't have proposed so soon. I know that now, Maggie. You aren't ready yet. You need to pursue your dreams. I get that. I do.

But why can't you pursue them here in Hillstone? You could teach at the studio. I even talked to Miss Miriam about it. Please, Mags. I miss you so much. Please come home. For me. For your parents. Come home so we can go back to the way things were. There's a hole in my life now where you used to be, and I can't fill it without you.

    I love you so much.
    Yours, Hank

I stared at the email. Then read it again. Then tried really hard not to chuck my phone in the lake.

Hank wasn't the one for me. He didn't get me. And he never would if he thought I could somehow pursue my dreams in Hillstone.

Yet I still felt a pull. A pull to return to what I knew. To people who loved me. I had Bronwyn and Nico now, but I still felt like a trespasser in their lives. I was working at a diner and taking dance classes, but really, life wasn't any better and way scarier here.

I still felt a pull to Hank, too. A yearning to be back in someone's arms. To feel lips on my own. To have someone tell me that everything would be okay.

The pull was tough to ignore. Which is why I let out a string of curses, saying all the words I hadn't been allowed to say growing up just so I wouldn't hear the little voice in my head saying, *just give up, you know you want to.*

I did kind of want to. But I didn't. But I did. No, didn't.

Back in Hillstone, after I'd graduated high school, my life had been frozen. Here in Vegas, I had a chance for more, but so far, I wasn't sure I liked where it was going.

    To: Hank Markham, hlmcowboy@mymail.com

    From: Margaret Hale, maggie-hale@mymail.com

Thank you for what you said, but I can't come home, Hank. I just can't. I'm sorry.

You'll be fine, I'm sure of it. I'm not who you thought I was. Heck, I'm not who I thought I was. You deserve someone who wants to live their life in Hillstone. Until then, know that I never wanted to hurt you and I'm sorry every day that I did. I know that doesn't make it any better, but I do want you to be happy. One day, sooner than you think, you will be.

Maggie

I paced the floor outside Nico's apartment, almost on the balls of my feet. From below, the voices of students in training created a low buzz, though not loud enough to drown out Bronwyn's screaming or the sound of breaking glass, even behind the closed door.

"Are you *trying* to make me walk away?" Bronwyn shrieked. "Do you want to be alone, is that it?"

Something smashed against the wall and I flinched. I should have left. Bronwyn and Nico were in the middle of an epic fight. But I couldn't go. Bronwyn had been there for me when I was at my lowest, I could be there for her, too. If she wanted me.

I'd stopped pacing and my feet were tapping, almost of their own volition. I took tap for a couple of years when I was younger but hadn't kept with it. I'd always preferred whole body movements versus crazy feet. But I would still find myself shuffle-ball-changing in random places.

"It was *one* drink," Nico shouted back. "Stop being such a—"

"One drink? *One drink*!" Another smash. "I'm not an idiot!"

"Bron—"

77

I closed my eyes. My feet moved through the audition piece I danced for EDT and soon I was doing it full out. The empty room outside Nico's apartment was just big enough and I used every inch of space. I moved to the music in my head, punctuated by Bronwyn's screams as if they were a drum beat.

"I'm so done with this!" she shouted as I pirouetted into a developé. The door slammed. My arms lowered and my feet stilled.

Bronwyn's eyes met mine. Her face was streaked with tears. "What are *you* still doing here?" she snapped.

I wilted. "I was... Are you okay?"

"Yeah. Peachy." She was down the stairs before I could respond.

I sighed. She didn't need me after all. I grabbed my purse and went to Nico's door. I knocked hesitantly.

"Bron?" Nico's face was so full of hope when he opened the door, I hated to be the one to make it disappear.

"Sorry. I just wanted to make sure you're okay." Behind him, broken glass littered the floor and spots of his brick walls were stained wet.

Nico scrubbed his black hair. He gave me a flat look. "Oh, I'm fine. Just redecorating."

"Right, sorry." I stepped back. "Well, if you need anything..."

His eyes dropped to the ground. "How about a broom?"

"Aren't you a janitor?" It was out before I realized how insensitive that sounded.

He let out a short laugh. "Right. Thanks for reminding me."

I shouldered my purse. "I'll go. Call me if you need anything." I started down the stairs.

"Hey," he said and I turned. "Tell Bron I'm sorry."

I nodded. Not that Bronwyn would listen to me. She was stubborn. If she was done with Nico, nothing would change her mind. Nor was I sure that I *should* say anything. I liked Nico, but I wasn't sure he was the best boyfriend.

I stuck to the edge of the gym so as not to get in the way of the class. About twenty boys and girls, ranging from maybe five to eight, were sparring with each other on the mats. I couldn't see their faces through their padded headgear, but their big red and black gloves didn't stop moving, punching and jabbing and swinging.

I stopped to watch for a minute, smiling at how cute they looked trying to act like tough little fighters.

"And *time!*" the teacher called and I stiffened. "Switch partners."

I hadn't seen Jay Thornton when I first came into the gym. Maybe I wasn't paying attention. But he was there now, wearing shorts that were too short for a man and a t-shirt that strained across his chest. He was a mix of intimidating and ridiculous in his undersized clothes and shoulders as broad as the river that ran behind my house back in Hillstone.

Jay lifted a girl's arms, showed her how to jab. Her head shook, like she was prepping herself, and then her arm shot out, hitting her partner's glove so hard the other kid stumbled back. Jay smiled and backed off. The girl bounced on her toes and then went at it again, punching right and left and then giving her partner a turn. I watched the exchange go on several times back and forth.

"Are you interested in taking classes?"

I jumped. When had Jay gotten so close?

"No, thanks," I said, keeping my eyes on the kids to avoid looking at him.

"Well, you always seem to be here, I just assumed..."

"Not my kind of thing," I said, harsher than I meant. My eyes travelled from Jay's chest to the tanned skin of his neck, to his curved lips, and finally to his eyes.

He raised an eyebrow. "You're against learning how to protect yourself?"

"Do I need to protect myself?"

He shrugged. "It's a good skill to have."

"Yeah, around here..."

"Not just here, anywhere."

A weird sound came out of my throat. "Where I'm from, a girl doesn't worry about knowing how to punch a guy's lights out, or accidentally wandering into a scene from *Fight Club*."

"Sounds boring."

My lips tightened. "Try safe. Or do you prefer a world where you're always looking over your shoulder?"

Jay looked at his students. His shoulder brushed mine, a dark heat, and I inched away. "You haven't lived here long, have you?"

"No."

"If you're so worried about your safety, why did you move to Vegas in the first place?"

I'd asked myself that more times than I could count. But I would never admit that Vegas wasn't everything I'd imagined it would be, especially not to Jay Thornton. He'd just laugh. It was mostly because of him I was worried about my safety, anyway. Him and his boss. It wasn't that he'd hurt me, necessarily, more that the people here weren't what I was used to.

I looked at him. He looked at me. Chills and heat erupted over my body, like the beginnings of the flu.

His head tilted. "What are you doing here, Maggie?"

I swallowed. "Leaving," I said. "That's what I'm doing." And I did just that.

CHAPTER 14

MAGGIE

BRONWYN WAS WATCHING SIMPSONS RERUNS; two empty bowls lay beside her and small popcorn bits dusted her black shirt. She didn't laugh at the jokes, just stared blankly at the TV like a hospital patient.

I moved one of the bowls, nothing left inside but the greasy kernel duds, and sat beside her. For a while, we did nothing but watch. Episode after episode of Bart getting into trouble and Homer doing stupid things. Midway through the fourth, Bronwyn finally grabbed the remote and turned off the TV.

I waited. Asking her if she was okay was not only a dumb question, but probably a bad idea. If Bronwyn wanted to talk to me, she would.

She wiped the crumbs off her shirt and sighed. "Sorry I didn't save you any."

It took me a second to realize she meant the popcorn.

"I don't like popcorn much anyway." I shifted on the couch so I could look at her.

"What planet are you from? I couldn't live without popcorn."

I shrugged. "It's the butter—grosses me out. And without it, popcorn is tasteless."

"Weirdo," she muttered.

I waited, my foot swinging up and down.

"I know what you're doing," Bronwyn said after a few minutes.

"What's that?"

"The whole patience thing."

"Do you *want* me to bug you?"

Her eyes lowered. I uncrossed my legs and recrossed them.

"He's had it rough," she finally said without looking at me. "When we first met, he wasn't like this. I mean, he's not *like* anything. He drinks more than he used to."

I'd thought the drink conversation had to do with another girl, but it was the drink itself that was the problem.

"I'm so sick of it," Bronwyn said. "I don't want to deal with this, you know?"

Then why would she keep going back to him? I didn't ask. She didn't say.

She ran a hand over her short hair. "But every time, I wonder, why? Why does he get passed out drunk? I know his life sucks right now, but can't he deal without forgetting his own name? Forgetting me?"

I didn't know what to say, didn't have any experience with this kind of problem. I wasn't qualified to give advice. "What will you do?"

"What I always do. Go back to him. He needs me. And I love him." Her eyes met mine. "What else is there?"

I looked away. What else? Everything. Or maybe nothing. I didn't know.

W e were at a little Italian restaurant called La-something-Italia. It had checked tablecloths and painted walls and it smelled like carb heaven. Brownyn had scarfed down almost the whole plate of garlic bread, the grease making her fingertips shiny.

"This is so good," she said, grinning at Nico. He grabbed one of her fingers and stuck it in his mouth, licking off the flavor. I looked away. Clearly, Bronwyn had forgiven Nico and taken him back, just like she'd said she would. I mean, the finger sucking was a dead giveaway.

"Did you want some?"

I realized Bronwyn was talking to me when she waved the empty bread bowl in front of my face.

"No, that's okay." Even though I loved garlic bread, I had to treat carbs like the eighth deadly sin. I couldn't let one ounce of fat chunk up my body. If I put on weight, Essence wouldn't even look at me come spring.

In fact, the entire menu of La-something-Italia wasn't good for my figure. But Bronwyn had practically dragged me out of the apartment by my hair, demanding I do something other than dance classes and diner shifts. I was starting to regret it as Nico and Bronwyn began to make out in front of me.

So they were *that* couple. The kind who break up and make up as regularly as a full moon. Misty/Melissa had been like that during high school with her boyfriend, Paco, all through junior year. They'd fight. Break up. Then be going at it in the janitor's closet the next day. Then fight. Then break up. And on and on.

Not that I could compare Bronwyn and Nico to that. Their problems were way more serious than any petty high school drama.

"I'm gonna go," I said, sliding my chair back.

Bronwyn came up for air. "Can't handle our sexy?"

"I don't want to see your sexy," I replied. "It's ruining my appetite."

She laughed.

"We'll save it for later then," Nico said. His lips were covered in Bronwyn's red lipstick.

"Thanks for making such a huge sacrifice."

He cupped the back of Bronwyn's neck. "You have no idea."

"Ew." I looked down at the menu. Even though I was seriously craving some arrabiatta, I'd have to go with soup and salad.

The waitress came, topping off our drinks and refilling the bread bowl. After we ordered, Bronwyn attacked the garlic bread again.

"What?" she asked, her mouth full. "I burned a lot of calories today. Besides, if you're not having any…"

"Don't like garlic bread?" Nico asked.

"Love it. Can't eat it."

"Why not?"

"She's starving herself for her art," Bronwyn answered.

"I am not." I'd never starved myself before but there was nothing wrong with being careful.

"If you start puking in the bathroom, this friendship is over," she said.

"Nice to know you're supportive."

Nico leaned toward me and lowered his voice. "You're not puking up your food, are you?"

"No!" I swatted at him, but he was too far away to reach. "I'm limiting my carb intake. It's the eleventh commandment: *thou shalt not carb.*"

"I can't imagine Reverend Hale preaching *that* from the pulpit." Bronwyn pushed the bread away.

Even though she had a funny way of showing it, Bronwyn did have my back. It was nice to know that someone here in Vegas cared. Two someones, since she and Nico were a package deal.

"How are your classes coming, anyway?" she asked. "Any more mean girl incidents?"

I shook my head. "No, I…" My voice trailed off.

Jay Thornton had entered the restaurant with two men. One was either Tweedledee or Tweedledum, I wasn't sure which. The other was Officer Ting, only without the uniform. Instead, he wore an expensive suit, a flashy red tie, and a dangerous expression. At the diner, I'd seen one side of this man, the police officer side. Now, I was afraid I was about to see the other. The ugly one.

Jay's eyes went from Nico, to Bronwyn, to me, in a matter of seconds. When he saw me, his jaw clenched.

Ting didn't waste any time. He came toward us.

CHAPTER 15

JAY

SIMON KNEW I didn't want to press Nico for the money but he ordered me to anyway. He was disappointed with everything I'd done lately. He made either Alonso or Alfonso tail me wherever I went, as if he didn't trust me anymore. It wasn't a good time to ask him to quit. Or maybe it was exactly the right time. Either way, I hadn't much choice but to follow him to the restaurant where he knew Nico would be that night, Alfonso in tow.

Alonso had wanted to come, but Alfonso was better for this job. Alfonso spoke less, but his gargantuan size was enough to intimidate anyone. Alonso—which wasn't his real name but it had stuck the first time Simon had screwed it up—was more about the physical show, and intimidation with weapons. But we were in a restaurant, not the best place for Alonso's brand of coercion.

When we walked in, I immediately tensed. Maggie was there, all done up for a night out and hot as hell. Why did she have to be there? She was going to mess up my whole night.

Simon snapped his fingers and a waitress came scurrying up. "Chair," he said. She jumped to his bidding, pulling an empty chair from a nearby table and dragging it over. She probably sensed danger.

The girlfriend, Bronwyn, glared daggers at me, her hand absently stroking Nico's arm. She might wear the pants in their relationship, but her glare was wasted on me.

Simon put the chair between Nico and Maggie and sat down. He didn't even glance at Maggie. Hopefully he didn't recognize her from the diner. Better she stayed off his radar. I would've asked her to leave if it wouldn't have drawn attention.

I stood behind Simon, close to Maggie. Alfonso stood on his right. Bodyguards, not like he needed them in a place like this, but you could never be too careful. Plus, it added to the presence, and the pressure.

Simon pulled a small leather journal from his suit pocket. He flipped through it. "Nico Higgins." He looked up from the book at Nico. "Your contract is overdue."

Nico blanched. Bronwyn squeezed his hand.

"You owe me thirteen. You've had more than enough time to pay your debt."

Maggie twitched. Her mouth had opened a little. Was she surprised at the amount? Thirteen grand was pretty low compared to most. Not something that usually warranted a face-to-face with Simon.

"I paid you a grand a couple of days ago," Nico said.

"It's not that grand I'm worried about. It's the rest. You're proving to be a bad risk for me, Nico. You pay a bit here and there, build up more interest, but never honor your commitment."

The restaurant moved around us while I tried to focus. I saw Maggie cross her legs, the hem of her dress rising on her thigh. The waitress sidled in with the food, setting plates and bowls on the table. No one touched them.

"I waste more time on you than anyone else on the Strip," Simon continued. "And that's bad for business. It's got others thinking they can slack off as long as they don't mind taking a few punches. I want them to learn the value of honoring one's debts, or what happens if you don't, and play me for a chump. That starts with you, one way or the other."

"I can't pay you the whole amount," Nico said. "I don't have the money."

Simon tensed. Nico was pushing it, he didn't realize. He could talk to me like that, but not Simon. "But you can enjoy a fancy night out, is that it? You signed a contract. Do you need a reminder of the terms?"

Maggie's eyes were on me, but I stared at the far wall. I was angry at myself for being here, still involved in this crap, but even angrier at Maggie for judging me. I knew she was, I could practically smell it on her.

"You don't honor our contract, I call in the full amount." Simon stretched his arms across the back of Maggie's chair, and Nico's. Maggie moved slightly so that he wasn't touching her.

Simon's eyes raked over her, then Bronwyn. "Two very pretty girls."

I stiffened.

"Not hard to tell which one is yours."

Alfonso moved behind Bronwyn. He rested his hands on her shoulders. Lightly, but the threat was clear.

"I doubt you need this kind of motivation," Simon said. "Do you?"

"Don't touch her," Nico said. His voice shook. He gripped the edge of the table.

Simon rubbed the back of Nico's head like he was scratching a dog. "Pain is a useful tool. People don't like to get hurt, but survival instinct kicks in and people can live through amazing things. They think they've become invincible."

Nico was visibly trembling now, crumbling like a day-old doughnut.

"Are you invincible, Nico?" Simon let go of Nico's head. "How about her?"

Bronwyn bristled but said nothing. Didn't even move. She hadn't let go of Nico's hand.

"I don't have the money," Nico said. "I need more time. Please."

And there it was. I wanted to close my eyes and pretend I was anywhere else but there, because I knew what was coming next.

Simon leaned back in the chair and crossed his legs. "Your time is up." He was the picture of a businessman slogging through a boring meeting. He wasn't there for Nico, he was there for me—testing me.

"Jason," he said. Using the name I hated, it was an order.

I didn't want to do this, not here, not anywhere, not anymore. But I couldn't say no. It wasn't that I was spineless, or afraid of what might happen to me. The loyalty I felt to Simon couldn't be shrugged off like some dirty shirt.

Bronwyn's face was set. Nico was biting his lip. But Maggie... She watched me as if daring me to be better than all this. Daring me to prove her right. Tension thickened the air in the room, as if one breath would set off an explosion.

"I'm waiting," Simon said, drumming his fingers on his knee.

I took a step forward. "Simon—" I started.

"I'll get you the money."

I froze. My eyes went to Maggie. Everyone's did.

She'd just screwed everything.

"Maggie," Nico said then snapped his mouth shut.

I willed her to look at me, so she would know what a gigantic mistake she had made. She had to take it back somehow. She had to look at me. She couldn't be involved in this.

"You'll get your money," she repeated. "All of it."

Simon's eyebrows twitched with surprise. He stared at Maggie, noticing her, remembering her, assessing her. Seeing her in a way that I didn't want her to be seen.

"Are you going to write me a check?" Amusement laced his words, but he wasn't smiling.

"Not today." She swallowed. "I need a month."

"A week."

"Two weeks."

"Done."

I blinked. I'd seen grown men try to negotiate with Simon before, and they'd wilt under his stare. And there was Maggie, not backing down, bartering like it was second nature.

"And here I thought you were just a waitress." Simon put his hand on the back of Maggie's chair and leaned in close. My hand clenched into a fist. "You won't let me down, will you, Maggie?"

She didn't back away, she stared him down like she was the one in charge.

Simon slid from his chair and stood. "I'll see you in a week, to check in."

"I'll take care of it," I said to Simon, too quickly. I composed my face to avoid giving anything else away.

Simon smiled, and it was genuine. "We'll see. It'll be interesting to see how this plays out." He turned and walked away, Alfonso on his heel.

I glanced one last time at Maggie, wishing I could turn back time and warn her not to get mixed up in all this. But it was too late.

Maggie had ruined any chance I might've had to walk away. She was my next mark.

CHAPTER 16

MAGGIE

"You shouldn't have done that," Bronwyn said, once the air in the room returned and we could all breathe again. She didn't call me an idiot or make a crack about what I'd done. If anything, that only emphasized how serious the situation was.

Nico was looking at me like I had landed here from another planet. They both were. I shook my head. My throat felt clogged and sticky. Bronwyn was right. What had I been thinking? I couldn't pay Officer Ting thirteen thousand or thirteen hundred or thirteen anything! But I'd promised him. I had two weeks to come up with this money and no clue how.

"Maggie," Nico said. "I'm not asking for it, but do you even have thirteen thousand dollars?"

"No," I replied. Nico drooped like a popped balloon. "But we'll figure something out."

"Don't be so naïve," Bronwyn snapped. "How are you going to get that kind of cash?"

I had no idea.

"You could've stayed out of it, but no. Now you're mixed up in our problems."

"What was I supposed to do, let Jay take you out back and beat the crap out of you, or worse? I mean, it didn't sound like it was going to stop with a beating this time." It's not like Nico had defended his girlfriend. Even Bronwyn hadn't stood up for herself —argued or begged or...or something.

"Jay wouldn't have hurt Bron," Nico said.

I tossed my head. "Now who's being naïve?"

Bronwyn put her hand over Nico's but she looked at me. "I could've taken it. Then we would've gotten more time and figured something out."

"I got you more time, without anyone getting hurt."

"But Maggie," Bronwyn said, her eyes hard. "Next time, it won't be Nico or me with the target on our backs. It'll be you."

I pushed my chair back. "I'm going home."

"Maggie—" Nico began but he didn't say anything else. What could he say? I'd saved his bacon, and Bronwyn's, and he cared more about that than he did about me.

"It's fine." I slung my purse over my shoulder. "Maybe some time alone will help me figure out how to come up with thirteen grand."

The corner of Nico's mouth quirked but Bronwyn didn't smile. "Let us know as soon as you do."

Like it was that easy.

Darkness had settled over Vegas while we'd been inside the restaurant. Lights down the street flashed neon colors, making everything look almost pretty. Magical.

I sighed and started down the sidewalk. There was nothing magical about Vegas.

Someone stepped into my path. I gasped and jumped back.

"What the *hell* were you thinking?"

Jay Thornton's mouth was set in a grim line, his hands buried in his pockets. Officer Ting and his other bodyguard were nowhere in sight.

"Leave me alone." I tried to step around him.

He blocked my way. "Do you realize what you've done?"

"Saved my friend from getting hurt?"

His face loomed near mine. "Made yourself the mark."

Threats, bullies, dirty cops, guys who beat people up for a living. What made this city so different from mine? What made its people do such awful things to one another? I'd been stupid to think Vegas would solve my problems. My problems had tripled since I'd moved here.

"Are you going to hurt me?"

He growled.

"Right. Not this week, then. I'll pencil it on my calendar."

"You have no idea what you got yourself into." He rubbed a hand through his dark hair. "Do you even have the money?"

"Why? Are you going to lend it to me if I don't?"

He let out a burst of laughter and then stifled it with pursed lips. He looked me up and down. "Never mind. You'll probably borrow it from Daddy."

I scowled. "You don't know anything about me." Truth was, my first thought *had* been asking Dad for help, not that my parents had thousands of dollars lying around. But there was no point anyway because no preacher, let alone my own father, would ever agree to pay off a loan shark.

"You think I don't know the pampered princess type?" Jay fingered the sleeve of my dress and I yanked my arm away. "Never had to work a day in your life, never struggled for anything. Never lost anyone. Never had a problem aside from what to wear to prom or what purse matches your shoes."

I gripped my purse strap. He looked down at my shoes and smirked. My purse and shoes were both red.

"I know your type. You have no idea what the real world is like because you've lived in a bubble your whole life. Then you come here thinking the world owes you something, or that you just have to snap your fingers to get what you want. And it doesn't happen, but you still cling to that bubble as if it'll protect you. It won't. It'll just pop."

I could feel my cheeks burning. Angry tears stung my eyes. He'd hit on so many truths that the things he'd gotten wrong didn't even matter. Something like regret flashed over his face and he took a step back but I closed the distance. He wouldn't get away so easily.

"I know your type, too. Mean. Angry. Power hungry. You think because you never hear the word *no* that you're strong. You think you matter because you can force people to do things. You probably plan on taking over for your boss one day, ruling this crappy city from whatever rock you live under. Is that why you teach at the gym? Building yourself a little army? Well, guess what? I'm not intimidated."

He grabbed my arms with both hands. His eyes flashed. "You don't know anything."

"Let. Go. Of. Me."

Jay's hands jumped from my arms as if I burned him, but it was my skin on fire where his touch had been.

"Find a way to come up with that money," he said.

I raised an eyebrow. "Or else, right?"

"*Please* find a way, Maggie. I don't want there to be an 'or else.'"

Despite his pleading tone, I didn't believe him. I twisted around him and walked away.

CHAPTER 17

JAY

I SLAMMED the door of my truck so hard the windows shook. My hands curled around the steering wheel and I let out a growl.

Stupid. Stupid, stupid, stupid. Maggie's words ran through my head, taunting me with their truth. But she didn't know anything. She didn't know me and she never would. I wasn't good enough for someone like her. I saw it on her face every time she looked at me.

The truck rumbled to life but I didn't drive away. Not yet. I was on the verge of smashing my fist through the windshield.

I should've told her about my plans to own the gym, proved to her she was wrong about me. That I wasn't interested in power or taking over Ting's business. That I wanted nothing more than to get out of that world. That she saw only what she wanted to see. She hadn't given me a chance to defend myself. Now I didn't want to.

My hands had been on her slim arms, squeezing, before I knew what I was doing. I hadn't hurt her, but it was no wonder she thought I wanted to. It's not like she'd seen any other side of me.

I pressed my head against the steering wheel and let out a

breath. My temper simmered below the surface. I'd never had good control over it. Not at times like this. I needed the gym.

The drive wasn't long but it felt endless. Rock music blasted from the stereo, but nothing could shake Maggie's words from my head. Or the sight of her in that short lace dress, her long legs pale in the dark street.

Maggie. If she didn't come up with the money, what would I do? I couldn't hurt her. But if it wasn't me, then Simon would send Alonso, or someone worse to do the job. That's why I couldn't leave now. Couldn't quit, couldn't ask to.

But if I did nothing to Maggie, Simon wouldn't forgive me. I'd never had to harm a woman before. I'd threatened plenty, but never gotten physical with one. I wasn't dumb enough to think Simon didn't have female clients, but he sent others to deal with them.

Someone darted in front of my truck and I slammed on the brakes. It was a man, weaving as he walked, completely wasted. I cursed at him out the window, but it had probably been my fault. I couldn't even remember the drive between there and the restaurant.

When I reached the gym, I unlocked the front door and flipped on the lights. Without bothering to change my clothes, I strapped on my gloves and went at one of the heavy bags. Tension, aggression—it all exploded out of my fists onto something that couldn't be hurt. I didn't stop until my shirt was soaked through with sweat.

I grabbed the bag, slowing its momentum, then rested my forehead against the leather.

Maybe Simon would leave me to it. I'd never volunteered for a female mark before, maybe that would squash any suspicions he had about me going soft. He'd trust me to do my job.

Or maybe I'd just put a bigger target on Maggie.

I wanted out, now more than ever, but Maggie had made that impossible. Unless I ignored my conscience and let Maggie sort this out herself. It was her fault she'd volunteered the money. Maybe Simon would go easy on her. She wasn't a criminal, after all. She had nothing to offer him. She wasn't the kind of person he'd ever lend to in the first place. Simon was a good man, or he used to be. I'd seen the kind of scum he'd put behind bars. I'd helped.

But lately, he seemed more interested in making nice with criminals than putting anyone away. Like his meeting with Aguda. Whatever Simon was up to, I couldn't be blind to it any longer.

The only way out now, without hurting Maggie in the process, was by going after Simon. My testimony alone might be enough to convict him. But if I took him down, he'd take me down with him. I could go to Aguda, but then I'd be owned by a man far worse than Simon.

Or I could talk to that cop who pulled me over then cornered me at The Wall. Hopkins. He said he'd help me if I helped him. But I didn't know him. I certainly didn't trust him. I had firsthand knowledge of how cops weren't always what they seemed. For all I knew, he just wanted to take Simon's place.

I went to the front desk, searching one of the cabinets for a water bottle. The message light on the phone was flashing. All of my anger disappeared when I heard the recorded voice on the line.

"This is Nurse Nevin, I'm calling from North Vista Hospital. We have admitted a Conall McCrary and he has your name listed in case of emergency. He's in stable condition now if you'd like to come in and see him."

I exploded out of the gym and back into my truck. North Vista was only ten minutes away. Five if I floored it.

I got there in four.

"McCrary?" I asked the front desk nurse, panting to catch my breath after running from the parking lot. "Conall McCrary. Where is he?"

She took an agonizingly long time to find the information, then yelled at me not to run when I booked it down the hall to the elevators.

McCrary had to be okay. Not because I wasn't ready to buy the gym, but because I wasn't ready for him to go. When Simon first took me in, he was the father I'd never had. But when I met McCrary, I realized that even though Simon loved me in his own weird way, he wasn't the kind of person to call family. I'd respected Simon because I'd feared him, and because of what he'd built out of his life. I'd respected him for using any means necessary to get the job done.

McCrary was the opposite of Simon, and I respected him for that even more.

I leaned against the doorframe outside his room. No one had ever accused me of being afraid, but in that moment, my feet didn't want to move. Conall was asleep on the hospital bed, his wrinkled face an ashy gray color. An IV fed into his arm. Drool made splotches on his hospital gown neckline.

I went inside and sat by the bed, closing my eyes against the sight of age catching up to someone I cared for. I pressed my fingers to the bridge of my nose.

"Where's my pajamas?"

My eyes flew open. McCrary was awake and glaring at me.

"You didn't bring them, did you?" he barked.

My lips twitched. I sat up. "No. I was too busy worrying about you, old man."

He laughed but it came out a wheeze. "You better bring them tomorrow. I hate these nightgowns. I ain't no lady."

"You'd make one ugly lady."

"Hey now," McCrary said. "Don't you give me lip." Despite his haggard appearance, his eyes were bright and alert.

"What happened? The message didn't say much."

"It's a fever, no big deal."

I glanced pointedly at the IV.

He let out a loud sigh. "And I'm dehydrated or some nonsense. They're making a big fuss over nothing."

At his age, any illness was something. McCrary wasn't one of those people who hadn't realized he'd gotten old, he was one of those people who knew and fought it every second of the day.

I leaned my elbows on the chair arms. "When do you get out of here?"

"They won't tell me. I need *further testing*." His voice went high on those last words, as if he was imitating one of his nurses or doctors. "That's why I need my pajamas. And maybe a couple of books. Bring me my Dostoyevsky, and maybe sneak in some Guinness while you're at it."

I snorted. The nurses would have a field day with McCrary if he managed to get himself some of that. "I'll bring the books and the pj's. No Guinness."

He groaned. "You're killing me, son, you're killing me."

The smile melted off my face. McCrary noticed. He shut his eyes for a few moments. I thought he'd fallen asleep until he said, "It's yours."

His eyes opened and he held out a hand for me. I took it reluctantly. His palm was cold, his skin so thin I worried my touch alone might crush it.

"The gym is yours. It's in my will."

I opened my mouth but he wouldn't let me say anything.

"I didn't want to tell you because I knew you'd pitch a fit. But in case something... In case this is worse than those blasted doctors are saying..."

"It's not." My grip tightened. He winced and I let go. "You'll get out of here in a day or two and when I have enough money to get the gym the proper way, you'll be able to go off to Mexico, or Hawaii, or wherever you want to go."

He sighed. "Ireland. I want to go back to Ireland."

"Ireland, then. That's the plan, got it? No screwing it up."

"I'll do my best," he said, his voice getting faint. He closed his eyes again. "But I always was a screw-up."

When McCrary fell asleep, a nurse kicked me out. I drove home, but instead of going to bed, I tackled the business books again. But I was distracted, worried about McCrary, worried about the gym, worried about Maggie, worried what I would do if Maggie couldn't come up with the money.

If I left Vegas behind for good, all my problems might disappear. Wishful thinking. Simon would send someone after me. I knew too much and I owed him. If it hadn't been for him, I probably would've ended up in prison, or dead.

Before Simon, I'd been a foster kid, but I hadn't felt like one. My foster parents had been the best parents a kid could've asked for. I'd been with them since I was a baby, I hadn't known anything else. Even when they had a child of their own, they didn't neglect me. We were a family, my little brother, my foster parents, and me.

And then they'd taken in a girl. I was twelve when she came, she'd been eight. From the start, she knew how to manipulate—our foster parents, teachers, other kids at school. She lied, twisted stories, got people in trouble and always ended up coming out the innocent one. When I caught her stealing money from our foster mom, I threatened to tell if she didn't fess up. Instead, she went to them with bruises on her wrists that she'd given to herself, telling them I'd done things to her. She was convincing, and they believed her.

They hadn't kicked me out, but they had to report it to social services. The problem was, no one believed me. They had to do something, distance me from my foster sister and brother. No one wanted to take me, and I didn't want to go to the group home, so I'd run away.

I'd been sleeping in an abandoned warehouse when Simon found me, hungry and dirty, two years without a real home. I walked right into the middle of something going down. I took one glance at the uniform and made a break for it.

A guy had grabbed me and I'd kicked and screamed and bit him, fighting him with everything a fourteen-year-old kid had. The guy, I couldn't remember his name, kicked me right in the face with his boot, breaking my nose. Simon had shot him in the leg and told him to get out of town, he was done in Vegas. Then he bent down to me, holding out one of those old-school handkerchiefs so I could stop the blood flowing from my nose. He'd told me I was strong, and smart. He'd told me he could help me.

I still didn't know why he did it. Maybe he'd always wanted a son. Maybe he saw someone who could be molded into what he wanted, who would do his bidding, no questions asked. Whatever the reason, my life had gotten better after that. He'd given me a home, an outlet for my anger, a purpose.

Later, I found McCrary and the gym, and that outlet, that purpose changed into something I loved. Something I respected myself for. Simon didn't understand.

The pages of the book on my lap blurred. Two paths spread out before me. Do things Simon's way, or McCrary's. It should've been an easy choice, but it wasn't.

It came down to Maggie or Simon. A girl I barely knew over a man I wanted to break free of. Neither would get me what I wanted.

I wasn't ready to choose.

CHAPTER 18

MAGGIE

I HADN'T HEARD from Frasier in weeks. I needed my brother. Needed someone to turn to for advice, even someone who'd never had a long-term job, didn't graduate from high school, and was basically a hobo. It's not like I could go to my parents. They were the absolute last resort.

I was preoccupied at the diner, which led to wrong orders, forgotten refills, and lousy tips. Not my customers' fault. I was the one with my head in the clouds: the money-shaped, unreachable green kind. I didn't have thirteen thousand dollars. I barely made my half of the rent and utilities, plus drop-in dance classes and groceries, with a little left over for dinner out sometimes or a bottle of shampoo. I wouldn't be able to save thirteen grand in a year, let alone two weeks.

One thing I knew, though—I couldn't go home. Not now. Not when I'd promised to help. It's not that I had planned to move back to Hillstone, but it had always been a possibility in the back of my mind. But now, that would be running away. Abandoning Nico and Bronwyn to a miserable fate.

The other thing I knew—if I were to come up with any money whatsoever—I'd have to quit dance classes. The whole reason for my move to Vegas had gotten run over by me and my big, prom-ise-making mouth.

I hurried through Eastside Boxing and up the stairs to Nico's apartment, hoping not to run into Jay Thornton on the way. The gym was empty.

Nico greeted me at his door with a hopeful smile. "Got the money already?"

If I hadn't been born and bred a preacher's daughter, I would've flipped him off. "No, sorry. And before you ask, I have no idea how, either."

"Yeah, I didn't really think you'd be able to." He slumped into the apartment and collapsed on his bed.

"Do you have anything saved at all?" I asked, not bothering to sit. His counter was piled with dirty dishes, clothes littered the floor, and the bed was unmade. The whole place smelled like sweat and alcohol.

He shook his head. "What I save, I hand over to Ting. But interest keeps kicking me in the butt. I can't get ahead of it."

"We'll think of something." I hoped he noticed my use of the word *we*. Not me. Even though I'd agreed to come up with the money, this was still Nico's problem. I had a feeling he was all too happy letting me sort it out.

"Does anyone use the room just outside?" I asked.

Nico frowned. "You mean that empty space? Don't think so."

"Can I use it then?"

"For what?"

"Dance space."

Nico snorted. "You gonna teach your way to thirteen grand?"

My lips tightened. "No. But I'll have to quit classes, so I thought maybe I could use the space to practice. Keep in shape. Bronwyn's apartment isn't big enough."

He lay back on the bed and stared at the ceiling. "Sure, why not? I'll run it by Old Man McCrary, but as long as you don't get in anyone's way or blast your music or something, it probably won't matter."

"I can stick to practicing after hours, as long as I'm not working." I put some dirty dishes in Nico's sink. "Who's Old Man McCrary?"

"The owner. He's not around a lot." His voice lowered. "Don't tell anyone, but he's *old*."

I rolled my eyes. Nico was still lying down so I took a peek inside his fridge. Bottles of Heineken, mustard, ketchup, and a huge jar of pickles. Nothing else. I made a note to tell Bronwyn.

"He's got health issues," Nico continued. "Don't know what exactly. Jay knows. He's been visiting him in the hospital lately."

I shut the fridge and turned around. "Are they related?"

"Naw, he just likes the guy."

I tried to picture Jay Thornton visiting an old man in the hospital, taking him flowers or a giant balloon that said, "Get Well Soon." The image wouldn't stick.

It was like a parallel universe, this place I was in now. One where Nico was kind of friends with the guy who beat him up. Or, if not friends, then at least friendly enough to know things about him. To work in the same place. Seriously, what kind of people thought this was a normal way to live?

Nico sat up, bracing his fists on either side of his legs. "Is Bronwyn mad?"

"No idea." I wasn't about to get in the middle of their relationship. "I better go. I've got to work. I'll be back tomorrow night to use the space, so text me before if I can't."

Nico got up and I thought he was seeing me out but he went to the fridge and grabbed a beer instead. "Right-o."

I headed down the stairs and into the gym. Sunlight streamed through the glass wall but the whole place looked lonely. It was still morning, classes probably didn't start until later. Someone moved near the front, at the desk, turning toward me as I picked my way around the mats.

"I'm starting to think you're stalking me," Jay said.

I hadn't noticed before how deep his voice was, or how it rever-berated through my entire body. "I was , thinking the same about you."

"I work here, remember?" He pointed to the Eastside Boxing shirt he had on. The shirt was sleeveless, highlighting his tanned and perfectly ripped biceps. I tried not to look.

"I have a friend who lives here, remember?"

"Friend?" Jay made it to the door before I did. He leaned against it, ever-so-casually blocking my way.

"I have to work," I said, ignoring his question. Nico was a friend, sort of. I felt sorry for him. And I liked Bronwyn—she *was* a friend. But maybe getting sucked into Nico's world hadn't been such a good idea.

Too late now. And nothing I wanted to discuss with Jay Thornton.

Jay crossed his arms, his biceps flexing. I *really* tried not to look. "I wouldn't think that diner paid you enough."

I tugged on my uniform's miniskirt, which only drew Jay's attention to my legs.

"To get Officer Ting's money, you mean?"

Jay didn't move. Maybe he liked having this bit of power over me.

After a few seconds, I decided to just push around him. He didn't let me. Instead, he grabbed onto my elbow. His fingers trailed the back of my arm, leaving me breathless. His eyes soft-ened. His whole face did, hard lines melting away as if he were becoming someone else.

"You don't get it. Simon Ting isn't someone to mess with." He paused, the silence punctuating my beating heart. "I don't want to see you get hurt."

"Then don't hurt me."

"I don't want to." It was practically a whisper.

I'd gotten closer without realizing. My hips flush with his. He smelled like soap and sweat. My eyes were on his lips.

Annoyed, I stepped back. Jay was doing his job. Making sure I paid. Instead of his usual beatdown, he was playing nice. Drawing me in. Anything to get the money I owed his boss. And I was falling for it.

"I'm not stupid," I said.

His lip curled. "Prove me wrong."

I moved his hand from the knob. "I don't have to prove anything to you."

S itting on the couch in the apartment, my feet up on the coffee table, a blanket covered my legs despite the lingering heat of the night. Behind me, Bronwyn was tinkering around in the kitchen.

"A bank loan," I said, staring at a black and white photograph hanging on the wall. It was of a couple kissing on the street. "That's all I can think of."

Bronwyn said nothing. A cupboard door slammed.

If the bank approved me, I could pay off the lump sum to Simon Ting and then Nico could pay me back in installments, which I could then pay back to the bank. Provided Nico paid me on time and didn't flake out. I wasn't confident in that.

"They might make me get a co-signer though," I said.

Bronwyn circled the table and sat beside me, a cup of noodles in one hand and a spoon in the other.

"Have you ever tried to get a loan?" I asked her. If anyone was doing this for Nico, then why not Bronwyn? Maybe it hadn't occurred to them. Maybe she couldn't get approved.

She buried her nose in her cup, steam rising around her face. "Nico won't let me." She met my eyes and her face was shiny. "He won't take a dime from me."

I tossed the blanket off my lap.

"I'm his girlfriend," she continued. "If he takes my money, he's worried people, or I, will think that's the only reason he's with me."

That was sweet, but stupid. Maybe Nico wouldn't be in this mess if he'd let Bronwyn get the money for him. But maybe their relationship wouldn't last with that kind of stress between them, either. Maybe Bronwyn didn't trust Nico to pay her back.

"I doubt my dad will co-sign," I said. Bronwyn took a big slurp, a noodle hung down her chin before she sucked it through her lips. "Not if he knows what it's for. And I don't have a good enough lie."

"I wish you hadn't done this."

"A simple 'thank you' will be fine."

She smacked me lightly. "Thank you. But I wish you hadn't done it. We never should have let you get involved in this mess." She went back to her soup, drinking straight from the cup, her spoon ignored. "If you need a lie, we'll come up with something."

"Do you think it's a good idea? The bank, I mean."

"I think it'll get that loan shark off our backs." She paused. "And if Nico doesn't pay you back, I will."

That hardly made me feel better.

"That was the first time I met Ting," she said. "Did you know—"

A knock sounded on the door. "I'll get it," I said, rising from the couch. I squinted through the peephole but all I could see was the back of a dark head. Nico maybe, but the skin below the dark hair was too light.

I cracked open the door. I was getting used to Vegas, but you couldn't be too careful.

The man turned around.

"*Frasier?*"

My brother grinned at me. I threw my arms around him and he lifted me with a grunt.

"Have you gotten taller?" he asked when he set me down.

"Not lately." I looked him over. His hair was longer but he'd shaved the goatee he'd been sporting the last time I saw him. He looked thinner than I remembered and dark circles shadowed his eyes, but his smile was just as bright.

"Are you going to let me in, or what?"

"Right!" I grabbed his arm and hauled him inside, shutting the door behind us. "Bron, I've got a surprise!"

Her mouth dropped open when she spotted Frasier. "You dirty rat," she said, putting her cup of soup on the coffee table and giving him a hug. She pulled away. "If you think you can mooch off me, think again. I've already got one Hale under my roof, I'm not taking another."

He laughed. "Come on. Just a few nights? You wouldn't keep me from my baby sister, would you? Especially since we haven't seen each other in years."

She groaned but slung an arm around his shoulder. It was weird to see them like this. I barely remembered Bronwyn from high school. Fraze had never invited her over. Despite him contacting her for me, and the whole make-out story, I never imagined they were that close.

"What are you doing here?" I asked, retaking my spot on the couch. Frasier dropped a duffle bag on the floor and then plopped down beside me.

"Passing through. But I'll stay a few days." He craned his neck over the couch and raised his voice unnaturally high. "Making sure my friend is treating my sister right."

Bronwyn snorted from the kitchen. "Maggie wouldn't have lasted three days without me."

"And Bronwyn wouldn't have lasted yesterday without me."

Fraze raised his eyebrows at me.

"You gonna crash on the couch then?" Bronwyn said before Frasier could ask what I'd meant.

"If that's okay," he said.

"Does it matter if it's not?" she asked.

"Nope."

She rolled her eyes.

"I haven't heard from you in forever," I said, pulling his attention away from Bronwyn. "How did you get here from Seattle?"

He shrugged. "Bus, train, car, feet, you name it. I met this girl in Boise who has a thing for road trips and the tall, dark, and handsome type." He waggled his eyebrows. "She drove me most of the way."

I rested my head on his shoulder. "I'm glad you're here." It wouldn't last. He wouldn't stay, he never did, so I would take what I could get.

"Me too, Mags." He patted my head while Bronwyn looked on, an unreadable expression on her face. "Me too."

CHAPTER 19

MAGGIE

"So you're telling me, *actually* telling me, you owe some loan shark thirteen thousand dollars?" Frasier stood over me, looming like he was trying to be the scary big brother. "For one of Bron's deadbeat boyfriends?"

"Watch it," Bronwyn snapped.

"They were going to beat her up. Maybe worse." I curled into the couch, my shoulders near my ears. Out of everyone I knew, Fraze was the last person I thought would berate me for this.

"How are you going to come up with that kind of cash?"

"Bank loan."

He scoffed. Loudly.

"Look, don't worry about it. I can handle it."

"So she keeps saying," Bronwyn said.

Fraze started to pace in front of me. Bronwyn yawned. It was late, and I had an early shift in the morning.

I stood up. "Seriously." I put my hand on Fraze's shoulder and he stopped moving. For now. "It'll be fine."

He gave me a half-smile but he was looking through me. "Sure." His brain was working on something. Fraze didn't have that kind of money either, he'd never held onto a job longer than a couple of months. But if I was in trouble, he would do anything for me. That's what worried me.

When I woke up the next morning, he was gone. Not for good, his big duffel bag was still on the couch, his toothbrush upside down on the bathroom counter. But he'd left the apartment—my brother, who usually couldn't muster enough energy to get up before noon.

I left him a note in case he came back before I did, telling him I had a shift at the diner and that I'd be going to Eastside Boxing to dance after. I wanted to see my brother, but I had to get back to practicing. My body was already getting stiff, weak. Frasier would meet me somewhere.

Sure enough, he stopped by the diner for lunch, ordering everything on the menu just so he could say the ridiculous names aloud before finally settling on a burger and fries. I begged my boss Craig to let me take my break early and we ate lunch together, laughing and talking about our parents, about Hillstone, my time in Vegas and his trip from Seattle. When he left, he didn't pay, but that was Frasier for you.

That night at the gym, I tucked my phone into my leggings, the chord of my earbuds snaking up my chest to my ears. Nico had replaced the light over the empty space so that I could see. He'd also slipped me a key to the place so I could get in. Other than me, Eastside Boxing was empty.

I warmed up in the middle of the room, my phone blasting a techno beat in my ears. Three times I knocked my earbuds out. I'd have to invest in some cheap speakers. Maybe Bronwyn or Nico had some I could borrow, because dancing like this was super awkward.

Once I warmed up, I sat on the floor and stretched. My muscles burned. One week off from dance and already my body was losing it. But I kept going, pushing through the pain but taking it slow so I didn't injure myself.

When I was done warming up, I pulled my phone from my

leggings and scrolled through the playlist. I needed a new audition piece, and a new song to go with it. "Adagio" by Giazotto? Too slow. A piece from Swan Lake by Tchaikovsky? Too ballet. Something from the Harry Potter soundtrack? Too Harry Potter. I needed something that spoke to me. *Was* me.

I considered "Amazing Grace." I'd always loved the song. Definitely me, the preacher's daughter. I played and replayed it, but it didn't feel right. I didn't feel found. I'd always had God in my life, that had never changed and never would. But I still felt lost. Didn't quite feel like myself, or even know who I was. Dancer? Trying to be. Diner girl? Definitely. Friend, sister, daughter. I was all of those things. But still not me. "Amazing Grace" was a finale, a closing act, and I was still just beginning.

I continued to scroll through and then stopped when a name caught my eye. I pressed play, closed my eyes and listened. This was it. "Song of the Caged Bird" by Lindsey Stirling. It started with a slow violin, mournful, but accompanied by a fierce beat. Perfect for mixing sharp hits with fluid motion. Then the violin grew into a frenzy, evoking the image of a caged bird trying to get free. My body was already moving to the beat, choreography swirled in my head.

Rising to my feet, I started the song over, and then just let myself go. I wanted to get the feel of it before I started choreographing myself. I stopped a few times, once to reposition my earbuds, but mostly I moved through the violin notes, dance steps going from my brain to my body in milliseconds. It wasn't good, what I was dancing. It wasn't *something*, not yet. I'd need to choreograph every beat, every *ba-da-da-dum*, to perfection. I'd need to make it my own.

And yet it was a beginning. My body moving, creating art on the spot. It was freeing and wonderful. It was forgetting everything else except this moment.

The song ended, one final note lingering until it died and my phone slipped into a jazzy musical number. I pulled out my earbuds. Sweat beaded around my hairline and the back of my neck. I turned my head to wipe it away and stopped.

Jay Thornton was standing near the top of the stairs in the dark, one hand on the railing.

CHAPTER 20

JAY

MCCRARY WAS STILL in the hospital, but Nurse Nevin had told me he'd get out tomorrow. His fever had been high, and he'd been seriously dehydrated. So much so that he'd almost passed out, and ended up dialing 911. I wish I'd been there. I could have helped. Yet another reason I could never leave Vegas. Not when I was the only family McCrary had here.

My phone buzzed as I pushed open the door to Eastside Boxing. I glanced at the screen, dreading to see Simon's name. He'd called three times already today to ask about the Nico/Maggie situation. He wouldn't get off my back about it.

It wasn't Simon, it was Annie. I pressed ignore. I hadn't seen her since the night we'd barely spoken at The Wall, before Lieutenant what's-his-nuts tried to get me to rat Simon out, but she'd called me a few times since. Not so many that it felt needy, but too many. I'd hoped my silence would be hint enough. I had no clue how to break up with someone I wasn't even dating.

A few lights were on in the gym, including upstairs. I headed to the front desk when I heard noises. Footsteps, or scuffling, I couldn't tell. In case it was a break-in, I followed the sound to the back of the gym and up the stairs. If Bronwyn and Nico were going at it outside his apartment, I'd lose it.

I paused near the top of the stairs.

Maggie was dancing—spinning and leaping around the room McCrary had set up for aerobics classes that nobody had wanted to take at a boxing gym. Her body moved in a way I'd never seen before. It was beautiful and strange. Compelling and sexy. There was no music, but earbuds snaked from her ears and into the waist of her skin-tight leggings.

Her movements slowed, she hesitated for a moment, breathing deep without looking my way. Aside from her leggings, she only had on a sports bra, showing off vast amounts of bare skin shining with sweat. Every curve and muscle of her body was visible, and I wanted it all under my hands.

She resumed dancing, swaying to a beat I couldn't hear, her arms making long lines, one leg reaching for the ceiling. Then she was on the floor, her body almost caressing it as she moved. I'd been to clubs, watching girls dance in far less than Maggie had on, writhing and swaying for money. The way Maggie danced was different, special.

Tension and desire moved through my body. I clenched the railing.

She stopped, freezing her last step for a moment before she pulled the buds from her ears. Wiping sweat from the back of her neck, she turned and finally saw me.

My lips parted.

"What are you doing here?" she asked. She was panting from the exertion, her chest rising and falling. Her face flamed under my stare. "So late, I mean?"

Blood pounded through my veins. I wanted nothing more than to close the distance between us and wrap my hands around her waist, caress her sweat-soaked skin with my fingertips. Taste her with my mouth.

I swallowed. "I had to grab the accounting books for McCrary."

She slipped her phone from her leggings, avoiding my gaze. "McCrary?"

"Conall McCrary. He owns this place."

"Oh, right." She pulled a hoodie over her sports bra, curves and skin disappearing under the bulky fabric.

"What are *you* doing here?" I asked.

She bent down and removed some kind of weird shoes, then stuffed them into her bag. "Nico said I could use this space for practice."

"Practice?"

"Yeah. I needed some space. He said he'd run it by Old Man... Mr. McCrary." She slung her bag over her shoulder. "I'll only come at night, when no one is here. So I don't interrupt classes or anything."

"Okay." It would be exquisite torture, watching her dance again. I already wanted it.

We headed down the stairs together. She smelled faintly of sweat and something sweeter. I moved closer.

"Is this some scheme to come up with the money?" I asked. "Because I don't know if it'll work. You'd have to get a lot more naked."

I'd meant it as a joke, but her face flushed again and her jaw clenched. I was an idiot.

At the bottom of the stairs, the gym was dark except the light over the front desk. Maggie tripped on a mat and I grabbed her arm, steadying her. She jerked away, whipping me in the face with her ponytail.

"My life doesn't revolve around Officer Ting's money, you know," she said.

"It should."

She stopped walking. We were near the front, close enough to the light that I could see her face, twisted with annoyance. "Would you leave me alone about it?"

My eyebrows lowered. "No." I would bug her and bug her

about that money until the deadline hit, anything to keep me from doing what I had to do if she couldn't pay up.

"No?" Her hands went to her hips and so did my eyes.

I grabbed the strings of her hoodie and tugged on them, bringing her closer. "I won't leave you alone until I see all thirteen thousand of those dollars."

She batted my hand away. "Right. Just doing your job."

I pulled her into me, our legs entwined. I didn't let the feel of her distract me. Her hands were on my chest but she didn't push me away.

"Maggie. This isn't just about my job. Simon will hurt you." My grip on her hips tightened, I couldn't help it. She needed to wake up. She needed to know. "Simon will *make* me hurt you. Don't you get it?" He would make me do something I couldn't do. But I didn't want to be faced with that choice, or the consequences if I refused.

"It's all part of the job though, isn't it? I mean, you must enjoy it. Hurting people. Otherwise you wouldn't do it."

Desire turned to anger, and it began to boil under my skin. Of course that's what she thought. I let her go. "Your life might be black and white. Mine isn't."

"God gave us this life," she said. "It's up to us what we do with it."

"Was that on an inspirational poster at Bibles 'R' Us?"

She made a face I couldn't read. "My dad is a preacher."

She was clueless. If her father was a preacher, her life had probably been all Bible Study and prayer meetings and choir practices. Everything boiled down to a belief in simple moral choices. As if my life, my choices, were so simple.

I crossed my arms. "Maybe some of us are doing the best we can."

"Maybe your best isn't good enough," she said, but her face softened, taking the bite out of her words. She was pitying me now, and that was somehow worse.

"I'm sorry," she said. My eyebrow twitched in surprise. "If I can't practice here, I won't come back again."

I turned away. "You can practice here." All the time and never.

She didn't move. I didn't move.

"Thank you," she said.

CHAPTER 21

MAGGIE

FRAZE and I were at Sunset Park, the scorching sun burning the tops of our heads. Sitting there with my brother, throwing rocks into the pond and scaring the geese, I felt like a kid again. Like nothing was as important as doing nothing in that moment.

I scuffed my sandal against the grass, flicking tiny amounts of dirt to the edge of the pond. Fraze had been in Vegas a week. He came to the diner every day when I was working, to see me and get a free meal. But what else he was up to, I had no idea. It was only a matter of time before he left again.

"Why don't you come to the gym with me tonight?" I asked while Fraze tried to skip rocks. "You can tell me what you think of my piece so far."

He took off his shoes and socks and rubbed his bare feet against the grass. "Nah. I don't know anything about that kind of stuff."

A cool breeze rippled the pond, raising goosebumps on my bare legs. I tugged my skirt down. I'd had an early shift at the diner today. Fraze had met me for lunch, disappeared, and then reappeared when my shift ended at four. We'd been walking around ever since, a bit aimlessly, but that didn't matter. Time spent with Frasier was never boring.

"Your deadline is coming up, isn't it?" He got up from the bench and inched toward the water.

"I don't know if you should put your feet in there."

Fraze took one look at me and grinned. He didn't even bother rolling up the ends of his jeans before stepping into the pond.

"I heard there are piranhas," I said.

He laughed. "Piranhas are people, too. Besides, I'm cooking."

I watched him wade around the pond, peering into the water as if he could see something in all that murk. It went no deeper than his knees, even in the middle. He waded back.

"I've only got a few days left," I said. "I have an appointment at the bank tomorrow."

He shook his head. "You can't take a loan out for that deadbeat. You'll never get your money back."

I crossed one leg over the other. "I don't have much of a choice. I'd rather be in debt to a bank than a loan shark. Unless you've got some bright idea you're not telling me."

One corner of his mouth tilted. "I might."

That's what I was afraid of. "Don't do anything stupid."

"I am never stupid." He stepped out of the pond, shaking his legs off. "Can't a guy help his sister out?"

"You're broke."

Again with the sly grin. "Not for long."

"What does that mean?" He wouldn't answer. "Fraze…"

He wouldn't let me talk. Wouldn't hear my arguments. Wouldn't even tell me what he was thinking. It drove me crazy. My brother wasn't stupid, but he was impulsive, and sometimes that led to stupid decisions.

"Come on," he said after I'd pestered him for ten minutes. "Let's go find some dinner. I'll pay."

"Sure you will."

L ater that night, I was a building away from East Side Boxing when Jay stepped outside, the door swinging shut behind him. Under the streetlights, I watched him take a deep breath and run a hand over his hair as I approached.

"Four days, Maggie," he said.

"Hi to you, too."

He put his palm against the door, keeping me from opening it. "*Four* days."

I rolled my eyes. "Yes, thank you, I have a calendar."

"It's the money that concerns me."

Like I didn't know that. Every time I saw him, Jay would bring up the money, and I saw him more than I wanted to lately.

"I've got it under control."

He tilted his head. "Why are you doing this?"

His question caught me off guard. I looked out into the street at the cars going by. A beater, a sedan, a mini-van, another mini-van, another beater, their lights bright in my eyes.

"He's not worth your energy," Jay said.

"You don't get to decide who's worth it and who's not."

"It must be exhausting, being you."

I gave him a pointed look. "Sometimes, it really is."

He turned his head and stared at the door, or at his hand, I couldn't tell which. "I know how it feels."

"Then get out of my way."

His eyes lowered to mine. "That's not what I meant."

"I know."

He dropped his hand from the door. An imprint of his palm remained on the glass.

"Maggie—"

A car screeched up to the sidewalk. It rocked back and forth when it came to an abrupt stop. The doors opened and five men poured out, all wearing big baggy jackets despite the Vegas heat.

MELANIE STANFORD

"Get inside," Jay said to me. His arm was in front of me like a shield, the rest of his body tense and coiled.

Fear, curiosity, and stubbornness all kept me rooted to the spot.

"Jay, my man," one of the men said. He was average height with a dark shaved head and thick eyebrows. One of his arms was in a sling. The other four flanked him on either side, all of them looking like they'd gotten on the wrong side of a bear recently.

"Rafael Antonio." Jay dropped his arm but stepped in front of me. "Come for another loan?"

Rafael shook his head. "My business with Ting is over."

Jay crossed his arms. He turned his head, putting his chin to his shoulder. "Get inside *now*," he hissed.

Rafael and the other men approached. As one moved, something flashed near his belt before he closed his coat. A knife? A gun? Definitely a weapon.

"I got unfinished business with you, amigo," Rafael said.

The entire line of Jay's back was rigid. "We'll talk, as soon as my friend goes inside."

Rafael laughed and some of the others joined in, but Jay ignored them. He turned around, yanked the door open and shoved me through.

"Go do your thing," he said. "This is none of your business." He shut the door in my face.

I stood there, bristling, but Jay had already turned his back on me. I didn't budge.

The men approached. I dropped my bag then shifted to the window to get a better view. Jay was saying something to them. Rafael was talking too, but it was too muffled by the thick glass to understand. Jay threw his head back and laughed. Rafael's face went dark.

They rushed Jay before I could blink. Four of them were on him while Rafael watched. Jay's head slammed into the window and I gasped.

Jay put up a heck of a fight. His fists connected with ribs and

122

jaws, anything they could find. He was an animal, scary and strong and wild, but it was still five against one. Jay didn't stand a chance.

I couldn't watch. I yanked the door open.

"Stop! Stop or I'll call the cops."

One of these days I really needed to call the cops first *before* threatening to, but I'd acted before thinking. Again. I didn't really expect it to work on these guys anyway, but they stopped, frozen and staring at me.

"Get out of here, Maggie," Jay growled.

I moved in front of him. "I said that's enough."

Jay grabbed me by the waist. I tried to push his hands away. He wouldn't let me go. "Get inside," he said, his voice rough next to my ear.

"This your girlfriend?" Rafael asked, assessing me. "It's alright chica, you can stay and watch. We're just giving your boyfriend back some of what he gave. With interest."

Rafael nodded. One of the other men pulled something from the back of his pants. A gun.

Jay's arms tightened around me. We spun. I screamed. A shot rang out. A flash of pain. I fell into him. Curses in the air. The rev of an engine.

Jay's eyes were wide, the first time I'd seen him afraid. He whispered my name right before my legs gave out.

CHAPTER 22

JAY

RAFAEL and his thugs had bolted, their car screeching off. Kneeling on the sidewalk, I held Maggie in my arms. Her gaze darted around, she gasped for breath. Blood seeped from her arm, below the sleeve of her t-shirt.

I put one hand on her cheek. "Maggie. Look at me."

"I've been shot, haven't I? Have I been shot? *Ohmygosh,* I've been shot."

I whipped off my shirt. "It's not that bad, but we should get it looked at." It seemed like the bullet had only grazed her skin. "I think you're going into shock."

"You're not that good-looking," she mumbled, her eyes on my chest.

I held in a smile, wrapping my shirt around her arm, tightening it just above the wound, then using the rest to try and stop the bleeding.

"Hold here," I said. She pressed the shirt into the wound and hissed. "I'm going to lift you now."

I scooped my arms under her back and lifted her. She was almost as tall as I was, but I had no problem carrying her around the corner to my truck. She could've walked, but I didn't tell her that. It felt nice to hold her without her yelling at me for once. Trembling, she pressed her face into my neck. I opened the passenger door and gently laid her inside, then hurried around to the driver's seat.

Maggie leaned her head against the glass. Her eyes slid closed.

"Hey, talk to me," I said, pulling into the road.

"I don't wanna." Her face had gone pale. Blood had already soaked through my shirt. Maybe I'd misjudged the wound. I sped up.

"Yell at me then," I said. "You seem to like that."

She pivoted her head against the window to look at me. "You deserve it."

Rafael had said the same thing. I deserved what I got. I'd never thought so before. Now, with Maggie bleeding in front of me, it felt true. "You're not the first person who's said that to me tonight." I glanced at her. "Not gonna pull a gun, are you?"

I smiled but she just blinked at me.

"Was he a client?" she asked.

Client made it sound so posh, as if I were some kind of lawyer.

"Not allowed to divulge that kind of information?" she asked when I didn't answer.

"Rafael was a client of Simon's," I said. "A difficult one."

"Meaning you kicked the crap out of him."

She was judging me again. But I couldn't argue, couldn't even defend myself. She was lying there in my truck, hurt because of me.

Maggie shivered and pulled her knees up to her chin. She started to close her eyes.

I didn't want her to pass out so I kept talking. "Him, his brother, his friends. There's always someone." I blasted the heat, turning the vents so they blew on her. She let out a sigh.

"If you don't keep those eyes open, I'll make you."

She popped them open and stared at me. I kept my eyes on the road but I could feel her watching me. I shifted in my seat.

"What are you going to do," she asked. "Hit me?"

Anger uncoiled in my belly. Anger and hurt. "I'll pretend like you don't know what you're saying."

"Whatever helps you sleep at night."

At a red light, I wanted to reach for her, but I settled for a look. "I wouldn't hurt you, Maggie."

"I know." She looked shocked by her own words, then quickly added, "Not for four more days."

I pulled up to Alfonso's, parking my truck in front of his garage. There weren't any lights on. Alfonso had better be home.

Grabbing a hoodie from the backseat of the truck, I threw it on, then opened the door for Maggie.

"Where are we?" she asked as I helped her get out. "Is this your house?" She looked at my hoodie and sighed.

"No. Alfonso's." I slid my arm around her back and helped her shuffle to the door.

"Shouldn't I be at a hospital? Who's Alfonso?"

"Hospital isn't such a good idea. Alfonso knows what he's doing." Usually.

I rang the doorbell multiple times, then pounded on the door for good measure. I didn't stop pounding until a light came on.

Alfonso opened the door a crack, peering past the chain of the lock.

"Open up," I said. He didn't hesitate.

I carried Maggie inside and laid her gently on the nearest couch. "She's been shot, but I think it's just a graze. Can you fix it?"

Alfonso nodded. "Let me get my stuff." He hurried away. Alfonso was a man of few words and I'd never appreciated it more.

On the couch, Maggie was shivering. I started to unzip my hoodie.

"Stop taking your shirt off," she said. "I'm fine."

I raised an eyebrow. "I thought you liked it."

She snorted, but her cheeks turned a faint pink. That was better than the pallor of a few moments ago.

I knelt beside the couch near her head. The sound of Alfonso rifling through cupboards echoed down the hall.

"Why did you bring me here?"

I shifted closer, sitting down, my shoulder next to her head. "Hospitals ask too many questions."

She gave me a reproachful look.

"Don't worry." A strand of hair had fallen across her face and I gently brushed it away. "Alfonso will take good care of you."

She leaned away from my touch.

I scowled. "Trust me, would you?"

She returned my scowl. "It's him I don't trust."

So she trusted me then? That was hard to believe.

Maggie was quiet, but her chest rose and fell rapidly.

"Hey," I said. "It's going to be okay."

Her eyes filled with tears and she blinked up at the ceiling. Her whole body tensed, and her face turned hard as if willing herself not to cry. I ran my fingers through her hair. I'd wanted to touch her, and hadn't wanted to, since the day I'd met her.

She reached for me with her good arm and I took her hand, pressing it against my chest. She seemed to relax.

Alfonso removed my shirt from her arm and checked the wound. Maggie didn't let go of my hand and I didn't let go of hers.

"Just a graze?" I asked. Maggie looked from me to Alfonso. He nodded.

"Won't need stitches," he said. "I'll clean and bandage it."

"Just a graze?" she asked, squeezing my fingers. "*Just?*"

I tried not to laugh. "Did you want worse? Hoping to get some street cred out of this?"

She shot me a dirty look.

"You should get a tetanus shot," Alfonso said. "Can't do that here. But drink this."

Her eyes narrowed on the shot glass he was holding. "What is it?"

"Vodka. It'll take the edge off."

"I don't drink."

I took the glass from Alfonso and held it in front of her. "It's gonna hurt when he cleans it. This will help."

She considered it, then grabbed the glass and chugged. She immediately started coughing. "That's disgusting! Why did you make me drink that?"

I tried not to laugh.

Alfonso began to clean the wound, digging at it with a cloth.

Maggie's eyes filled with tears. "Ow."

I held up the empty glass, silently asking if she wanted another. She nodded.

When Alfonso was done, he left the room, taking his supplies with him.

"I don't think the vodka worked. That still hurt," Maggie said as I helped her to stand. "Except that I'm all warm inside. Warm and fuzzy. Like a teddy bear. Wait, am I drunk?"

"Probably not." Although she let me lead her outside by the hand, so maybe she was after all. We climbed into the truck. "Where do you live?"

"Crampton Oasis."

I pulled out of the driveway.

"But I don't want to go home."

I glanced at her in surprise.

"Actually, I do. No, I don't." She let out a frustrated growl. "I don't know what I want."

My fingers tapped the steering wheel as I drove out of Alfonso's neighborhood. At a stop sign, I turned to look at her. She was staring at me.

"What about seeing the sights?"

"I see the sights."

"What?"

"I don't know."

She really didn't drink if two shots of vodka had affected her this much. My truck idled at the stop sign. "I promised I would show you the great parts of Vegas. Remember?"

"I already found the park. I don't think there's anything else."

I raised an eyebrow. "You have much to learn, my young grasshopper."

She pointed to herself. "Maggie. My name is Maggie."

I drove. "We'll start with the strip, Maggie."

We didn't get out of the car, but there was always traffic on the strip, giving Maggie enough time to look. We drove past the Wynn, the Venetian, and Treasure Island. She caught a glimpse of the fountain show in front of the Bellagio, then whipped her head around to look at the fake Eiffel Tower on the other side of the street.

"I can't believe I haven't come down here before now," she said, her eyes wide as she tried to take in everything. "It's all so...shiny."

The streets were full of tourists despite the hour. Bass pumped from a car nearby. Maggie rolled down the window and nodded her head to the beat.

"You'll have to walk it one day, when it's not too hot out," I said.

"I will."

"Just don't take anything people are handing out to you."

She glanced at me. "Why not?"

"Trust me." She was so churchy, she'd be horrified at the ads for the seedier side of Vegas.

At the Mandalay Bay, I turned around and we drove it again. Then I took her to Fremont Street, where the neon lights were so bright, it was like daytime. We idled outside the Springs Preserve, and the Neon Museum.

"What's this place?" she asked as I pulled in front of a large, pale brick building.

"It's the Mob Museum." I switched radio stations to something a little softer.

"It's no wonder *you* like it," she said.

"Yeah, it's *fascinating*."

She looked at me with her eyebrows raised.

"No, really, it is." I hadn't meant to sound sarcastic, but her comment bugged me.

"Is Al Capone your hero or something?"

I frowned. "I don't kill people, Maggie."

"At least there's that." She continued to stare at me. "That, and you're hot."

I blinked, surprised. And then my lips spread into a smile.

She closed her eyes. "Pretend I didn't say that out loud."

"Nope. You don't get to take that from me." She'd defended me tonight, plus she thought I was hot. Progress.

"Stop looking at me like that," she said. I smirked. "Can you take me home now?"

Maggie rested her head on the window while I drove to her apartment, my phone telling me the way. She'd fallen asleep and I didn't want to wake her. I parked, then lifted her from the truck.

"I can walk, you know," she mumbled, but I didn't put her down.

"Just tell me which apartment it is."

"Fifteen." She nuzzled into my neck, her breath hot on my skin. Her fingers played with the ends of my hair; she probably didn't realize it.

I knocked on number fifteen but there was no answer. "Where's your key?"

"Bag."

I cursed. I didn't have Maggie's bag. We probably left it at the gym. Hopefully not on the sidewalk. "You're going to have to stand." I put her down and she slumped against the wall.

Sometimes, when helping Simon get what he needed to put a bad guy away, a little B&E was required. But smashing a window or kicking in a door only leads to more questions and loose ends, so Simon had one of the cons who owed him one teach me how to pick a lock. Given my size it probably looked comical to see me fiddle with tiny torsion wrenches on a tiny lock, but it turned out I had a knack for it. I always kept the wrenches in a hidden part of my wallet, in case of just such an emergency.

It took only a couple of minutes to pick the lock, then I swung Maggie into my arms again and carried her inside. She didn't object.

There were two rooms, but it was easy to tell which was hers— it smelled like her, fresh and fruity, like an orchard. I laid her on the bed, and she fell asleep instantly. I pulled off her shoes and covered her with the sunny yellow blanket, bright, like she was. Her face was smooth and peaceful as she slept, no trace of the anger or the superiority that always seemed to be there when she looked at me.

Tonight had been different. She'd stepped in front of me with no fear of Rafael and his thugs. She might have even saved my life. That had to mean something.

Did I mean something to her? It was impossible, but why else would she have done it? Why not let me fend for myself? She'd made it clear she despised my way of life, my job, my boss. So why put herself in harm's way for me? She'd said she trusted me. She'd actually wanted to spend time with me.

I wanted to believe she felt something. Believe it would be okay if I climbed in bed beside her, stretched my body against hers, breathe in her scent until I fell asleep. I wanted to wake up next to her, feel her skin and her lips against mine.

But mostly, right then, I wanted to thank her. For doing what no one else in my life would have, except maybe McCrary. Not even Simon would've stepped in front of a gun for me. If I was ever going to be the right kind of man for Maggie, I had to go straight. Leave Simon behind for good.

After I left, shutting the door quietly behind me, I pulled out my phone and looked up LVMPD's Internal Affairs department. There he was on the contacts page. Hopkins. It was time to give him a call.

CHAPTER 23

MAGGIE

I woke in my bed. My eyelids felt weighted down, my head throbbed. I still wore last night's dance clothes. I couldn't remember going to sleep.

Then it all came back. Jay Thornton. The fight. Five against one. Stepping in front of him. The gun. The pain. The heat. Jay's arms around me.

I looked down. A thick white bandage circled my upper arm, the whole thing felt stiff. A strange sound came out of my nose, half gasp, half snort.

I'd been shot. For Jay Thornton, of all people. It's not like I'd stepped into the line of fire or deliberately blocked him, but still. They hadn't been aiming at me. I'd been shot by accident instead of someone who probably deserved it.

Shamed, I leaned my head against my pillow. No one deserved that, not even Jay. Not five against one, not one against one.

"You're awake!" Frasier popped into my room and sat on the edge of my bed. He held a coffee cup in one hand and a cell phone in the other. Bags rested under his eyes, even heavier than before, but he was smiling.

He noticed my bandaged arm and his smile faded. "What happened? Are you okay?"

Jay had taken me to some house. He'd stroked my hair, held my hand before some big Mexican used a cloth as a torture device. Then we'd driven around Vegas, I couldn't remember where. All I remembered were neon lights, the warmth of his truck, and the feeling that Vegas was a lot prettier than I had come to think. It must have been the vodka. Only alcohol could make Vegas seem pretty after what I'd seen.

"Maggie?"

My brother's voice brought me back to the present. "It was outside the gym," I said. "Five against one—a guy I know. I couldn't just... They weren't aiming at me."

"Do you have a death wish?" Fraze yelled.

"I didn't ask to get shot! Besides, it's just a graze." I grimaced. Now I sounded like Jay.

"Oh, swell. That makes it *so* much better. Seriously, Mags, I never knew how messed in the head you were."

I pursed my lips.

"Don't give me that look," he said. "You could have been killed. And for what? Some guy who probably had it coming? Who is he anyway?"

"Nobody," I said in a small voice. He had a point. What had I been thinking? I hadn't been thinking, that was the problem. I just acted, and things could've turned out much worse. They were already bad enough. Some sketchy guy had fixed me up. Would my arm heal properly? When would I be able to dance again?

"It's not the first time, either." Fraze took a swig from his coffee cup. "Bronwyn told me how you broke up the fight between Nico and the loan shark's enforcer."

Probably best not to point out that the enforcer was the same guy I'd just defended.

"You're not in Hillstone anymore, Mags. You keep forgetting that."

Bronwyn busted into the room, her face pale. "Are you okay? Jay Thornton was here, he brought this." She tossed my bag on the floor. "He told me what happened."

Jay had been here? "I'm fine."

"Yeah, right," she replied. "And your boss called, by the way."

I groaned. I couldn't possibly go into work today. I called the diner while Fraze and Bronwyn whispered to each other.

I didn't tell Craig what happened—how could I explain why I hadn't gone to the cops?—only that I was injured. He was allowing me this one sick day but he wasn't happy about it.

"Do you think you're Wolverine or something?" Bronwyn asked, her arms crossed.

"Who's Wolverine?"

She rolled her eyes. "Hugh Jackman. *X-Men*. Fast healing?" When I didn't respond, she said, "Never mind. I guess I know what movie we're watching next."

"Well, I've got the day off." A day where I'd rather be doing anything other than thinking about the stupid stunt I'd pulled.

"Sorry, I don't." She had on her spandex shorts and a bright yellow bike shirt. "Duty calls."

"Maybe later?"

Bronwyn nodded. "I'm almost afraid to let you out of my sight. I mean, what's next? Throw yourself in front of a bus to save a pigeon?"

I never used to get in trouble in Hillstone, but I refrained from pointing that out.

CHAPTER 24

JAY

WHEN I CALLED LIEUTENANT HOPKINS, I made sure to do it from the gym phone. Stupid to use my cell when Simon got the bill.

Hopkins didn't answer, which was just as well. I left him a message: "This is Jay Thornton, calling from Eastside Boxing. I'm calling to confirm your beginner adult Muay Thai class this Thursday at eight-thirty pm. Gloves and headgear will be provided for you." Hopkins would be smart enough to come.

He showed, five minutes early, wearing basketball shorts and a t-shirt that strained over his gut. Captain Internal Affairs obviously needed to get away from the desk more often. That became increasingly clear when he barely made it through the warm-up. Even McCrary could've run circles around this guy.

"Split into pairs," I called out, after we'd done some technique exercises. I caught Hopkins's eye. "You, with me." He stood in front of me and I lifted my gloves. He did the same.

"What am I doing here?" he asked in a low voice, after ducking my jab.

"Sparring."

He shot an uppercut to my chin but I blocked it. I moved in

close and adjusted his hands. "Simon has a lot of connections. It was safer to meet here."

I stepped back.

"You're going to help me then?" He swung. I swung. Our feet shuffled against the mats.

"Depends on what you want." Louder, I said, "Right, left, right, uppercut."

He did what I said. "I know how to box, you know."

I dodged easily. "Looks like it's been awhile."

I turned away and called a switch-up of partners. We didn't speak again until class had ended. As the other students filtered out, Hopkins approached me at the desk.

"Enjoy the class?" I asked as one of my regulars passed, nodding a goodbye.

"Verdict's still out," Hopkins replied. He took a drawn-out swig from his water bottle, no doubt waiting for the place to clear out.

I pulled out an information sheet and pushed it across the desk to him.

He bent over it, speaking low. "I want to hear about Ting, not beginner Muay Thai. What is your relationship with him?"

"It's complicated." Talking about it meant dredging up my past, my old foster family, the charges against me, and I had no interest in going there.

"Look, you called me," Hopkins said. "Which means you want something."

I wanted freedom. And the only way to get that was by putting Simon behind bars. But selling him out wasn't so easy. Loyalty was a hard thing to shed.

"Officer Ting is a good cop. He's put more than his fair share of criminals behind bars." Hopkins pointed to a place on the sheet, showing me.

This ruse might have been unnecessary but I didn't want to risk it. I took the paper from him. "Then why are you investigating him?"

"I've had my eye on him for a while. His arrests are too clean. Not to mention that mansion of his outside the city. Apparently, it was inherited, but something seems off. And then I came across this."

He put his gym bag on top of the desk, rummaging around inside before slipping out a picture and laying it on the desk by the bag so that anyone outside wouldn't be able to see. The picture was of Simon getting into a sedan, the windows tinted.

I gave him a questioning look.

"That car belongs to Rance Aguda." He paused. I said nothing. "Why would Officer Ting get into a car with Rance Aguda?"

"Is Aguda in the car?"

"That's not the point."

"What is the point?"

Hopkins quickly shoved the picture back in his bag. "I'm not lead on Aguda's case. Organized Crime Bureau is handling that. I got this photo surveilling Ting."

Hopkins stumbled onto something bigger than he expected.

"They met," I said. "But I don't know why or what for." Which was the truth.

"Can you find out?"

I hesitated.

"Listen, if I nail Ting *and* Rance Aguda, it'll be my chance to get out of Internal Affairs." He leaned toward me. "But I'll get fried if I go anywhere near Aguda. Simon's the key, and I know you work for him. What exactly does he have you doing?"

I pressed my lips together. He wouldn't leave that question alone.

Hopkins shrugged on a sweatshirt. He kept his face pleasant as he spoke. "I've got evidence of Simon meeting with a number of known criminals. What's he got going on the side? Drugs?"

"No. No drugs."

"What then?"

I didn't answer.

"I know Aguda is the big fish here, but there's something off about Simon Ting. I don't like dirty cops. I don't respect them. And it looks to me like he's been rolling around in the mud. But I need evidence."

I handed him the Muay Thai info sheet. "I'll think about it."

Frustration crossed his face, but I wasn't about to pledge myself right then and there. When I had something to share, something I knew wouldn't get traced back to me, then I'd take it to Hopkins. For now, all he needed to know was that I was considering his offer.

"Thanks for the class," Hopkins said. "If I come again, maybe you'll have a bit more for me."

I shrugged. "Come again and we'll see."

CHAPTER 25

MAGGIE

My arm ached. When I changed the bandage, it didn't look too bad. I got the tetanus shot, anyway, and I didn't go into work for a few days. Craig yelled at me over the phone. Even though he didn't fire me, I figured I'd better get off my butt. The wound had pretty much healed aside from a scab, and I had a job to get back to and a dance routine to choreograph.

After an exhausting day of work, my arm only stinging a bit, I decided to head to the gym. Even if I couldn't push myself, I could still stretch and work on a few more bars for my audition piece. It was only October, I had months until my audition, but I wouldn't blow it this time.

Nico gave me a quick hello before he disappeared, mumbling something about mopping. I went upstairs and shrugged off my hoodie. Bronwyn had a small speaker shaped like a pig that she let me borrow, so I brought that along, plugging in my phone and turning on the music. I stretched for about fifteen minutes, being careful with my arm, then I got to my feet, switched the music to "Song of the Caged Bird" and got to work.

I'd already choreographed the first sixteen bars, and I went through them a couple of times, but I wasn't happy with it. I replayed the music and paced, lost in my choreography. What I had was too sterile, emotionless. I closed my eyes and marked it again, tweaking a few steps. I was scared of moving my arm too much, so I kept it down by my side at first. Then it came to me, how to use that in the choreography, at least for a few bars.

I went over it again, added another eight bars, and repeated the steps until they felt natural. Until I didn't have to think about what I was doing anymore. By now I was sweating, and I went to my phone to restart the music one last time. I caught something out of the corner of my eye, something that hadn't been there when I started.

I turned and there was Jay Thornton, arms crossed, leaning against Nico's door. He was looking at me with an unreadable expression.

"Are you here to see Nico?" I didn't know how long he'd been watching me, but it was unnerving. When I danced, I got lost in my own world and barely noticed anything else going on around me.

"No."

Silence stretched thin between us. I didn't know what to say. Didn't know what he wanted, if he wanted anything, or if he was just there to intimidate me. And then I realized.

"The money." Of course it was about the money. I'd missed the deadline. But no one had come to my door. No one had followed me down the street when I went to work this morning. This was it though, he was coming to collect and I couldn't pay. I'd missed my bank appointment convalescing.

Jay pushed himself off the door. "I talked to Simon. He gave you another two weeks."

I tried not to show my surprise. "How kind of him."

Jay was right in front of me. I rubbed the sweat from the back of my neck.

His eyes went to my arm. He reached out and rubbed his

thumb over the scab, what was left of my bullet graze. "I never thanked you for saving my life."

I turned away. "I didn't save your life."

He was behind me, his breath on the back of my neck. "If you hadn't gone outside, I would've been shot. And they would have been more careful with their aim."

I didn't want his thanks. I didn't want to feel the hardness of his chest on my back. Definitely didn't want to lean into it. I moved away again but turned to face him. "It wasn't a big deal. I would've done it for anyone."

He let out a short, wild laugh. "Maggie, you got shot. Because of me. Don't act like it's nothing."

He was taking this way too personally. I tightened my ponytail, then winced at the twinge in my arm. "I thought it was *just a graze?*"

He snorted. "You got lucky. It could've been much worse."

"Not lucky. Blessed." I said it before I could stop myself.

He raised an eyebrow. "You think God saved you?"

I walked to my bag. My body had gone cold, sweat freezing on my skin. I pulled my hoodie back on. I didn't want to talk about God with Jay Thornton. "Speaking of thank yous, I never said thank you for making sure I got fixed." I waved at my arm. "And taking me home." I barely remembered that part, but I was pretty sure it involved me inhaling the scent of his skin as he carried me to my bed. My cheeks burned.

"Maggie." Jay was there again, right in front of me. Too close. He took my hand. Both our palms were slick with sweat. I looked up at him.

"Maggie Hale," he repeated. His other hand cupped my cheek. There was an expression on his face I'd never seen before. Hopeful, unsure, and something else. Desire?

My lips parted in surprise. And then his head tilted and his mouth merged with mine. Just like that, he was stealing my breath. His lips were soft, practiced. My heart was in my throat.

The taste and feel of him was intoxicating. My whole body tingled, wanting to give in. I pushed him away with my good arm.

"What are you doing?"

He blinked. "I—"

"Your thanks was enough."

"Are you serious?" His eyebrows lowered. "You think I kissed you because I'm grateful?"

Wasn't that why he was here, looking all mournful at my scab like it was his fault I'd been shot? Which it sort of was. But I didn't need his gratitude, and I definitely didn't want his lips.

Without thinking, I grabbed my bag with my bad arm then hissed at the sharp shock of pain, dropping the bag to the floor. Jay was there, bending down to pick it up. He placed it over my shoulder and my lips tightened.

"I appreciate having more time," I said. "But if you think getting me a longer deadline means I owe you something—"

"Excuse me?" The words came out like he'd been slapped.

"I'll get you the money as soon as I can and then *this* can be done." I waved between us.

His whole face went dark. "You mean me."

I'd never liked Jay Thornton, he had to know that. I went for the stairs.

"You're a real piece of work," he said to my back.

I spun around. "What did you think was going to happen here? That I'd jump into your arms because you extended my deadline? Or because we spent a little time together the other night?"

"That's really what you think of me?" His voice became hard, dangerous. "Just because I work for a man like Simon doesn't mean I'm anything like him."

"Could have fooled me."

He rubbed a hand through his hair. "I thought, after—"

"You thought wrong."

Pain flashed in his eyes, his jaw clenched.

Despite who he was, I didn't want to hurt him. "I'm sorry if I gave you the wrong idea."

"It wasn't an *idea*. I'm capable of real, actual feelings, you know." His face closed down.

I didn't know what to say. Of course he had real feelings, but had I allowed them? I hadn't seen Jay as anything other than someone who hurts people for money. I didn't want to think there was anything else to him than that.

"I…" I hesitated.

"It's okay, Maggie. I get it." He brushed past me down the stairs.

He was gone and all I felt was relief.

CHAPTER 26

JAY

I WENT straight for the nearest bag, not bothering with gloves. Every word Maggie had said to me went through my fists and into the leather as I tried to work things out in my head.

She'd stepped in front of a bullet for me but acted like it meant nothing.

She'd assumed the kiss was because I thought she owed me something.

She'd thought I wanted sex in exchange for a longer deadline.

She wanted nothing to do with me.

And I wanted her. Still.

Sweat poured down my neck and my knuckles were in agony, but I kept going. Punching, my teeth gritted to keep from screaming in frustration.

Maggie didn't want to see me anymore, that much was clear. She couldn't believe I had feelings for her, or that I had feelings at all. And yet I did. I loved the way she argued with me, even though it drove me crazy. I loved the way she didn't back down one second, then leaned on me the next. I loved her courage, her faith, the fire in her eyes, and that body I couldn't get out of my head. She'd become a light in my dark world. But she would never know because I couldn't be that light for her.

I collapsed to the mats, wiping my raw knuckles across my forehead. The light above the gym was off. While I'd been taking out my aggression on the bag, Maggie had gone.

The skin over my knuckles was cracked and bleeding. I found some gauze in the bathroom and began to bandage my hands, Maggie's words still playing through my mind.

Not lucky, blessed, she'd said, so certain God had a presence in her life. As if she deserved to be blessed when someone like me didn't.

I let out a growl, itching to get back to the bags, but I took a deep breath and calmed myself. As much as I wanted to, I couldn't fight the bags all night. Like with Maggie, it was a fight I could never win.

Inside Pearl of China, I grabbed a bowl of wonton soup from Mingyu and headed to Simon's office. Alonso let me in with a salute and a smirk.

Simon was arguing with someone on the phone so I took a seat and slurped my soup. I didn't look at him as he talked because he didn't like that, so my eyes roamed over the framed photos on his wall, most of them of him with various local celebrities and people he deemed important. Squeezed between one of him and the mayor of Vegas, and another of him with some Asian man I didn't recognize, was a small 4x6 of the two of us, taken when I was sixteen.

I had a pronounced black eye and a cut lip but I was grinning, Simon's arm slung over my shoulder. That had been after he'd set two of his enforcers on me without warning. He was one of those guys who, if you couldn't swim, they'd throw you in the deep end and either you learn quickly, or drown. That's what had happened on that day. I'd learned quickly, using my speed to my advantage against men bigger and stronger than me.

Simon hung up the phone and stood. "Let's go." He buttoned his suit jacket and left the room. I followed, dropping my bowl off in the kitchen. We climbed into Simon's Lexus out in the back lot.

"Where are we going?"

"We have a meeting with Aguda."

I tensed. I had no desire to see Rance Aguda ever again. But this could be something to take to Hopkins.

"What's it about?" I patted my pocket to make sure my cell phone was there. If I was lucky, I might get a recording of this meeting.

Simon's lips thinned. "He wouldn't say. But when Aguda calls, it's unwise not to answer."

Simon drove at his usual snail's pace through the darkened streets of Vegas. Despite jumping to Aguda's call, it didn't seem to affect Simon's driving speed. His Lexus was his baby, after all, and nobody put his baby at risk.

"Do you have something on him that will put him away?"

The corners of his mouth curled. "We'll see."

Simon pulled up to a random office building somewhere in the north. One other car was parked in the lot—a black Lincoln with tinted windows, just like the one in the picture Hopkins had shown me. Simon got out. I reached for my phone to find the record option when my door flung open.

Someone grabbed my arms and pulled me from the car. "Out, now!"

My muscles tensed, ready to fight. The man who'd grabbed me was strong despite his size. But that didn't mean he knew how to use those muscles for anything other than weights. I grabbed his forearm, put my foot behind his ankle, and down he went.

A gun cocked. I looked up. Aguda had exited the Lincoln, but it was one of his goons pointing the .45 at me.

I put my hands up. "Whoa, now. I don't let anyone grab me."

147

"What's going on here?" Simon asked, stopping beside me. "You called us. You asked for Jason. I wouldn't have come if I knew my son would be treated like this."

I glanced at Simon. What the hell was this?

Aguda came toward us, his bodyguard following on his heels, gun at the ready. "Jason, is it?"

My whole body was coiled, ready. "It's Jay." If Aguda had asked for me specifically, I was in trouble. But I had no idea why. Plus, with his focus on me, I would never be able to get evidence of this meeting.

Aguda turned to Simon. "You've done me a lot of favors lately, Officer Ting." He said 'officer' like it was a joke. "So I'm here to do one for you."

Aguda cocked his head. The man who'd pulled me out of the car handed something to Simon. A picture.

"I've got a posse of detectives following me around," Aguda said, then looked to one of his men. "Is posse the right word? No matter. They take pictures of me. I do the same. You never know what you might find."

The picture was of me and Hopkins at the gym.

"Who is this?" Simon asked. Despite the danger in the air, he was the picture of ease. I admired him for it.

"Yes. Who is that, Jay?" Aguda asked.

I shrugged. "Somebody Hopkins. He came to one of my classes last week. So what?"

"What your *son* is failing to tell you," Aguda said, "is that Hopkins is a cop."

"I don't recognize him" Simon said.

"He's I.A."

Simon looked at me. I shrugged like I hadn't a clue. Simon returned the picture. "Lots of people take boxing classes," he said. "Cops get soft and look for a tune up once in a while."

"Perhaps," Aguda replied. "Or perhaps it's not so innocent as that. In any case, I would never allow something like this among

my boys, innocent or not. If you don't have the stomach to properly chastise your *son*, Joseph here would be happy to do it." He
motioned to the bodyguard who pointed the .45 at me again.

My fingers curled into fists. I stared Joseph down, daring him
to do it.

Simon's laughter pierced the silence. "Quite the drama you're
putting on here, Rance, but it's not necessary. Jason is loyal."

Aguda glanced between me and Simon. He adjusted his coat
sleeves. "I don't share your unwavering faith."

Simon's smile died. His voice went cold. "Thank you for
bringing this to my attention, even if it was for nothing. We'll be
going now."

Aguda snarled. He grabbed Simon by the arm. Instinct kicked
in and I moved to break them apart. Joseph pointed the gun in my
face. I froze. We both loomed over our bosses, protective, waiting.

Aguda had regained his composure. "When I see a threat, I
don't waste time with questions." He let go of Simon and glanced
at me. "I've done you a favor tonight. I won't do so again."

S imon seethed the entire drive back to Pearl of China. Chinese
curse words were hurled in every direction. I stayed silent.

I'd dodged a bullet, almost literally. I'd been worried about
Simon catching me with Hopkins, but it turned out Aguda was the
bigger threat. Simon had believed me. He trusted me. He thought
my loyalty still lay with him.

Shame covered me like sweat after a double class.

Simon's muttering had turned to English. "To threaten you like
that. To threaten *me!* I thought he wanted you for a job, I thought
he was borrowing you. Instead he wanted to demonstrate his
power over me. He was testing me. But I'm not playing. That's
what he doesn't understand. He thinks I'm just a cop looking for
some easy money. He has no idea."

I stared at Simon. He was going to lend me to Aguda for some job? Suddenly, I didn't feel so ashamed about my fading loyalty.

"What have you done for him?" I asked. Aguda had mentioned favors, plural. Just how deep had Simon gotten in with him?

"This and that," Simon said. "Nothing to warrant pulling this power-play on me. He's built an empire here in Vegas and what does he do with it? Wastes it! On drugs and prostitutes, illegal fighting and gambling rings. Nonsense."

Simon sounded genuinely upset, as if he would do so much more with Aguda's "empire" if he had the chance.

We pulled up to Pearl of China and Simon parked. "He doesn't deserve what he's built. Not anymore. And I won't let his threats go unchecked." He looked at me, the kind of stare down that usually got clients to spill the truth. "Even if you have been a bit of a disappointment lately."

My hackles rose. "You think I was lying about that cop?"

He shook his head. "No. I worry that you've been distracted."

"Has there ever been a time when I haven't done my job?"

Simon's eyes narrowed. "You spend more time at that boxing place these days."

I relaxed. This was about my day job, nothing more. "I like teaching."

He scoffed. "Son, you won't get anywhere in life *teaching*. I don't understand why you waste your time over there. I've indulged it up till now, but if it gets in the way of your real job, then you won't be going any longer."

I kept my breaths even, but it wasn't easy. Simon was dictating my life. He'd done it since the beginning. I hadn't noticed at first, and then when I did, I didn't mind because I owed him. I'd liked working for him. Just as Maggie had said, I'd liked the power it gave me. Now, I had no interest in that. I wanted something different, something he wouldn't let me have.

Hopkins was my way out, but I'd gotten nothing from the meeting tonight, except Aguda's mistrust of me, and Simon's unwavering faith. Simon wanted to hold me in place, but he'd laughed in the face of one of the most dangerous criminals in Vegas when my loyalty came into question. He'd protected me. Once again, I was torn. Freedom or loyalty. I couldn't have one without giving up the other.

We both climbed out of the car. "Did you talk to the Hale girl?" he asked. "I still can't believe she stepped in front of a bullet for you." He couldn't believe it because he would never do it himself. But he had given her the extension because of it.

Maggie. She'd been another reason for wanting to get free of Simon, but she'd shot me down as easily as she smiled. The taste of her lips, the feel of her soft curves pressing into me when I'd kissed her. The moment when I'd imagined she could be mine and I could be hers—it was painful to remember now.

I rubbed the bandages over my knuckles. "I told her you extended the deadline."

"She better make the most of it," Simon said.

Wanting Maggie was as pointless as wanting my freedom, but I didn't know if I could stop fighting for either.

CHAPTER 27

JAY

SOMEONE WAS TAILING ME. A few times I'd caught a souped-up Mazda with blue rims in my rearview mirror. Not exactly inconspicuous. Not Hopkins style, either. Probably one of Aguda's lackeys, checking to see if the cop showed up near me again.

Simon thought it was Aguda too. "I'll take care of it," was all he said. A few days later, he got on a plane without telling me where he was going or when he would be back.

I relished the taste of freedom. Teaching without having to worry about being interrupted by some shady job. Spending time with McCrary, who was back to his old self. Pretending to ignore the Mazda hovering at the corners of my vision. Pretending to ignore Maggie whenever she came into the gym. Doing my best not to think about kissing her again, running my hands through her hair, pressing her hips into mine.

But with Simon gone, I had to keep an eye on things, so when Alonso told me he had a meeting with a potential client, I had to show.

"Why don't you wait until Simon's back?" I asked Alonso.

He'd taken up Simon's spot behind the desk in his office at Pearl of China as if it belonged to him.

"This guy's perfect—in a hurry for money, desperate." Alonso adjusted the chair until it was up so high you couldn't tell how short he was. His feet didn't reach the floor. "I don't know when Simon's going to be back anyway. Did he tell you?"

"No." Simon didn't usually keep secrets from me. It was stupid that this bothered me now, given my feelings toward him. "Still, send the guy somewhere else. What if Simon doesn't approve?"

"Are you kidding?" Alonso checked his reflection in one of Simon's picture frames, rubbing his hand along his pasty white cheek. "This is easy money. I could tell on the phone the guy is a patsy." He cracked his knuckles. "Patsies are great for compounding interest."

Alonso just wanted to knock someone senseless.

The appointment arrived. It was a younger man, probably around my age, with longish dark hair and an easy grin. He was skinny, with dark circles under his eyes. An addict, maybe? He held out his hand for Alonso to shake. He didn't seem nervous at all to be there. Most people usually were. I stood against the wall where I could observe his profile, his hands, his feet, anything that might reveal some kind of tell. Simon would want these details later. Alonso wouldn't see past an easy target.

"Fred Madsen," Alonso said, giving him a pointed stare. It had nowhere near the same impact as Simon's. "Are you sure you want to be here?"

Fred didn't even twitch. "Of course."

"Why?"

His eyebrows rose the tiniest bit. "Because I need the money."

This Fred guy needed to watch his tone or Alonso would prove his strength before he even signed the papers.

"Do you really need it so badly?" So far Alonso was following Simon's script exactly. Simon always made it very clear to each of his clients what would happen if they didn't pay up. Yet they always seemed surprised when an enforcer came calling.

"I have a solid investment plan but I need the start-up capital."

He cracked a slight smile. "It's the sort of thing a bank wouldn't want to be connected with, but still, all above board. I have all the necessary paperwork."

I tensed when he opened a briefcase, but he only pulled out a stack of papers and handed them to Alonso.

Alonso looked over the documents, taking his time, trying to make Fred sweat, but the guy inspected the office and stared at the pictures as if he had all day and no cares at all. It made me suspicious. Either he'd fallen from the stupid tree and hit every branch on the way down, or he was up to something.

"Seems to be in order," Alonso said finally. He folded his hands over the papers. "I'll have to check your references, of course."

"Of course," Fred replied with a smile.

Alonso's eyes narrowed. "I don't lend fifty thousand to just anyone. I'll be doing some digging."

Fred shrugged. "Go for it."

Now I was really suspicious. Fred didn't seem desperate like Alonso thought. But there was something off about him. He was too young, too sure of himself. That kind of confidence comes with experience and Fred didn't look like he had any.

"Can I talk to you for a second?" I asked Alonso. Fred gave me a once-over as if noticing me for the first time.

Alonso ignored me. "You'll owe two grand a week, plus ten percent interest. You miss a payment, interest goes up. You miss two payments, we start taking a more personal interest."

Fred winced. Finally, he was showing something real. "I understand."

Alonso rifled through Simon's desk drawers. Messing up his desk would be another thing on the list of what Simon would be upset about when he got back. But that would be nothing compared to this mess.

"I think we should talk now," I said.

Alonso grit his teeth but ignored me. He handed the paperwork to Fred. "Go ahead and read it over. If you're happy with the terms, sign."

Fred paled but he bent over the papers and scrawled a signature. When he was done, he handed them back to Alonso, his grin gone. Maybe his nonchalance had been an act, something he couldn't keep up anymore.

"My errand boy here will be in touch, once I've made sure everything is in order."

My knuckles itched, begging to knock some sense into Alonso.

Alonso and Fred stood, shook hands.

"Excellent," Fred said, his grin back in place. "It was a pleasure doing business with you."

Alonso gave him a malicious, pencil thin smile in return. No doubt he was squeezing the life out of Fred's hand. "You too."

Fred swallowed. When Alonso let him go, he left the room, shaking out his hand as he went.

"That was a mistake," I said as soon as he was gone. "There's something shady about him."

Alonso rolled his eyes. "Everyone who comes in here is shady. If they weren't, they wouldn't be here. He's just stupid. That investment might pan out but it'll take a while. Which means lots of cash coming our way." He held out Fred's papers to me. "Check on these, just in case."

"I don't work for you."

He smirked. "You might, one day."

No chance of that. Alonso was too stupid and too greedy to run this place on his own. He'd screwed up with Fred today, I'd bet on it. I wasn't going near this deal.

"Your bed," I replied. "You lay in it."

"Simon's gonna give me a big fat bonus for this deal when the money starts coming in. You'll see. And if I get to mess up Fred Madsen's face a few times first, all the better."

"Just remember whose office this is," I said. Alonso didn't listen to me this time either.

CHAPTER 28

MAGGIE

EVER SINCE I got myself shot, my brother had been acting weird. Weirder than usual. Secretive. He went out at night, had hushed conversations on the phone, and changed the subject every time I brought it up.

A few days after the Jay incident—which I wasn't thinking about, no matter how confident his kiss had been—Fraze had gone out and still wasn't home when I got back from the gym. I waited up but finally called it a night at one in the morning. Tossing and turning, I woke at the click of the door. Footsteps crept down the hall and into the bathroom. I got out of bed.

"Fraze?" I said into the bathroom door.

"Yeah," he said from the other side. "You okay?"

"I'm fine. I was about to ask you the same thing."

"It's all good. Late night, is all. Go to bed, Mags."

I hesitated. "Okay. See you in the morning."

It took a while for me to fall back asleep. What could Frasier be doing out there all by himself? Maybe he had friends I didn't know, or he'd met new ones since coming here. Fraze made new friends as easily as picking produce at the grocery store. Still, I worried. Couldn't help myself.

In the morning, I woke to the smell of frying bacon. Rubbing my eyes, I shuffled into the kitchen. Frasier was at the stove, three pans in front of him.

"What are you doing?" I leaned over his shoulder to check out the bacon, scrambled eggs, and fat sausages. "Trying to give me a heart attack?"

He showed the barest of smiles, but didn't say anything.

I checked the time on the stove. Eight in the morning and I had to be at the diner in an hour. "I gotta jump in the shower," I said. "Save me some?"

When I got out, my brother had set the table with two heaping plates, two glasses of orange juice, and two forks. After twisting my hair into a wet bun, I took a seat at the small kitchen table.

"What is this?" I said, suspicious. Frasier never cooked when he was at home.

His eyes met mine. "Consider it a goodbye breakfast."

"No." It was too soon.

Frasier dug into his eggs, shoveling them into his mouth like it was his Last Supper. I ate a few bites, had one piece of bacon, then pushed my plate away.

"Where to this time?" My voice wavered, my nonchalance falling flat.

"A friend of mine has a job lined up. We've been working out the details these last few days."

I raised an eyebrow.

"Working in a recording studio," he said. "Sounds like a pretty sweet deal, I couldn't pass it up."

"Doing what?"

He shoved a sausage into his mouth before answering. The only words I understood were 'music' and 'boss.'

I scraped the rest of my food onto his plate, then took my dishes to the dishwasher. "Sounds…" I didn't know what it sounded like. "Where?"

Fraze didn't answer. My hands braced against the counter, I watched him eat, clearing his plate in five minutes.

He grinned at me around his last bite and I laughed. "Pig," I said. I checked the time. After eight thirty. "I've gotta go. When are you leaving? Can you stop by the diner first?"

He went to his duffel bag, which was already packed. The pile of clothes that had graced the floor by the couch was gone. He bent down, grabbed an envelope, and then came to me.

"I've got a present for you."

"What is it?"

He grabbed my hand and put the envelope on my palm. His eyes were wide like they used to get on Christmas morning when we were kids, before he stopped getting along with our dad. Back when he still believed in something.

I opened the envelope. Inside was a stack of bills. Hundred dollar bills. I gasped.

"You can cancel that bank appointment. Thirteen thousand plus a little extra thrown in for you."

He looked so pleased with himself but my heart was pumping faster than when I auditioned for EDT. I was more scared than I'd been outside the gym with Jay and the guys who wanted to kill him.

"How much?"

"Fourteen."

A thousand bucks could cover a year's worth of drop-in classes at Fluidity. "Where did you get this?"

He shrugged, like fourteen grand was no big deal. "It's an advance for my new job."

"Seriously?" I put the envelope down.

He waggled his eyebrows. "Don't you trust me?"

"This isn't a game, Fraze."

"I know, Mags." His gaze went to my arm, the scar currently covered by my gold work shirt. "I was supposed to settle in with this money. Get an apartment, a car, that sort of thing. But you know me, I can crash on couches and bum rides until things take off. I told you this job's a big deal."

I shook my head. This was exactly what I'd worried about. I knew he would try to help me.

"Just take it, Maggie."

I met his eyes. "I'm scared."

He pulled me into a hug. "Hey. There's nothing to be scared of." He let go. "It's completely legit. Okay? I've already talked to Bron and she's going to make sure Nico pays me back. If I could, I'd give the money straight to this Ting guy so you wouldn't have to see him again. But I can't stay."

I nodded, a lump still in my throat.

"Besides, how can you be scared of this? You stepped in front of a bullet."

It hadn't gone down quite like that but I didn't say anything. My brother shoved me toward the door. "Get to work. I'll stick around so we can have one last lunch together and then I'm outta here."

I swallowed. "Promise?"

He grinned. "I'm the king of keeping promises."

I didn't buy that lie any more than his others.

I had to beg Craig for one last lunch break with Frasier. His patience with me was wearing thin, but he allowed it, as long as I changed out of my uniform first. I took off my apron, pulled my hoodie from my dance bag and slipped it over my ugly gold shirt. Good enough.

We sat by the window and people-watched while Fraze downed the Fishers of Men platter and I picked at a Garden of Eden salad. My brother was leaving. I'd had him for a short couple of weeks and then in a few minutes he would be gone again, probably for years. As much as I wanted to, I couldn't ask him to stay.

He wouldn't anyway. Not for me, not for anyone. It was like he had wings on his shoes, always flying away, never staying put. Or as Fraze liked to say, he had a rocket under his butt that never burned out.

"Don't stop the emails." Frasier licked the grease off his fingers. "Even if I don't reply. It means my phone is dead or I don't have access to wi-fi."

"No excuses," I said, pointing at him with my fork. "Or I'll come down there myself." I frowned. "Where are you going again?"

Fraze scooted from the booth. "I'm gonna check out some sights along the way, but I better go before I miss my bus."

I didn't fail to notice that he wouldn't tell me where this so-called job was. But I didn't push it. Fraze would be a lot more forthcoming in an email.

He was already at the door, his duffel bag slung over one shoulder. I looked at our empty dishes on the table and sighed. Another meal coming out of my paycheck. I wouldn't complain though. Because of Fraze, fourteen grand was hidden in my pillowcase.

We stepped into the sunlight. The street outside the diner was busy with people on their lunch break.

My brother pulled me into a tight hug. We were the same height, and I rested my chin on his shoulder. He smelled like grease and shave gel, not familiar but not strange either.

"I'm glad you came," I said.

He pulled away. "Be good." He tugged on my ponytail. I batted his hand away.

"When am I not?"

He hugged me again, lingering. We both knew it would be a long time until we saw each other again. When he let go, his parting smile was bright and confident. "I'll see you." He shouldered his bag and headed down the street, turning once and waving goodbye before disappearing around a corner.

When he was gone, I turned back to the diner. Jay Thornton was standing on the sidewalk, his feet wide apart, his arms crossed, staring at me. A scowl darkened his face. He was angry. Even though I'd seen him fight, he looked truly dangerous right then. Dangerous to me.

I hurried inside the diner, my heart beating faster than my footsteps.

CHAPTER 29

JAY

I'D SEEN HER. Maggie. With Fred Madsen. They'd been hugging on the street outside her diner. I'd seen the way he looked at her before disappearing around the corner. They were obviously together. He'd borrowed fifty grand. I knew something was off about that guy but I never thought Maggie would be involved. And what were they doing with the thirty-seven left over?

My anger mounted the entire day until Hopkins showed up at beginner Muay Thai, distracting me. I didn't expect him to show so soon, not when I hadn't given him a sign that I had anything for him.

"What are you doing here?" I said through my teeth. I was hanging up a poster on the bulletin board and he'd come to stand beside me, perusing the board as if he were interested in the upcoming junior competitions.

"We need to talk," he said.

"This isn't a good idea. I'm being tailed." I hurried away, scanning the street outside the window for the Mazda with the blue rims. It wasn't there. But if he was smart, he'd switch up cars every so often anyway.

Hopkins followed me. "Gloves?" he asked, giving me a meaningful look.

We went to the bin of extras. Both of us bent over it, rummaging through to find a pair that fit him.

"Who's tailing you?" he asked, his mouth barely moving.

"Aguda. He had pictures of us, last time you were here. Tried to get Simon to turn on me."

"Aguda's dead."

I froze.

"How about these?" Hopkins said, loud this time. I straightened. He tried the gloves on.

"You sure?" I said, then louder, "Nope, too small."

We went back to the bin.

"We think Ting did it."

I almost laughed. Simon? Killing Rance Aguda? Simon was resourceful, smart, and dangerous. But to kill Aguda? He wasn't dumb enough to try that. Aguda would be too well protected.

"How do you know?"

"That's confidential."

Of course it was.

"Was Simon in town this past week?"

I glanced at him. "No."

"Where did he go?"

"No idea. Wouldn't tell me." If Simon really had been responsible for Aguda's death, was it because of me? When I told him Aguda had someone tailing me, he promised to take care of it. Then he left town. Now Aguda was dead.

Hopkins tried on another pair of boxing gloves. "Doesn't matter. We already know where he went, and the purpose of his trip."

"Then why are you here?" What could he want from me now? If Simon really had killed Aguda, they'd arrest him. My problems would be over. I'd finally be free.

"Right now, we don't have a case. Some of our evidence will

get thrown out because of how we got it. Unlike Ting, we have to do things by the book."

Snorting, I tightened the Velcro around his wrists. "If he really killed Aguda," I said through tight lips, "then you should be thanking him."

Hopkins held his gloves in position, ready to punch me in the face. "Not if he plans on taking over."

During the next class, I couldn't stop thinking about what Hopkins said. Simon's thing had always been putting bad guys behind bars using any means necessary. Killing Aguda, taking over his operation, that was unlike him.

But he'd said himself how Aguda had wasted all he had built. Did Simon really want Aguda's empire? Aguda's boys wouldn't transfer their loyalty to the person who'd killed their boss. It made no sense. If Simon had killed Aguda, it seemed to me that it was because he knew he'd never get anything on him to put him away. Simon had said he'd been working on it. Maybe he came up with nothing. Aguda had connections, and he'd weasel out of any jail sentence.

Simon might've done it because he thought there was no other way to get rid of someone like Aguda. And to protect me. That, I understood. But if it was true, I could never sell him out to the cops now.

CHAPTER 30

MAGGIE

THIS TIME, as I headed to Eastside Boxing, I actually wanted to see Jay. I could give him the money and be done with him forever. It was wishful thinking—being done with him, because I couldn't avoid him. Not when I was using the top floor of the gym for dance practice. Not when I couldn't forget that kiss.

I went a little early so I wouldn't miss him. He was there, teaching an adult class, all men. They were sparring together in pairs and he was circling the room, yelling at the top of his lungs.

"Harder!" Jay shouted. "Gloves up, Manny."

I hesitated by the door. I didn't want to go upstairs because Jay might leave before I could give him the money. But I felt weird standing there watching like a creeper. I shouldered my bag and shifted from foot to foot.

I caught his eye but he quickly looked away. He wouldn't acknowledge me. Last time he had, outside the diner, he'd looked like he was about to murder someone.

When he moved to the outer edge of the mats, I approached him. He turned away when he saw me coming. I almost laughed. The world had gone topsy turvy if I was the one chasing Jay Thornton.

I grabbed his arm before he could escape. His muscles tensed under my grip. "I've got your money," I said. "Come up when you're done."

He scowled. Not at all the reaction I'd been expecting. I let him go.

Upstairs, I knocked on Nico's door. He answered almost immediately.

"Hey," he said, smiling.

"Can I come in?" I asked. He pushed the door open and I stepped inside. The apartment was scrubbed clean, it smelled of bleach and lemons. Music played, something old and jazzy.

"Bron's coming over." He waved a hand. "She said we had something to celebrate but she complained last time about how messy the place was getting."

"It looks great." I dumped my bag on the table. It felt unnaturally heavy, maybe because of all the cash I was carrying. "Perfect for celebrating."

"Do you know what it's all about?" Nico opened his fridge and pulled out a bottle of orange juice. I didn't see one can or bottle of alcohol in there. Bronwyn would be happy.

"I've got the money. I'm giving it to Jay as soon as he comes up here."

His face broke into a wide grin. He started hopping around and I thought maybe he had to go to the bathroom until I realized he was dancing.

"Your brother came through, then?" he said, doing a poorly imitated Michael Jackson spin. I laughed. "Yeah, baby."

"How did you know?" I asked.

He shrugged. "He said he had a plan, but I never heard if it worked."

"Do you know anything about it?" Nico shook his head and I sighed. "Ting won't be on your back anymore," I said. "No more late night beatdowns from Jay."

He finally stopped dancing. "He likes me. It wouldn't have been so bad."

Yeah, right. No matter what he thought, the important thing was Nico remembering he still owed my brother the money. He wouldn't have someone hounding him, but it didn't mean he didn't have to pay up.

"Well, anyway, I've got practicing to do," I said, going for the door. "Have fun with Bron."

He said goodbye as I left. Jay was in my practice space, waiting. He stood in the middle of the room, arms crossed over his chest, muscles bulging in his sleeveless shirt. His hair was slick from sweat, and a scowl pulled down his brow.

I rifled through my bag for the envelope, having a mini panic attack when I couldn't find it at first. Finally, I slipped it out from inside a ballet shoe where I had tucked it for safe keeping.

I held out the envelope. "Thirteen thousand dollars, as promised."

Jay didn't move. I didn't move. The envelope hung in the space between us until my arm began to shake and I lowered it.

I knew things would be awkward between us after the kiss, but I didn't think it would make Jay like this...whatever *this* was.

"What's the problem?" I asked, breaking the silence.

He grabbed the envelope from my hand. He pulled the cash out and counted it before replacing it. "Where did you get this?"

I frowned. What did that matter?

He took a step toward me and I took one back. "*Where* did you get this?"

My mouth tightened. "That's none of your business."

His eyes narrowed.

"I got you the money. Nico doesn't owe Officer Ting anymore. It's done."

He stuffed the envelope in the back pocket of his shorts and then looked at me, his gaze like a winter blizzard. "This is a dangerous game you're playing."

"What are you talking about?" My eyes went to his lips, then darted away.

"Don't think you can screw over Simon Ting," he said. "It won't end well."

"Is it not all there?" I reached around him and yanked the envelope from his pocket, my arm brushing his. My nose filled with his scent of sweat and soap but I ignored it. I'd counted the money three times already, just to make sure, but I would count it in front of him so he couldn't accuse me of skimping.

He grabbed it back from me. "It's all there."

I looked at him in confusion. "Then what's the problem?"

But he didn't answer. He gave me one last cold look and left.

I understood why he was angry with me, why he radiated a chill toward me now—I'd rejected him. What I didn't understand was why he thought I would screw over Ting.

I shed my sweater and shoes and turned on some music. There was no point worrying about it. I'd done what I'd promised—I'd paid off Nico's debt.

It was over now.

CHAPTER 31

JAY

I HATED that my suspicions turned out to be true. Maggie and Fred Madsen concocted up some scheme to borrow money from Simon, and now she was paying him back with the same money.

It should have blown up in their face, ending with both of them in the hospital. Except Fred had gotten lucky and met with Alonso instead. If Simon had been there, he'd have listened to my suspicions and never lent to him in the first place. But Alonso was stupid, and now Maggie was paying off Nico's debt with Simon's own money.

How Fred thought he'd get away with this, I didn't know. I didn't care about Fred Madsen. It would be a pleasure to put my fist through his face when I tracked him down. It was Maggie who'd disappointed me.

Her music echoed above me. My whole body tensed, I wanted to go back up there and watch her dance. But I wouldn't. It wasn't the same anymore.

I'd thought she was different. Honest and real and good. Better than me, better than everyone I knew. I'd put her on a pedestal, and it turned out she didn't belong there. She was the same as everyone else. Screwing over Simon and pretending like she had no idea what I was talking about. She wasn't who I thought she was, and that hurt worse than any rejection.

The gym phone rang and I answered. My next class was stretching on the mats.

"Get over here, now." It was Simon, back from his mysterious trip. "You have a mess to clean up."

"What's going on?" I asked.

"The deal Alonso made? It was bogus. There is no Fred Madsen."

Big surprise. "Alonso was supposed to check him out. I told him not to go through with it."

"You didn't tell him hard enough. I had Alfonso track down the address and no Fred Madsen ever lived there. Even the landlord's name was a fake. Fred Madsen—whoever he is—has disappeared."

I clenched my teeth. Simon was pissed, and that meant we were all screwed.

"Every reference he gave was forged. There is no investment." Simon's voice was steel, his anger barely contained. "And now I'm out fifty grand and an employee."

My body went cold. "Alonso?"

"His employment has been terminated."

I slammed my fist into the table and one of the girls in the class looked up at me. My chest heaved. If Alonso had listened to me, he wouldn't be dead and I wouldn't be in this mess.

"Once that's dealt with, you have work to do. Track down this Fred Madsen right away, whoever he really is. Someone out there thinks they can mess with me. That's a message that can't be allowed to get out."

I hesitated. Now was not the time to push Simon. But, "I have a class."

The silence on the other end was long. "As soon as you're done, then. Alfonso can take care of the mess."

If I had doubted he'd done in Aguda, I didn't any longer. "Okay."

"This is your top priority," he said. "I expect you to fix this."

"I will."

"And son," Simon said. "If that gym gets in the way even a little bit, you're out of there."

"I understand."

The line went dead.

I hung up the phone, breathing deep to keep control. Because I was practically his son, Simon was giving me a chance to fix this. Otherwise, I might have been another body for Alfonso to dispose of.

I had to find Fred Madsen, and my only clue to where he'd gone was upstairs dancing.

Find Fred Madsen, or else Simon would take away the gym.

Find Fred Madsen, and put Maggie in Simon's crosshairs.

It was my future on the line, or hers.

CHAPTER 32

MAGGIE

OCTOBER HAD DISAPPEARED, leaving a drab November in its place. Vegas went from brown to even browner as the grass died, the leaves fell from the park trees, and even the palm trees looked decayed and sad.

I worked at the diner and finished choreographing my audition piece, although I was never satisfied with it. It was good, but not quite there yet. With Nico's debt paid, and that extra cash from Fraze, I resumed drop-in classes at Fluidity. I barely saw Jay Thornton and I was pretty sure he was avoiding me.

Life was back to normal for me, but not so much for Bronwyn.

"I'm so sick of this," she said, stuffing a handful of caramel popcorn into her mouth. Bronwyn didn't drown her sorrows in ice cream or chocolate like most girls, or alcohol like Nico. Bronwyn's kryptonite was popcorn of every possible flavor.

I reached for some but her hand beat me to it.

"Why do you hold on?" I asked, leaning away so she wouldn't whack me. I never knew with her.

She'd just gotten out of an hour-long shower that probably sucked the hot water from the whole apartment building. I wouldn't be able to get clean until morning. But she had good reason. Despite paying off Nico's debt, he'd sunk into himself these past few weeks. He never left his apartment, and I was pretty sure his main food group was Heineken.

"I don't know, but I'm done this time." She slammed the bowl on the table and some of the popcorn jumped. *"Done.* I can't sit around and watch him drink himself to death."

I sighed. I didn't know what to say or how to help. Nico's black moods were a mystery. Why she stayed with him was even harder to understand. I was grateful that love had never held me in its grasp so tight that it hurt this much to try and break free.

"I got him an interview at CJ Lynch, did I tell you that?" she said.

I shook my head.

"They need an accountant. I found it in the paper." She leaned her head against the couch and closed her eyes. "I thought with his debt gone, things would turn around. He wouldn't go. Didn't even get out of bed. When I tried to make him, he…"

"He what?"

She opened her eyes but wouldn't look at me. "Doesn't matter."

I put my arm around her. It didn't feel natural, trying to comfort Bronwyn this way, but she leaned into me and rested her head on my shoulder.

"I've never understood why people stay with people who aren't good for them," I said.

"No, you wouldn't."

I didn't take it as an insult, even if she meant it as one. I didn't want to understand. Didn't ever want to be in an unhealthy or toxic relationship. It hadn't been like that with Hank. It had been wonderful, while it lasted. It just hadn't turned out to be a forever thing. Even now, months later, I knew I had made the right choice. When I last talked to my mom, she told me he'd moved on and was now dating Ashley Valenti, my friend Stace's little sister. I was happy for him.

My thoughts turned to Jay and the kiss we'd shared. So brief. So different from kissing Hank. Probably because I hadn't been expecting it. Not because his lips had tasted salty like potato chips, or because even in that few seconds they seemed more practiced and sure than Hank's had ever been. Not because of those reasons at all.

I pushed Jay from my mind. He was probably beating someone up right then, either at the gym, or for real. That was all Jay knew how to do, kiss and fight.

Bronwyn raised her head off my shoulder. "I've gotta go over there."

"Where? Not Nico's?" She didn't answer. I pulled my arm away. "Bron, you said you were done. Isn't this where I'm supposed to say you need to cut the cord or something? Should I hide your bike lock key?"

She stood up. I followed her out of the living room and into her bedroom. Bronwyn had painted the exposed brick an off-white color. Her headboard was pale lavender and she had small vases of flowers on her bedside table. A total girly room, except for her black bike helmet sitting on top of the ruffled duvet, covered in little metal spikes.

"You can't go over there," I said.

"What if something happens to him? No one will check on him. He'll be one of those guys…one of those people that sit there for days and days before anyone notices. Then they'll notice the smell, that's the only reason they'll check."

She was talking crazy. Her hands shook as she pulled off her long sweater and replaced it with a coat.

"I'll go with you."

She didn't say no so I hurried to change from my leggings into some jeans, and then threw on my coat. I didn't want her to leave without me.

We took a bus to the gym, neither of us speaking the entire ride. It was eight at night on a Sunday but the streets were just as busy as if it were rush hour. The cold was nothing compared to winter in Hillstone, but people huddled against the wind that swept garbage from the streets into pooling corners. I would've rather been back at the apartment watching Netflix. When I looked at Bronwyn, at the blank look on her face as if her insides had left her outsides, I knew I was supposed to be there.

At Nico's, I didn't go in with her. I could tell as soon as he opened the door and slurred his hello that this was way out of my depth.

"I'll wait out here," I said, "but I'll be here if you need me."

Bronwyn didn't respond. Nico had stumbled so she had wrapped her arm around him and was helping him to the bed.

"I can walk myself," Nico shouted. He pushed Bronwyn away. "You're not my mother."

"I'm not going to be your anything if you keep this up," she said.

Nico shuffled toward the table. He grabbed a bottle and began to swig, looking at Bronwyn out of the corner of his eye the whole time.

"You have to make a choice, Nico," she said. "Me or the booze?"

I turned away, but the door was still open and I could hear everything. Every insult they hurled at each other, every hateful word. Nico was a mean drunk and Bronwyn wasn't about to take it lying down.

I went to the window and looked out on the street. I shouldn't have come, and yet I needed to be there for Bronwyn when this was all over. If only to be beside her, to make sure she got home. So she wouldn't be alone.

They were screaming now and I desperately wanted to cover my ears. My parents had never been like this. Sometimes they yelled at Fraze and he yelled back, but it was never this bad. None of my friends' parents had either, at least not while I was around. This screaming was unbearable. It wasn't love, it was torture. They were torturing each other and I just wanted them to stop.

There was a loud crash and the sound of something shattering. I spun from the window and ran to Nico's door. Pieces of glass littered the floor. Bronwyn was frozen, her hands over her mouth. Nico was on the floor, his cheek pressed to the wood.

"What—?" I started, moving toward Nico.

Bronwyn grabbed my arm. Nico groaned. He pushed himself off the floor.

Bronwyn gripped my hand. "I can't watch you do this anymore," she said, near tears.

Nico took a step forward and winced. He jumped back, hopping on one foot and swearing.

Bronwyn started to back away.

"Bron, don't go," Nico said. He was examining the bottom of his foot. When she didn't answer, he looked up. "Bron. Baby."

She kept backing away, taking me with her.

"Bronwyn!" Nico shouted.

"Goodbye, Nico," she said.

He continued calling her name but didn't follow. She clutched my hand, pulling me with her until we were outside. And then she broke down. Bronwyn, who was the strongest woman I'd ever met, didn't stop crying until we made it back to the apartment.

CHAPTER 33

MAGGIE

I AVOIDED Eastside Boxing and Nico's apartment. I wanted to practice my audition piece, but I was scared of being near him. Scared he was going to ask me to help him get Bronwyn back. Scared that he'd be so far gone that he wouldn't. Bronwyn wouldn't talk about him, wouldn't let me mention his name, not that I wanted to. She was better off without him. She deserved better. But she wouldn't listen when I said that. She spent her days biking off to work, biking home, and sleeping. That's all she did. I tried the tough love approach she'd used on me but it didn't work. Guess I didn't have the touch.

At one of my drop-in classes at Fluidity, I showed Robbie my audition piece. She was critical, and it hurt, but I needed to hear it. I had known all along it wasn't there yet. More importantly, she had some solid advice on how to tighten the piece up. So I decided to brave the gym, go back to the still empty space and get back to work. It was December now and I only had a few months until my spring audition.

When I arrived at Eastside Boxing, a class was just letting out. This one was female-only, the girls ranging from early twenties to late thirties. A few were shrugging on coats while a group of three chatted loudly in the middle of the mats, clearly not ready to leave.

I took off my boots and left them near the front door. Vegas had gotten colder, but it was mild compared to Hillstone. A couple of days ago, I'd received a big package in the mail—my winter boots, scarf, hat, and heavy mittens sent from my parents who were obviously clueless about Las Vegas weather.

I tiptoed around the shoes near the front door, passing a woman leaning over the front desk talking to Jay.

"It's my favorite place," she was saying. "The food is fab. You should try it."

"Maybe I will."

She was smiling and he was smiling and I averted my eyes because watching a girl flirt with Jay Thornton was just plain weird. Then again, there was something intensely attractive about him, and there was no denying his deliciously muscled body, especially after a workout.

Not to mention those lips...

My cheeks grew hot and I hurried by so Jay wouldn't see, equally relieved he couldn't hear my traitorous thoughts.

Upstairs, a light glimmered under the door of Nico's apartment. Hopefully he wouldn't try to talk to me. I put some music on, the beat echoing from Bronwyn's pig speaker, and stretched, did some middle of the floor exercises to get warmed up, then pulled off my long-sleeved shirt because I was starting to sweat.

I decided to work on some of my jumps before going back to my audition piece. Robbie had said I should use my long legs to my advantage, showcasing my extension and the height I could reach in my leaps.

I went to one corner of the room, waited for the music, then chaséd into a grand jeté. In the space, I only had room for one. I went to the opposite corner and did the same thing on my other leg. After a few more times, I switched to a tour jeté. I wasn't getting enough height, so I tried again, pushing off hard. Too hard.

My legs did a perfect switch in the air but it all went wrong when I landed. My left foot twisted and I went down. Catching myself with the palms of my hands, my left knee hit the floor hard and I let out a yell.

I got up slowly, but when I tried to put weight on my left foot, a sharp pain went through my ankle and up my calf. I stifled a moan. So much for improving my audition piece. I'd just screwed myself for the next couple of weeks.

Hopping on one foot, I slipped my shirt back on and slung my coat over one arm. I gripped each side of the stair rails with both hands and hopped down. My bag kept banging into my leg as I went. My coat fell off my arm and I had to sit down on the step and kick it down the stairs, cringing at the dirt. It landed a few steps up from the bottom.

When I finally made it to my coat, I bent down to pick it up. With only one hand on the rail, I lost my balance and put my left foot down without thinking.

I let out a yelp as I almost fell again, managing to catch myself and lower my butt to the stair. Pain throbbed from my ankle. I covered my face.

"Need some help?"

I looked up. Jay stood over me, his face a cautious mask. Other than him, the gym was empty. The girls from the last class were gone.

"Thanks," I said, "but I think I got it." I grabbed my coat and put the hood over the back of my head. Jay's lips twitched. I held onto the stair rail and lifted myself up, then hopped down the last few steps, avoiding Jay's eyes.

"What happened?" he asked.

"Twisted it." I kept to the edge of the wall so I could hold onto something while I hopped. "Occupational hazard."

"Come on, Maggie, just let me help you."

My gaze flicked between Jay's outstretched hand and his face. At the rate I was going, it would take me half an hour to hop my

way around the edge of the gym to the front door. And then what?
I'd have to get a cab and I hated the expense.

"Okay. Thank you."

He pulled me close. I wrapped one arm around his waist and
he did the same to mine, helping me hobble through the gym. I
clutched his shirt, the hardness of him both intimidating and
comforting. He smelled of sweat, but also vanilla, which seemed
strange on a guy like Jay. When he helped me into my coat, I
caught that whiff of vanilla again coming from his hands. Soap,
probably.

We stopped at the door and he lowered me onto a bench.

"These yours?" he asked, grabbing my leather boots. I nodded.
He bent down on one knee in front of me, lifted my leg and slid
my uninjured foot into my boot, one hand on the back of my calf.
His hair had gotten longer, dark strands fell over his forehead.

"Better take this one slowly," he said, holding up my left boot.

His hand was hot on my leg as he carefully slid my boot on,
then zipped up the side. I couldn't take my eyes off him. When my
boot was on, he put my foot down and looked up at me.

"Now what?"

There was something formal and cold about the way he was
talking to me, as if I were a stranger and not someone he'd kissed a
few weeks ago. I didn't want to ask him for help, especially after
the things I had said, but I also didn't want to brave the streets
with a twisted ankle.

"I think I better go see a doctor." I hesitated. "Could you drive
me? I can't really afford a taxi."

He got to his feet. "I'll get my truck."

He cleaned up some papers from the front desk, flicked off the
lights, and then pulled on a hoodie.

"Don't move," he said before leaving me in the dark. A minute
later, the rumble of his truck pierced the silence. Back inside, he
lifted me to my feet, and helped me hobble outside and into the

passenger seat. After he locked the gym, we took off down the road.

"Where is your doctor?"

I didn't have a doctor in Vegas—I hadn't needed one so far, not counting the bullet graze. Also, it was late, and no doctor's office would be open now. Going to emergency over something this minor seemed silly. But what if it wasn't just a sprain? "Maybe you should just take me home. Or..."

This whole thing was weird, being with Jay in his truck again. Accepting his help when things were so awkward between us. We'd been carefully avoiding each other for the past month. It was easier that way.

"Or what?" Jay asked.

"That guy you took me to before." I paused. "Maybe he could check to make sure it's just sprained? He did a surprisingly good job on my arm."

I'd always have a scar from the bullet graze, but it was nothing more than a red splotch now. The scar itself didn't bother me, but having this connection to Jay, a constant reminder of him, I didn't like that so much. No matter what I did or where I went in life, he would always be a part of me now.

"Okay." Jay didn't say anything more and we spent the rest of the drive in uncomfortable silence.

CHAPTER 34

JAY

WHILE ALFONSO CHECKED Maggie's ankle, I stretched out on the couch. My thoughts were a brawl. I hadn't found one clue to who Fred Madsen was or where he'd gone, nothing that didn't involve the girl sitting across from me, wincing at Alfonso's touch. I didn't know what the hell I was doing taking care of her. She'd proved she could take care of herself. And yet I still wanted to. Wanted to be the one with her foot on my knee while I felt her skin under my fingers. Wanted those fingers to trail further up her leg and—

I squeezed my eyes shut. This girl was doing a number on me. She was trouble—the kind of trouble that could get me killed. I needed to forget her and do my job. Simon was losing patience and I had to come up with something soon.

Find Fred, find something on Simon to take to Hopkins. Then my life could be my own, not Simon's and not Maggie's.

"Jay."

I twitched. My eyes snapped open. I'd fallen asleep. Maggie was standing above me, a tensor bandage wrapped around her ankle.

"All done?" I asked, sitting up.

"Thanks for waiting." She bit her lip. "Could you drive me home?"

I rose from the couch and she started to hop after me. "Do you need crutches or anything?"

"He doesn't have any."

Of course not. I slipped my arm around her waist and helped her out of the house, ignoring the smell of apples in her hair and the desire to be even closer. To pull her into me and taste her lips again, deeper than before.

Inside my truck, Maggie lifted her bad ankle and rested it on the dash. "Ice and elevation," she said. She leaned her head against the seat and looked at me. "The usual."

I put on the radio, hoping she'd take the hint that I didn't want to talk. My fingers tapped along to the beat as I drove. I was antsy with Maggie so close, nervous and angry, my heart beating inside my chest from desire and disgust.

"Thanks," she said. "For the help tonight."

"No problem." Which was a lie, it *was* a problem. She didn't want to be around me, and I couldn't be around her anymore. Not when I knew what she'd done. Not when I still had feelings for her and hated myself for it. Not if it meant Simon might find out about her connection to Fred.

The silence was a thick barrier between us, like boxing gloves, protecting one of us from getting hurt. Problem was, I didn't know who. She'd already hurt me. But I'd never let Simon lay a finger on her.

"Can I ask you a question?" I said. With my eyes on the road, I massaged the back of my neck with one hand. "That guy you were with—"

"What guy?"

As if she didn't know. "On the street outside your work. About a month ago, I saw you with someone. You were hugging."

I glanced at her in time to see realization dawn on her face. "What about him?"

She was trying to contain a smile. My fists tightened on the steering wheel.

"Are you still seeing him?"

"Is that any of your business?"

"I'm afraid it is."

She folded her arms over her chest and huffed. I cursed her stubbornness. If she told me the truth, it would be easier for me to protect her.

I parked in front of The Crampton Oasis. She lowered her ankle from the dash and leaned down to grab her bag.

"That guy," I said before she could open the door. "He took out a loan."

"What?" She snapped her mouth shut. Even in the darkness, a flush was visible on her cheeks.

"A *sizable* loan," I said.

She shifted in the seat. "So?"

"He disappeared. Do you know where he's gone?"

"No."

"Look at me, Maggie."

Her eyes met mine, she didn't blink.

I put my arm over the back of the seat and leaned toward her. "Simon won't let this go. Your friend, Fred, screwed him over. He had references and a complete cover story that turned out to be a sham."

She swallowed. "References?"

"All fake."

"How much?"

"Fifty thousand."

She gasped. But was her surprise genuine?

"I need to find him," I said. "It's my job to find him. You get that, right?"

Her eyes narrowed. "I don't know where he is."

"You're lying."

"No—"

"You looked pretty cozy on the street that day." I'd seen the way he looked at her, like he'd do anything for her. I knew that stupid look. "Don't think I don't know he gave you the money to pay off Nico's debt."

She didn't reply but she started blinking as if struggling not to cry.

"I didn't tell Simon." I clenched my fist, trying to hold onto my anger. It was better than the alternative. "Simon doesn't know you know Fred. He doesn't know Nico's debt came from that loan. If he did…"

Her eyes widened, welling with tears.

"Just tell me where he is, Maggie, and this will all go away. It won't have anything to do with you."

She clenched the strap of her bag, her hands in fists against her chest. "I can't," she whispered.

"Maggie, please." Why was she taking the fall for this guy? Did she love him that much?

"I can't," she repeated, firmly this time.

I reached across her and opened the door. "Fine."

"Are…are you going to tell Simon?"

My jaw tightened. She was right to worry about her own skin. "No. But if he finds out from someone else, there's not much I can do."

She looked away, staring at the dashboard, then slowly nodded. "I understand. Thank you, for tonight." She slid from the truck.

I didn't reply and I didn't help her get out. I kept my hands on the steering wheel and my eyes on the road. As soon as she shut the door, I peeled away.

CHAPTER 35

MAGGIE

I HOBBLED up the steps to my apartment, anger and fear twisting my insides into knots. *Frasier, you idiot!* I wanted to shout. He hadn't gotten the money from his new job, he'd borrowed from Officer Ting so I could pay back Officer Ting, then made off with the rest. No wonder Jay had accused me of screwing over his boss when I gave him the money. He'd *known*.

He'd known and still taken me to Alfonso, waited for me, driven me home, all for nothing and after I'd rejected him. I didn't understand it.

Didn't Fraze realize what he'd done? The trouble he'd put me in? Simon would never let the debt pass with his own money if he found out. He would never let this go. With Fraze gone, I would be the target. The only way I was safe was if Jay decided to keep his mouth shut.

I gnawed on my lower lip. Could I trust Jay to keep his word? He clearly hated me now, so why he'd helped me at all tonight was a mystery. He thought I'd concocted this whole plan with "Fred," that I was actually capable of that kind of deceit and manipulation.

Grabbing my pillow, I pressed it against my face and screamed. A few times. What a mess. Fraze hadn't told me where he was going, only that he had a job with a record producer, which was obviously a lie. He hadn't told me anything to protect me, but it didn't matter, because Jay had seen us together. That had never been part of Frasier's plan.

I clutched the pillow like a lifeline, like the teddy bear Fraze had given me for my fourth birthday. The teddy bear I'd slept with until I turned fourteen but still kept on my bookshelf, a reminder of the brother I loved but rarely saw. It was one of the few things I'd brought with me to Vegas. I glanced at it, sitting on my dresser by a framed family photo. Now I wanted to strangle the stupid thing.

I lifted my swollen ankle and put the pillow underneath. Jay and Officer Ting weren't my only problems, though they were definitely the most dangerous. There was no way I'd be able to hobble around the diner on one foot, even with crutches. Craig would never allow it. This was the second time in a month I'd have to take sick leave and I might get fired over it.

And what about my dancing? A couple of weeks to recover was a couple of weeks without practicing. I couldn't lose that time. I needed every second I could spare or my audition piece would never be good enough for Mallory Hugo and Essence Dance Theater.

I'd thought it was all over, that with Nico's debt paid I could finally get back on track. But life was an even bigger mess than before.

Craig fired me. Apparently, I wasn't even a good waitress, which took my list of talents down to zero. I searched online for job openings, but with my sore ankle, I could barely get around for interviews. Bronwyn borrowed a pair of old crutches from a friend, but suggested, in her latest dead voice, that I wait until I healed before braving the streets of Vegas.

Despite where he got it from, that extra grand from Fraze was a blessing.

Christmas was only three weeks away. Bronwyn hadn't put up a tree or lights or anything festive. I couldn't afford to go out and buy a bunch of decorations so I settled for a dancing light-up tree I found at a local thrift store and Christmas movies on Netflix.

I missed my parents. Missed the snow that blanketed Hillstone in a sea of clean white. Unlike Vegas, where everything was brown and dead and dirtier than normal.

I turned on *White Christmas* just as Bronwyn was coming home from work. She put her bike away and disappeared into the shower. By the time she got out, I was already at the Minstrel number.

"What's this?" Bronwyn asked.

"*White Christmas.*" She gave no sign of recognition. "You haven't seen it?"

Bronwyn sat beside me on the couch. "Doesn't look very Christmasy."

"It gets there, eventually."

We watched the rest of the movie in silence. I wanted to say something, wished she'd talk to me, but at least she was there. With me and not shut up in her room all alone.

When the movie was over, Bronwyn scrubbed tears from her eyes.

I didn't ask if she was okay because she obviously wasn't. I didn't push her to talk. Instead I said, "Do you want to watch another?"

"Sure." She rose from the couch. "You pick while I make popcorn."

I scrolled through the list while she poured kernels into the popper. *It's A Wonderful Life* seemed like a good pick, but it might have been a bit much for her right now. So I decided on *Elf*.

A few minutes later, Bronwyn was back, placing the bowl

between us. I took a handful and popped a piece in my mouth and was hit with a sour blast to the throat. I started to cough.

"Oops, sorry." She grabbed the bowl. "Salt and vinegar. I guess I didn't mix the flavoring good enough." She expertly tossed the popcorn inside the bowl without spilling a piece.

Turning on the movie, I ate the rest in between sips of water. The next handful wasn't as strong.

"Nope, not this one," Bronwyn said. She grabbed the remote.

"What's wrong with *Elf*?" I asked.

"I hate Will Ferrell."

I laughed. "Why?"

"Don't know, just do. I can't watch him in anything."

"Okay then."

To my surprise, she settled on *The Nativity Story*. "Gotta get my religious fix in," she said. "Right, church girl?"

I squirmed. "I haven't gone to church since I came here." It wasn't that I had lost my faith, I just hadn't made time for it. With Sunday diner shifts and no preacher father breathing down my neck, it'd been easy to skip. Now I felt guilty.

Bronwyn gave me a wry smile. I was so happy to see it, I didn't care that she was mocking me. "Don't worry," she said. "I won't tell."

"Who, God, or my dad?"

"Either or."

"Well, thanks for that, but maybe you should be more worried about *your* immortal soul than mine." I grinned and stuffed more popcorn in my mouth.

She paused the movie. "I will, when it's necessary."

Maybe it wasn't necessary, for her. She'd put up with Nico for so long it practically made her a saint in my book.

She grew quiet. I waited.

"I got him a Christmas present, a while ago." She looked at me. "Do you think I should give it to him?"

"That depends. How expensive was it?"

She sorta smiled. "I still love him, you know."

"I know."

"When do you think that will stop?"

I sighed. "I think that's up to you."

She threw a piece of popcorn at me. "Not the answer I wanted, Hale."

"It's the only one you're gonna get." I threw a whole handful at her. She gasped then immediately began snatching the popcorn on her lap and eating it.

"You waste one kernel and I will murder you," she said.

I laughed. "Then I guess you better start worrying about that soul of yours after all."

CHAPTER 36

JAY

AT WORK, McCrary was needling me even worse than usual about buying the gym. "I won't be around forever, you know."

"So I just gotta wait out the clock."

"Oh, is that how it is?" he asked, though he knew I didn't mean it. "I can always give the gym to the Girl Guides, you know. They could use a new clubhouse. Maybe they'll make you their new den mother."

"Get off my back, old man," I said. "I'm working on it."

He slapped a paper down on the front desk. "You're taking too long." His face softened. "I don't want to sell it to some random eejit who won't love it like you do, or tear it down and turn it into another strip mall."

Bergin was warming up my class and I needed to get over there, but I hesitated. McCrary deserved to know the truth. Not about the money, or Simon, because he knew about both. But what was really holding me back. I lowered my voice. "I can't run this place. I don't know how."

McCrary scoffed. "Son, you're the best teacher I've ever met."

The compliment meant a lot, but I'd embarrass us both if I said so. "Not that. I have no clue how to run a business, and this gym is a business."

His mouth worked.

"I know you've tried to teach me, and I'm grateful, but if I take over now, Eastside Boxing will fold in less than a year."

"Then whaddya gonna do?"

"I'm working on it." Simon was more of a problem than me learning how to run a business any day. I could read books for the one problem, but there was no *Quitting Your Psycho Boss/Pseudo-Father For Dummies* for the other.

A cop car pulled up in front of the gym and Simon climbed out. Speak of the devil. I tensed. Simon never came to see me here. But there he was, adjusting his uniform as he stepped onto the sidewalk.

"What's he doing here?" McCrary asked.

I met Simon at the door, blocking him from McCrary's view. The old man wouldn't be able to keep his mouth shut, which would only get us both in trouble.

"What do you need?" I asked. "I have a class in a couple of minutes."

"Everyone needs to leave."

"Everything okay here, son?" McCrary said, standing beside me.

I wanted to push him back. He wasn't helping. "Everything's fine."

Simon narrowed his eyes at McCrary. "Get everyone out of here. Now."

McCrary bristled. "Excuse me? This is my gym, you can't go about—"

Simon yelled over him. "For your safety, I'm evacuating the premises. Everyone grab your things and leave now."

"What's going on?" I asked. Simon started herding Bergin and the students to the door, ignoring their questions and complaints. He was in full-out cop mode, something I rarely saw anymore.

"What is this?" McCrary asked me, but I didn't know any more than he did.

Bergin followed the last student out. Simon peered down the street before closing the front door. He turned. "We had a tip-off at the precinct."

"A tip-off about what?" McCrary demanded, pacing back and forth, cracking his knuckles.

"A gang of armed and highly dangerous men have been targeting specific sites. I believe this gym will be next."

"Why here?" McCrary asked. Simon didn't respond. "Fine. Let's go then."

"Jason is staying with me," Simon replied.

McCrary looked around. "Who's Jason?"

I shot him a look. He was doing it on purpose, trying to get under Simon's skin, but now was not the time.

"Just go," I said to him. "I'll be fine."

McCrary pulled me aside where Simon couldn't hear him. "I don't know what shady thing he's got going on, but you shouldn't hang around for it."

"I have to."

McCrary shook his head. "That man is trouble. It's better to be a coward for a minute than dead the rest of your life."

"I'm not scared of some gang," I snapped.

"Not what I'm talking about." He squeezed my shoulder before he left.

With McCrary gone, I turned back to Simon. "What's really going on?"

Simon's lips tightened. "It's like I said. We got a tip-off. They've already ransacked Pearl of China."

I started flipping off the lights. "Are they going after you, or me? Or both? And who is it?"

"Aguda's gang, under new management, and they're after me. We need to hurry. I don't know if they'll go to my house, your apartment, or come here first. I wanted to get this place clear of civilians, just in case."

I grabbed my bag and hurried to the front of the gym. "Why are they after you?" But I knew why.

Simon put his hand on my shoulder. He had to reach to do it. "Aguda never would have left you alone, and a conviction would never stick. He needed to be taken out. I thought I covered my tracks, but they must have found a connection."

"What did you tell the other cops?" They could protect Simon if they knew he was being targeted, but he'd never be able to explain why.

"A couple of units are chasing them down as we speak. It's a slim chance they'll be caught, though—these guys are sloppy, but we both know how useless cops can be."

The door opened. We both turned. Simon drew his gun.

Bronwyn froze inside the gym, instinctively putting her hands in the air. A gift bag hung from one finger. "What—"

"Get out of here, now," I said.

She didn't listen but went for the stairs. "I've gotta see Nico."

"Grab her," Simon said, but he didn't need to. I already had her by the arm and was dragging her to the door.

"What are you doing?" she shrieked. "Get off me."

"Stop struggling," I said through gritted teeth. "Nico's not here. You need to leave. You're in danger if you stay here."

She scoffed, but stopped fighting. I hustled her back to the front of the gym. Simon was near the glass wall, staring out into the street. His gun dangled in his grip.

A car slowed down on the street, the windows rolled down. Faces, then hands holding guns.

"Get down!" Simon dropped as the sound of gunfire and exploding glass erupted all around us.

I pulled Bronwyn to the floor, covering her with my body. Glass rained down on our heads like pricking snowflakes.

In seconds, it was over. Tires screeched away and then silence.

I didn't move, and neither did Bronwyn. Until Simon groaned.

"Jason," he called. His voice sounded weak.

I lifted myself off Bronwyn, about to ask her if she was okay when my eyes went to her face. Her stare was blank.

"Bronwyn?" I scanned her body but saw nothing. "Bronwyn!" I put my ear near her mouth. No breath. And then I saw it, the blood pooling under her head. The gift bag had fallen near her outstretched hand.

"*Jason*," Simon repeated.

I scrambled to my feet and away from Bronwyn's glassy eyes. Maggie's friend, Nico's girlfriend. Dead. Picking my way over the glass, I made my way to Simon.

His hands were pressed to his side, blood soaked his fingers. "Call 911."

I already had my phone out.

CHAPTER 37

MAGGIE

A CHILL in the night air pierced my sweater and I hurried inside the apartment, shopping bags balanced in both arms. Bronwyn wasn't home, which I hoped was a good sign. She seemed to be getting better every day, less depressed, closer to her normal self. When she came home last night and told me I smelled like a frat boy's bathroom, I knew she was almost there. I wouldn't worry so much about her when I went home for Christmas in a week.

I dumped my bags on the bed, then perused my Christmas purchases. A planner with a black leather cover for my dad—he wanted a new one every year. A collection of Fred Astaire/Ginger Rogers musicals for my mom. For Bronwyn, I found a black and white photograph of the London blitz during World War II. It was of a woman drinking tea and sitting on a pile of rubble. The picture was a little sad, but there was also something hopeful about it. As if ordinary life can go on even when everything gets destroyed. I thought it would go nicely with her collection.

Fraze had been a little harder to buy for, but I'd finally decided on a cheap silver money clip with a note attached that said, "For all your newfound cash." I would never turn my brother in, but I wanted him to know I knew what he'd done.

I also wanted him to know how much trouble he'd put me in, but that wasn't something you put in a Christmas card. Not that I had anywhere to send it at this point.

Worry gnawed at my insides. What if Simon found out that I knew Frasier? Would Jay tell him? What would Simon do?

That last question had my stomach roiling. My mind conjured up images of answering a knock at the door and Simon jumping me, or one of his goons I'd seen at the gym with Jay. Or Jay himself.

I'd open the door, and Jay would be standing there. He'd grab me, pull me close, his lips would meet mine, his hands in my hair...

I shoved that image away. What was I thinking? I didn't want that and neither did he anymore.

My phone rang and I answered. "Hello?"

The voice on the other line was intelligible. My heart began to race.

"Who is this?" I asked.

"Nico... it... It's Nico."

I let out a breath. For a second, I'd been worried it was Fraze, that somehow Simon had found him.

"What's wrong?" I stared at my ankle. It looked swollen after I'd hobbled on it all day.

"Just come," Nico said in between sobs. "Please."

I slipped off the bed. "What happened? Are you okay?"

"No. Bronwyn. She..."

I froze. And then I moved into action. "Are you at home?"

He choked out a yes.

"I'll be right there." I hung up the phone, threw on my coat and shoes, then limped down to the street, leaving my crutches behind. I didn't want them getting in my way.

A cab took me to Eastside Boxing and I gnawed on my fingernails the entire way. What had happened? Why hadn't Bronwyn called? I hoped against hope it was something minor, but Nico's hysterical sobbing suggested otherwise. I urged the cab driver to hurry.

The gym was surrounded by police cars, lights flashing. A small crowd had gathered, as well as some news cameras. I exited the cab on shaky legs. The entire front glass wall of the gym was gone, jagged edges sticking up around the sills.

I tried to get inside but a policeman held me back. "I'm sorry, ma'am. No one can go inside right now."

"But my friends... I think they're inside."

The look he gave me almost stopped my heart.

I spun away from him, searching for a sign of Nico, or even Jay. Someone I knew who could tell me what happened. All I saw were brown uniforms, strangers, and blinding lights.

A familiar voice penetrated the fog around my brain and I stumbled toward it, ignoring my throbbing ankle.

"Jay?"

He had his arms folded across his chest as he spoke to a policeman. He turned toward me as I came close.

"Maggie? What are you doing here?"

"Nico called. What happened?"

The policeman stepped up before Jay could answer. "Lieutenant Hopkins, ma'am. You should go home. We—"

"Where's Bronwyn?" I wasn't interested in going home, or listening to whatever brush-off Hopkins was going to feed me.

The emotionless mask that had been Jay's face fell away. He shook his head, his eyes full of sorrow.

"I'm sorry, Maggie."

No. I didn't want to believe it.

Nico pushed through the crowd of police. He fell on me, clutching me, sobbing into my shoulder. Tears pooled in my eyes— I couldn't stop them—but I wouldn't let myself break down. I stood stock still while Nico hung off me, crying and muttering Bronwyn's name.

The cop said something low to Jay and then walked away. Jay stood there, never taking his eyes off me.

"What happened?" My voice wasn't very loud but Jay must have heard because he came closer.

"Drive-by."

Even with Nico holding onto me, his hot tears soaking my coat, I still felt icy all over. Drive-bys weren't real things, they only happened in the movies, between gangs. Not a boxing gym and my best friend.

"Bronwyn came to see Nico," Jay said. Nico moaned.

"But why?" Why would someone shoot up a boxing gym? "Have they caught the person who did it?"

Jay shook his head. "They're working on it."

Nico let go of me and a cop pulled him aside, probably for questioning.

A cold wind blew open my coat and I shivered. I shifted toward Jay and his body heat. "You were there?"

"Yeah." He zipped up my coat, his hands lingering. I barely noticed. "So was Simon. They've taken him to the hospital."

My eyes shifted to his. He gripped my coat. "Were they after Simon?"

"Yeah."

"So Bronwyn—"

"She wasn't supposed to be there. I tried to get her to leave, before…" His voice trailed off.

My lips trembled, then my whole body. Instead of anchoring me, keeping me still, he let go of me.

"I'm sorry, Maggie."

It was the second time Jay had apologized. But it wasn't his fault. It was Ting's.

Right now, it didn't matter whose fault it was, because Bronwyn was dead.

Bronwyn was dead.

L ater, after Nico had calmed down and Jay disappeared, I went back to the apartment. Bronwyn's apartment. Everything about the place was her, from the framed vintage photographs on the walls to the rows of popcorn flavorings in the cupboard. I stood in her doorway, staring at the girlie purple comforter. My eyes moved to a small bookshelf full of CDs. I hesitated, as if I wasn't allowed to go in. As if Bronwyn might come home at any moment and catch me going through her stuff.

But she wasn't coming home. Ever.

I went to the bookshelf and checked out the CD titles. Metallica, Guns 'N Roses, Nirvana, Bon Jovi. Some band called The Red Jumpsuit Apparatus. This was so Bronwyn. Girlie on one side, total boss on the other. Yet at the same time, I felt like I barely knew her. She had been my best friend here in Vegas, but we'd never spoken of her family. I didn't know about her other boyfriends or if she'd gone to college. I thought I had time.

Time was a cruel trick. I'd had weeks of nothing but time—sitting on my butt and letting my ankle heal so I could get a new job and resume dancing. Now time had been yanked away from me, from Nico, but mostly from Bronwyn. It was gone and she was gone and I could never get either back.

Time took my tears.

CHAPTER 38

MAGGIE

BRONWYN'S FAMILY, who had moved away from Hillstone a few years ago, appeared in Vegas and took her. They were having the funeral and burying her somewhere in South Carolina, so they could be close to her. I wouldn't be able to attend. I wouldn't be able to say goodbye.

They took her things, leaving behind the furniture, the dishes, the photographs on the walls. And me.

I wanted to go home. The apartment without Bronwyn was unbearable. I wanted to see my parents and have Christmas and forget about everything else. But before I could do that, I had to see Nico. Bronwyn would want me to.

It took five minutes of incessant knocking before he finally answered.

"What?" he slurred. His eyes were bloodshot, his face pale and gaunt. He smelled like I felt. I glanced behind him at the disaster that had become his apartment. I pushed past him and went inside.

"Go away."

I ignored him, bending down and picking dirty clothes and garbage off the floor. He slapped them from my hands.

"I don't want you here!" he shouted into my face, his breath a vapor going up my nose. "Leave!"

I backed away, but didn't go, despite my fear. I gathered up a stack of dishes with molding food on them and put them in the sink.

Nico's arms were crossed over his chest but he was swaying slightly on his feet. He swore at me as I continued to tidy up, throwing his clothes in a hamper and getting rid of empty pizza boxes and take-out containers. I filled up a huge black garbage bag with empty beer bottles.

"You can't do this," I said.

"Can't what? Grieve?"

"You can grieve," I said, not looking at him, "but you can't live like this. She wouldn't want you to."

I didn't know if his legs gave out or he'd just given up on life, but suddenly Nico was on the floor curled into the fetal position. I put aside the garbage bag and knelt down beside him.

"Don't talk about her," he said, but there was no anger in the words, just despair. "You don't know…"

"You'll kill yourself this way," I said. "Is that what you want?"

He put his hands over his ears like he didn't want to listen.

I removed his hands and held them in my own. "She's watching you right now. And she's crying."

He squeezed his eyes shut.

"She should be up there, rejoicing. There's no more pain, no more suffering for her, only joy. But instead, she's watching you destroy yourself and I bet you anything she's wishing she could be here to help."

"But she's not," he whispered.

"No, she's not." I didn't know if Bronwyn's tough love had ever worked on Nico, or if she had even tried it. But I had to help somehow. "You have to do it on your own now."

It took him a long time to reply. "I can't."

"You have to." I gave his hands a tug and he sat up. "You can still be sad. You can cry. You can be angry and you can miss her until it feels like you might break." I let go of his hands and waved them at the bag full of bottles. "But you can't do this to yourself. She wouldn't want this."

He stared blankly and didn't respond. After a few minutes, I got to my feet and finished tidying the apartment. When I left, with two full garbage bags in my hands, he still hadn't moved.

I headed down the stairs, my mind still on Nico. It wasn't enough. He would keep drinking himself into a stupor, or worse. Bronwyn had worried that he would die and no one would know. It seemed even more likely now. But I couldn't stay, couldn't take care of him like Bronwyn had. He needed to figure this out on his own.

Down in the gym, I waited until I caught Jay's eye. He looked about as pleased to see me as Nico had been. That didn't stop him from coming over, his scowl smoothing as he got closer.

I tugged on the garbage bags. "Is there somewhere I can throw these?"

He motioned his head to a back door. I headed for it but he beat me there, holding the door open. He followed me out, then grabbed the garbage bags from my hands and tossed them into a dumpster.

"Thanks."

He nodded. His mouth seemed to be glued shut.

A faint smell of rotting vegetables wafted from the dumpster so I went for the door. Jay held it open for me again.

"Are you okay?" he asked when I was right beside him.

I glanced at him and my body started to tremble. "I'm going home."

He rocked toward me, then back. "You won't come back. Will you?"

Tears stung the corners of my eyes. I lowered my head. I had to get out of there before I broke down in front of him. "Check on Nico once in a while."

"Maggie, I really am sorry."

He wasn't lying, I could hear the sincerity in his voice. I moved away from him before I did something stupid, like grab onto him, hold him. Feel someone else's strength holding me up. Walking through the gym, I kept my head down, I couldn't bear to look at anyone.

That was the last I talked to Jay Thornton that year.

CHAPTER 39

JAY

I DIDN'T SAY goodbye to Maggie. I followed her inside, watched her walk away. She was leaving Vegas and wouldn't come back. I'd never see her again.

Look back at me, I silently begged her. She didn't.

It was better if she didn't come back. She was safer that way.

I visited Simon in the hospital. He'd had surgery to remove the bullet lodged in his side, barely missing his kidneys. He had to stay and recover, but he'd be fine.

"Do you have any leads on Fred Madsen?" he asked, wincing as he shifted in bed.

I shook my head. "I've been scouring the internet for any trace, but there's nothing. We don't have a picture of him to use facial recognition software. We don't know his real name so we don't know who we're looking for."

"I won't let some punk get one over on me, and I've got other problems."

His eyes flicked to the security guard stationed outside his door. I'd told Hopkins that Aguda's gang had targeted Simon. He'd set a watch on him for his protection, although he was pressuring me more than ever to get evidence on Simon's criminal activities. With Simon in the hospital, it would be easy to go through his things at home and at his office in Pearl of China for some hard evidence. But I hadn't. Not yet. Simon was in the hospital, partly because of me. He didn't have to come and warn me, or evacuate the gym. It didn't feel right betraying him now. Although I knew, if I wanted my own life, I'd have to do it soon.

"I almost regret Aguda," Simon said. "He had the resources for this kind of thing."

My blood ran cold. Regret the murder, not the man—that's how Simon *should* feel. Aguda was better in the ground.

"If Aguda's boys didn't want to kill me, I'd recruit them." Simon tugged at the blankets over his legs. "I could have used you to get them on my side if it weren't for this Fred Madsen mess. I need that fifty grand."

I leaned forward in the chair. "You really want Aguda's boys working for you?" They made Alonso's rough streak look like playground games.

Simon lowered his voice. "I want *everyone* working for me." His eyes glittered "You can only go so far as a cop, and even at the top the rewards are minimal. It's time to branch out."

"How?" I held my breath.

"I've made contacts over the years. People from all spectrums, criminal and legal, people who know I'm a man to be trusted and feared. It's taken a long time, but I'm close. I was sloppy with Aguda, but I'll get his boys on my side, and then I'll be able to carve out a piece of this city for my own."

My knuckles tingled. "You want to take Aguda's place."

Simon smiled. "That's right, son. And you'll be my right hand. They will bow to you as they bow to me."

I should've seen this coming. But I couldn't believe the man who'd been my father had wanted this. He was supposed to put men like Aguda behind bars, or keep them under control, not become them.

Simon leaned his head against the pillow. "It will take longer now, because of this, but it will happen. Until then, take care of the Fred Madsen problem. Because I'll need you when it's time."

CHAPTER 40

MAGGIE

MY PARENTS WERE glad to have me back. My mom and I watched Christmas movies and delivered hampers to those in need. I went to church and listened to Dad's sermon on the birth of Jesus.

I cried at church, I cried when a single mom broke down over the diapers we'd given her, and I cried watching *The Grinch*. Bronwyn would've laughed at my blubbering. I cried when I thought that, too.

The day after Christmas, I was reading a book my dad gave me, a novelization of the life of Ruth, when Mom came into my room.

"We're so happy to have you home." She climbed into bed beside me, smoothing the comforter over her legs. I put the book down.

"It's been quiet around here without you." Mom put a bookmark in my book and closed it. She never did like it when the spines got cracked with spindly white lines. "I always thought your father talked a lot, but with you gone, I've realized he doesn't talk nearly enough." She let out a low laugh.

It was comfortable to be home, with my mom beside me and Dad out on church errands. I knew what to expect. The colors of my walls and the view outside my window were familiar. I'd missed it all when I was in Vegas.

Now I found myself missing the brick of Bronwyn's apartment. The way her morning showers would always wake me. I missed dancing in my small space above Eastside boxing.

I missed Bronwyn. I missed my life.

"Are you—" Mom started. I looked at her out of the corner of my eye. "When are you going back?"

"I'm not sure." I had nothing to go back to. Bronwyn was gone. I couldn't afford her apartment, not for long anyway. I didn't have a job, and I would never make it into Essence Dance Theater. If Ting ever found out about Fraze, he'd hurt me to get to him.

I thought of Bronwyn. How she'd called me out and told me to run back home. To give up because she thought I was that person. But was I still that person? Hadn't I proved her wrong?

If I did it all over again, this time I'd be proving it to myself.

CHAPTER 41

JAY

EVEN THOUGH AGUDA wasn't a threat anymore, I had Hopkins meet me at Eastside Boxing. The glass window still hadn't been replaced; plastic covered the gaping hole, amplifying the street noise and letting in cold air.

Hopkins didn't bother taking a class this time. He strolled up to the front desk and said, "What have you got for me?"

I handed him a thick manila envelope. "Simon runs a lending business. I've made copies of all his contracts from the past ten years." It hadn't been too hard, smuggling the paperwork from Pearl of China, making copies at the local Kinko's, and then putting it right back where it came from. Simon would never know.

Hopkins peeked inside. "So he's a loan shark. That explains a lot." He looked at me. "Past ten years. There's more?"

"He's been at it a long time."

"This isn't much."

"What do you mean? He's running an illegal business. That's plenty."

He gave me a withering look. "He's a veteran officer and

people like him. At most, he'll get a slap on the wrist, that's my bet."

"Your problem, not mine."

"I need more than this."

"He killed Brian Morris." Alonso's actual name, though none of us had ever called him Brian.

Hopkins sucked in a breath. "You have proof?"

I folded my arms over my chest. "That's your job."

"Anything else?"

"Your hunch was right. He wants to take over Aguda's empire."

"Again, proof?"

"He told me. It's not like he signed a confession." I glanced at Bergin handling my class. "He can't do anything right now. But when he gets out of the hospital, his priority is to win over Aguda's gang. They're leaderless. If they can get over the fact that he killed Aguda, he might be able to do it."

I'd been thinking a lot about this lately. When Simon put his mind to something, he followed through, no matter the trouble or cost. This time, the cost would be me, he just didn't know it yet.

Hopkins tucked the envelope into his jacket. "I'll take this for now, see if I can do anything with it. And I'll look into Morris. With this and his injury, we can slow him down at least. But I want to nail him before we have another Aguda on our hands, and illegal lending won't do it."

I followed him to the door. "He has connections on the force. People looking the other way, even helping him. If he gets the manpower and money he needs, then he'll be untouchable." Hopkins was right, he could bribe his way out of whatever conviction came about over the lending. But he wasn't invincible— Aguda had proved that.

"With your help," Hopkins said, pushing the door open, "I'm certain we'll get him."

I didn't share his certainty. Hopkins didn't know Simon like I did.

I spent a quiet Christmas with McCrary. We had pre-cooked turkey and mashed potatoes and a pie from the grocery store. I was preoccupied, and McCrary knew it, but he didn't push me. There was nothing I could tell him. If things turned sour, I didn't want Simon to think he had anything to do with it.

I visited Simon in the hospital a few days after Christmas. The ward was still decorated with cheap tinsel and paper snowmen, a smiling Santa was pasted on Simon's door.

"Merry Christmas," I said, setting a present on the bedside table. It was a tie—I always got Simon ties. I never knew what else to buy for him.

He cursed at me in Chinese. I didn't bother sitting. If he was in a mood, I wouldn't stay long.

"Have you found Fred?"

"No." I retreated from the bed. "But it was Christmas and—"

"No more excuses." Simon tugged at the neck of his pajamas. "I want it taken care of by the time I get out."

"It's not as easy as—"

He held up a hand and I snapped my mouth shut.

"Let me rephrase that. If it's not taken care of by the time I get out of this cursed hospital, I will find something to motivate you." He raised an eyebrow. "Margaret Hale, perhaps?"

I kept my face blank. "Why should she be motivation?"

He laughed. "Don't think I haven't seen your tongue hanging out around her." My fists tightened. Simon noticed. "Exactly."

"I'll take care of it," I said.

I decided to take a trip to Hillstone. Maybe I could persuade Maggie to give up Fred Madsen. Although I couldn't use Simon's threats as motivation, not when the reason for them was me.

Hillstone was surreal. A place out of a movie, or out of my childhood dreams. I drove down Main Street, parking beside a fifties-style diner with an American flag hanging out front. The whole street was filled with quaint shops, the old brick buildings well maintained. Snow covered the streets, an old man who reminded me of McCrary was shoveling the front step of a post office. Christmas decorations hung from the street lights and most of the shops had window displays made for the season.

I hunched in my rental, completely out of place. Like a crack needle sticking out of a Norman Rockwell painting. I'd grown up in Vegas and never left. I didn't know anything other than the modest suburb I'd called home until I was twelve, the dirty down-town streets after that, then Simon's mansion outside the city. Where Vegas swarmed with vice and sin, this town was a postcard for down-home Americana.

I checked into a bed-and-breakfast nestled between a colonial and a rundown red barn. After taking a shower, I plugged Maggie's address into my phone and headed over.

Maggie's house was a two-story with a wraparound porch and shutters surrounding the windows. I parked down the road a bit so I wouldn't look suspicious, but couldn't make myself get out of the car. This was where Maggie grew up. I could picture her as a child, running around the lawn, rocking in the porch swing, carefree. No wonder life was so easy for her.

Hours went by and still I sat in the car. My excuse was that Fred Madsen might show up, then I could nail him and leave Maggie alone. But he never appeared. If I were him, I'd stay away from Maggie, too, for her safety. Although depending on the nature of their relationship, he might not have wanted to stay away. Hell if I could. There I was in her hometown, practically stalking her.

Maggie stepped out the front door, wearing baggy sweatpants, boots, and a huge coat. Her hair was thrown up in a messy bun, her cheeks turned pink from the cold. I'd almost forgotten how beautiful she was.

She climbed into a car and drove away. I followed her to a pharmacy, parking a few cars away so she wouldn't see me. I tracked her as she headed for the store, her mouth moving and her head bobbing as if singing to herself.

I hadn't realized I was smiling until it melted from my face. Shame and disgust itched at my skin. Maggie, this whole town, it was all too good for me. I didn't belong, not in Hillstone, not in her life. She would hate it if she knew I was here, invading her home and her privacy. Not only would she not give me anything on Fred Madsen, what little trust she had in me would evaporate.

I left. I'd never find Fred Madsen without Maggie's help, but she'd be safe enough from Simon here. Once he was out of the hospital, he'd be more consumed with Aguda's boys than threatening Maggie. And hopefully I could nail him before his thoughts turned to her.

CHAPTER 42

MAGGIE

A FEW DAYS after Christmas I went to the local pharmacy to pick up some supplies. I was browsing the aisles, all three of them, looking at the country knick-knacks, figurines of mice playing instruments and garish 'designer' purses, when someone made a loud and fake coughing sound.

I turned. "Hank!"

He reddened. "Hi, Maggie."

Hank wasn't wearing a cowboy hat for once. His hair was cut different, more stylish than it used to be. His tan had faded a little and his cheeks were red from the cold. Or maybe from running into me.

I hid the box of jumbo size tampons behind my leg. "How are you?"

"Good. Great. Yeah, fine." He rubbed at the top of his head. "You?"

"Fine." I probably didn't look fine in my sweats, knock-off Uggs, and my dad's giant parka. I wasn't even wearing mascara. Hank looked hotter than he used to, but my heart didn't flutter, not even a bit. Still, it felt comfortable to see him again. "I heard about you and—"

"Ashley?" He looked away. "Mags, I—"

"It's great. I'm so happy for you." I didn't sound happy. But I really was. For him. Just not in general.

"Oh." His shoulders lowered. "Well, good. She's really nice."

"I'm sure she is."

He looked at me. I hadn't meant that to sound sarcastic or condescending. Hank wouldn't pick any other kind of girl. He wasn't interested in the girls who got around, the party girls or the ones with bad reputations. He didn't want lying or cheating or boozing. Even though he was only twenty, he wanted a wife.

I hadn't wanted that a few months ago, and still didn't. I barely knew what I wanted anymore, aside from getting into Essence. Jay Thornton flashed in my head and I almost laughed. I didn't want Jay, I was only thinking about him because he'd been the only one who'd been interested in me.

"Anyway—" I started.

"I should—" Hank said at the same time.

We both let out a nervous laugh.

"Yeah, I should go," I said. "It was nice seeing you, though. I'm glad everything worked out." I moved past him to the front counter.

"Did it?" he asked.

The lie slipped easily off my tongue. "Of course."

W hen I got home, there was a giant package sitting near the front door.

"What's this?" I asked when Mom appeared at the top of the stairs. She hurried down.

"It's from your brother!" she said. "Can you believe it? Frasier never sends gifts."

Frasier never had the money to send gifts before. I examined

the box. There was no return address, just his name in the top left
corner in big bold letters.

"I was waiting for you to get home so we could open it together." Mom called my father who materialized from his office. He
picked up the box with a grunt and carried it to the Christmas tree.

Mom handed Dad a kitchen knife and he sliced through the
tape. Inside was a pile of crumpled newspaper. Dad took it all out,
and Mom immediately placed it in recycling. When she was back,
Dad lifted out the presents. There were four, all wrapped in Santa-
themed paper.

Mom opened hers first. It was an exquisite porcelain statue of
Mary holding the baby Jesus. "Oh," my mom breathed. She held it
tenderly in her hands.

Dad's present was a collection of books on doctrine and scripture study. Dad's mouth dropped open. These weren't the kind of
presents typical of Fraze, and not just because of the cost. He
usually got us gag gifts—like the time he got me a Santa that
pooped M&Ms. Or when he got my Dad a card that said, "You're
old enough to be told that the Easter Bunny and Jesus aren't real."

Dad did not like that one bit.

I opened mine, tearing off the paper and hoping my brother
hadn't gotten me a golden cross or something. My package was
much smaller. I lifted the lid off the box and stared.

It was a pair of Undeez—contemporary dance shoes made of
leather strips. I'd made mine and they looked dreadful. Now I had
a real pair. How had Fraze known?

"These are quite the gifts," Mom said. My parents exchanged
glances, probably wondering how Fraze could afford it all.

Dad handed Mom the last box. There were also two envelopes.
One he handed to me, it had my name on it. The other he opened.

"Dear fam," he read. *"I hope these get to you by Christmas but I was
cutting it a little close. Sorry if they're a few days late. It's the thought
that counts, right? Anyway, I have a great new job and I wanted to get
you guys some good stuff this year. But I couldn't help getting one of* my

gifts. You know what I'm talking about. Merry Christmas to you all, and to all a good night! Love, Frasier."

Mom unwrapped the present and I tried not to laugh. It was Cards Against Humanity. "A game for horrible people," my mom read. Dad's mouth tightened. It would go straight in the dumpster. Dad wouldn't re-gift it because he wouldn't want anyone else to be corrupted.

Mom put the game aside and picked up her statue. She ran her hands along the off-white porcelain. "This really is beautiful," she said, probably trying to distract my dad from the game. "I wonder how he could afford it?"

I slipped off my fuzzy socks and tried on my Undeez. They were a perfect fit. "His job sounds pretty good." How had Fraze known the size of my feet? "He said he's working for a record producer or something." I didn't meet their eyes; I didn't like to lie. But maybe it wasn't a lie. For all I knew, he could've taken that job, if it existed.

Who was I kidding?

"So he says." Dad sat down in his chair, the stack of books on his lap. He started flipping through one.

My brother's letter to me sat unopened on my lap. I took it, and my new dance shoes, and slipped out of the room.

Upstairs, I went into Frasier's old room. All of his stuff had been cleared out, either taken by him or boxed away. The furniture was still the same, but empty. Only his navy blue plaid comforter reminded me of him. I sat down on the edge of the bed and tore open the letter.

*"Hey sis. Hope you like my present. I had to do some reconnaissance before I left to figure out what you might want. I went through your stuff multiple times, even your unmentionables. GROSS. Anyway, I found your taped up pieces of crap that I assumed were shoes in your dance bag, and that's when I knew. It wasn't hard to charm the girl at the dance clothes store to help me out. *wink wink**

I hope you have a great Christmas, but don't get trapped there. Go back to Vegas, get Bronwyn away from that soul-sucking boyfriend, and give Dad a heart attack by getting into that dance company. Got it? These are things you have to do and I expect you to do them. ~~Get a better job while you're at it.~~ Never mind that last bit. I want free food when I visit again. Love and stuff. F."

A storm of emotions swirled inside me. An ache over missing my brother. Annoyance that he thought the food had been free. And sadness at the mention of Bronwyn. He didn't know. How could he? I hadn't emailed him since he left.

I sighed, scrubbing away the tears at the corners of my eyes. I'd have to tell him, but not yet.

I refolded the letter and put it back in the envelope. Fraze, Bronwyn, they all thought I could do it. Be more than the girl from Hillstone. More than Hank's wife or the preacher's daughter.

I'd gone to Vegas thinking the same, but it hadn't turned out the way I thought. I'd become more, in some ways, and also less. But I still didn't know who that person was, or who I was supposed to be.

The only way to find out was to go back. To try again and again, like Bronwyn had said. When I'd been in Vegas before, I'd made a start. It was time for me to finish.

CHAPTER 43

MAGGIE

I ONLY SPENT two weeks at home, but it was hard to return to Las Vegas. My mind tugged in both directions. Stay in Hillstone where everything was safe, but static. Return to Vegas, to an apartment without Bronwyn and back into the world of Jay Thornton and Simon Ting. I was going back to nothing but trouble. Or nothing *and* trouble.

The apartment was cold when I stepped inside, cold with the breath of a thousand ghosts. Or just one. The first night back, I flicked on all the lights and didn't turn any of them off, even when I went to bed. I'd been lonely when I first came to Vegas, but Bronwyn had saved me from it. Now I had nothing and no one to keep the loneliness away. So I kept myself busy.

I searched for a job. I ate Cup-o-Soup and walked everywhere to keep expenses down. Bronwyn's bike still rested against one wall in the apartment, but riding it didn't feel right. Dad had lent me some money and I didn't bother telling him I didn't need it right then. I would eventually, plus I was grateful for it. Not just the cash, but the meaning behind it. That he was starting to support my decision. If only he knew about Officer Ting.

I went back to Eastside Boxing to check on Nico, and hopefully to practice. The lights were on and Imagine Dragons blasted from a stereo somewhere inside. Jay was going crazy on a punching bag, his shoulders hunched near his ears, his dark hair slick with sweat. He wore low-slung shorts and no shirt, the muscles on his back rippling.

He didn't spot me staring, which was probably a good thing. I couldn't help myself. He had the kind of body I'd only ever seen in movies, and it was breathtaking. I never thought I was the kind of girl to get all hot and bothered over a six-pack, but I was *this* close to fanning myself.

I crept past him. When I reached the stairs, I looked back. Jay was holding the punching bag, his eyes on me. There was something in his face, but I was too far away or I didn't know him well enough to understand what it meant. I turned away.

Nico wasn't home when I knocked, or he wasn't answering. I sincerely hoped he wasn't passed out in there...or worse.

I put in my earbuds and did some laps around the small space next to his apartment. I did jumping jacks, ran in place with my knees up, and did some chasés around the room. My ankle had healed up over the holidays; it didn't twinge at all. I was in the middle of stretching on the floor when Nico came up the stairs.

His mouth moved, but I didn't hear him. I turned my music off.

"Hi," I said, giving him a hesitant smile. He was pale with dark rings under his eyes, but at least he looked sober.

"I didn't think you'd come back." He opened his apartment door.

"You and me both." I rose from the floor and followed him in. "Do you think Jay...McCrary will mind if I keep practicing here?"

"Nah, I'm sure it's fine." His apartment was clean. Not one beer bottle. Nico must have seen me looking because he said, "It's all gone."

I raised my eyebrows.

"At first, I thought I could cut back a bit and still be fine." He set his keys on the kitchen table. He stared at it as if afraid to face me. "But that's what they all think, don't they? Then I'd wake up in the morning, or the afternoon, and not remember a thing about the night before." He looked at me. "All or nothing. I've always been that kind of guy."

"How's it been?" I asked gently.

He pulled out a chair and sat down. "Hell." The table was covered in books and a laptop.

"Project?" I asked.

He shrugged. "I've gotta do something to keep busy."

"I know what that's like. I need a job. Know anywhere that's hiring? *Not* a diner? Or fast food. Or food of any kind."

"If I did, I'd be working there instead of here," he replied. "What are you looking for?"

I flipped through the books. "I'd prefer somewhere cool, you know? Like a kitschy shop or a boutique that sells great clothes. Something interesting. But I'll probably have to settle for whatever I can get." I held up a book. "Accounting?" The other books were about managing a small business, entrepreneurialism, and Managing Debt for Dummies.

"Trying to brush up. It's been awhile."

I hid a smile. Bronwyn would be proud. And more than a little annoyed that he hadn't gotten his butt in gear when she was alive.

I swallowed the sudden lump in my throat. "I'll leave you to it."

At the door, Nico called my name.

"Thanks," he said. "For the pep talk before Christmas, I mean. I needed it."

At least I'd done something right.

My audition piece wasn't right. No matter what I did, what I danced, what I added or took away, it was missing something. But I still had a couple more months to dig deep and choreograph something amazing. YouTube videos might help, or past seasons of *So You Think You Can Dance*. Maybe they'd inspire me.

I hurried down the steps of the gym and almost collided with Nico at the bottom. He was mopping the floors. It was the first time I'd actually seen him do any janitorial work.

"See you later, Maggie," he said, giving me a wave before bending back to his mop.

"Bye."

Jay was sitting behind the front desk, brows furrowed, a spread of papers in front of him. He'd put a hoodie on, zipped to his neck. He rubbed his forehead with one hand, the pen between his fingers almost poking him in the eye. I tried not to laugh.

He looked up at me as I passed and my eyes darted away.

"You came back."

I put my boots on, dug a hat out of my bag. I couldn't tell if he was happy that I was back or not.

"I didn't think you'd come back," he said, his voice flat.

He didn't mean the boxing gym. "I thought about staying home, in Hillstone."

"Is that where you're from?"

I nodded. Of course he wouldn't know that. We'd barely had a real conversation before. Not about anything normal.

"It's small. You've probably never heard of it." He wouldn't want to go to a place like Hillstone. Too tame. Too boring for a guy like Jay.

He looked down at the papers on the desk. "What's it like?"

"It's beautiful. Green in the summer. White in the winter. Like a painting." I tried to picture Jay there, walking down Main Street, or sitting on the porch swing at home, but I couldn't see it. He wasn't meant for anywhere but Vegas.

"Why didn't you stay?" His tone was harsh and a little offensive.

My anger flared. "Sometimes I really don't know."

Truth was, I'd missed Vegas. At first, I assumed I was missing Bronwyn, but it wasn't only that. I'd grown used to the noise, the bustle, the constant activity of strangers around me, the lights from the strip. I'd missed the possibilities I hadn't taken advantage of yet. There were no possibilities in Hillstone, just dead ends. But I didn't want to tell Jay that. Didn't want to give him the satisfaction.

"See you later," I said. I was a little hurt when he didn't say anything back.

CHAPTER 44

JAY

MAGGIE WAS BACK IN VEGAS. I thought she'd be smart and stay away, especially after Bronwyn. But there she was, pushing her way out of the gym, a beanie perched on the back of her head, her hair falling down her shoulders. Back to complicate my life, and her own.

I wanted to toss her all the way back to Hillstone and tell her to stay put. Simon would be out of the hospital any day now. If he wasn't consumed by taking reign of Aguda's gang, he might remember to threaten me by threatening her. I needed hard evidence on him before that happened.

Maggie disappeared from view and I looked away, only to catch Nico's eye. He had a mop in hand but he was standing there, smirking at me.

"What?" I barked.

He hitched his shoulders before bending over his mop. "Nothing."

Nico had been taking better care of the gym this past week than he had since he'd started. The place was always spotless now, even the bathrooms. The guy had been a borderline alcoholic before, but lately I hadn't caught so much as a whiff on him.

I tried to organize the front desk as best I could—McCrary would be in tomorrow to check the books. I filed away receipt copies, paper clipped a stack of permission forms for an upcoming tournament, then went through the messages blinking on the phone. One of them was from a parent who'd sworn they'd paid the yearly tuition up front but they'd received a statement for a balance owing. I searched through the filing cabinet for their name or a receipt of payment, but found nothing. I slammed the door shut with a growl.

"Old man McCrary really should get a computer." Nico leaned over the front desk, peering at the messages I'd scrawled.

"You know how many times I've told him that?" I massaged the back of my neck. "I have no clue how he's got everything organized, how am I supposed to find one client's payment history?"

Nico tapped the desk. "If you ever convince him, I can help him go paperless."

"You?"

"I didn't go to college to be a janitor, you know."

"I didn't know you went to college at all."

"Accountant." He must have read the disbelief on my face because he said, "No really. I am."

"Then what the hell are you doing here?"

"Bad luck and Simon Ting." He played with the mop, switching the handle between both hands. "Can't just blame that, though. It's my fault too. Wrecked my own life, brought Bronwyn down with me."

Not that I didn't respect him for fixing his life, but I didn't need to get this personal with the guy.

He lowered his forehead against the top of the mop handle. "She told me, over and over. But I wouldn't listen. Now she's gone and…" He looked up at me. "Anyway, she'd be proud I'm getting my act together. At least, that's what Maggie says. I don't really believe in all that heaven, afterlife, God kind of stuff."

"That sounds like Maggie."

"Yeah. Before Christmas, she told me to shape up. Said Bron was wasting her afterlife being disappointed in me, or something like that. I figure, I screwed up her life enough, I shouldn't screw up her death, too."

Maggie was so full of belief in something other than herself. I didn't know how to be like that.

"I didn't think Maggie would come back," Nico said.

My eyes flicked to his.

"She had nothing to come back to, with Bron gone. I wasn't exactly the greatest friend, letting her pay off my loan like that. And she doesn't even have a job now. She got fired from that diner."

I fiddled with the papers on the desk. "Do you know where she got the money?"

"No clue."

He didn't blink. I might've called bull, but why would he know? Simon was off his back, that's all he cared about. Maggie and Fred had whipped up the scheme on their own.

"I owe her one," Nico said. "Wish I could help her, but I can't even find myself a decent job."

I shoved a drawer closed a little too hard and met his eyes. Why was he babbling at me? There was a knowing smirk on his lips and I wanted to punch it off his face.

"You need something?"

"Just saying. Hint hint."

"Hint hint what?"

"That Maggie is looking for a job. A store or boutique or some-where 'cool,' she said. I don't know any places like that."

"And you think I do?"

Nico shrugged and walked off, carrying the mop over his shoulder and whistling like an idiot. He disappeared upstairs and I went through the gym, turning the lights off.

Who cared if Maggie needed a job? Wasn't my problem. I sure as hell didn't owe her anything. Besides, she wouldn't want my help. If she didn't find a job, maybe she'd go back home again. That would solve both our problems.

Except, I *did* know of a place along the lines of what Maggie wanted, and the owner's husband owed me one.

I was dialing his number before I'd even made the decision to help.

"Sam? It's Jay." I balanced my phone against one ear as I locked up the gym. "I've got a favor to ask. Your wife Lacey's store. Can she use another employee?"

The deal was done before I reached my truck.

CHAPTER 45

MAGGIE

I'D DROPPED off my resume at a handful of places, but never heard anything back. How did people land their dream jobs anyway? Or did they? Was gynecology anyone's dream job? What about managing a fast food joint, or cleaning roadkill off the highways, or being a mortician? Did people choose those things, or just get pulled into them somehow and never end up leaving?

If I'd never been fired from *Holy Diner!* I might've been stuck there for the rest of my life, taking orders, getting to know the regulars, maybe earning a half dollar raise. Yuck. I didn't want to be stuck anywhere, didn't want my future mapped out like that.

I decided to drop off resumes to places I wanted to be, even if they weren't hiring. I handed them out to all the kinds of shops I'd want to work in, wearing my best outfit and brightest smile. It might come to nothing, but it was worth a shot. I'd never get a job at a place I wanted if I didn't try.

When my cell phone rang a few days later, I didn't recognize the number.

"Hello?"

"Is this Maggie Hale?" a woman asked.

"Yes."

"Hi, Maggie. You don't know me, my name is Lacey Benwick and I own a store just off the strip. We need a sales associate and I wondered if you'd like to come in and interview."

"Oh." I paused. I didn't hand out resumes anywhere near the strip. I hoped this wasn't a scam. "Did you get my resume?"

"No, you were referred to me by a close friend."

I blinked. Referred? Close friend? "I would love to come in. What's the name of your store?"

"We're called Maquitte. We sell a combination of clothing, accessories, and home decor."

She told me the address and I jotted it down on my arm. "That sounds great. When would you like me to come in?"

We arranged a time and I hung up, excited but also confused. Who could've referred me to this place? I barely knew anyone in Vegas. Except Nico, who I'd just complained to about my job situation. Did he know someone at Maquitte?

The next day I walked into the store and gasped. Modern décor covered the walls, a glass chandelier hung from the ceiling. My eyes roamed over a mix of country and urban pieces. Soft leather purses dangled from racks and antique style jewelry nestled in bowls. And the clothes—my goodness, the *clothes*. I wanted to take every piece home with me.

A woman greeted me at the door, her hand stretched out. "I'm Lacey, nice to meet you."

Lacey was beautiful, sporting a trendy angled bob and light tan. She seemed older than me, though not by much which was a surprise since she owned the store. She put me right at ease and I ended up nailing the interview. She hired me on the spot. I went back to Bronywn's apartment—I'd always think of it as hers—with a smile on my face and a bounce in my step. I owed Nico, big time.

I went to Eastside Boxing that night with a couple of large pizzas from the place Nico and Bron used to order from, plus a six-pack of ginger ale. Nico was surprised when he answered the door.

"We're celebrating," I said, while Nico cleared the books from the table.

"Celebrating what?"

I put the pizzas down, then cracked open a can. "My new job." I held it up like a toast. "To you!"

Nico opened his own soda, but he gave me a weird look. He sipped, then made a face. "Disgusting."

"Better than beer any day." I took a slice of pizza, the cheese dripping off the top.

"Are you checking up on me?" he asked, motioning with his slice. "Is that what this is? Not that I'm complaining."

"I wanted to say thank you," I said, "for helping me get my new job."

He pressed his lips together, like he was trying not to laugh. "I didn't do anything."

"What?"

"I've barely left this building since Christmas. I've been too busy with all this stuff, and cleaning, and before…"

He didn't need to talk about before, I already knew about that. But if he didn't refer me to Lacey, then who had?

"Let's celebrate anyway." I'd figure out who referred me later. Maybe Lacey would tell me.

He smiled. Maybe he was lying about the referral, but I didn't push it. I was happy to see the smile there in the first place.

"I never say no to free food," he said.

Now that sounded like the Nico I knew.

After dinner, I took my stuffed self to my dance space and tried to work on my audition piece without vomiting. I'd eaten way too much. I gave up after less than ten minutes. I hadn't brought my dance clothes anyway and it was awkward trying to dance in jeans.

I headed down the stairs, my hand over my aching stomach. I'd have to be extra good tomorrow to make up for everything I'd eaten tonight. Essence wouldn't let me in if I gained twenty pounds.

On the mats, Jay was putting away some dummies, pushing them against the far wall. His arm muscles bulged with the effort.

"Need some help?" I bit my lip. Why had I offered?

"No." He shoved the last dummy against the wall and I went for my boots at the door. "Unless you want to clean the bathrooms."

I shuddered. "No, thanks. I had enough of that at my last job."

He came closer. "You don't work at the diner anymore?"

"Getting fired from that place was the best thing that happened to me."

"Why?" He crossed his arms. It made his biceps bulge, which is probably why he did it all the time. To intimidate men and make women drool.

"I got a new job. A little boutique near the strip. Haven't started yet." I slid my feet into my boots. "Anyway, isn't cleaning the bathrooms Nico's job?"

"When he gets around to it," he said. I straightened, making a face, which he noticed. "Don't worry, he will. He's been a lot better."

When Bronwyn was around, it didn't seem like he did anything at all. It was a good sign that even Jay noticed Nico was doing better.

"And that's thanks to you, I hear." Jay was close to me now, so close I could feel the heat coming off his body. I wanted to lean into it before I remembered who it was and what he thought of me.

"Me?" Why did my voice sound so breathless? And why was I looking at his lips?

"You." Jay's head tilted, and he leaned in.

CHAPTER 46

JAY

MAGGIE STARED at my lips like she wanted to kiss me. I could give her what she wanted. It was hard not to when every muscle in my body was tense, begging for some kind of release. I leaned in and her lips parted in surprise. I pulled a piece of fuzz off the shoulder of her coat and flicked it away. She blushed. I hid a smile.

"What do you mean, thanks to me?" she asked, stepping back.

"Sounds like you talked Nico off his ledge."

"I don't know about that. I just didn't want to see him hurt himself. Worse than he already was, I mean."

No one cared about people as much as Maggie. It was probably a preacher's kid kind of thing. I'd never gone to church so I didn't know a lot of religious types. Maggie wasn't in-your-face about her beliefs, but there was something about her that I hadn't seen in anyone else.

Of course, that something didn't matter after she'd lied to Simon, screwing him and trying to get away with it. *That* I'd seen a lot of, just never to Simon Ting.

Maggie was studying me, a crease between her eyebrows. I met her stare, daring her to speak first. I should've known Maggie wouldn't back down from a challenge.

"Why do you work here?"

The question caught me off guard but I answered honestly. "I like teaching."

Her eyes widened, as if she couldn't believe I wanted a normal life as much as anyone.

"I don't want to work for Simon Ting forever."

"Really?"

Right there, that said it all. All she saw in me was a fighter, a lackey. She couldn't see past that to who I really was. She hadn't ever tried. I leaned closer. "One day, I'll own a gym of my own, this gym, and I won't have to answer to Simon, or to anyone but myself. So you can get off your high horse and stop judging me."

She opened her mouth but I didn't let her speak.

"I used to believe you came from another world, one that I had never, and would never, be part of. But deep down, you're just like all the rest. You and that friend of yours manipulated and lied your way out of Nico's debt. Plus a nice little bonus to boot. Is your cut of that paying the rent?"

Heat rose in her cheeks.

"I've met plenty of lowlifes and criminals, the kind of people who'd come up with something like that. I never expected it from you. Bravo."

"I didn't—"

"*Don't* lie to me. I'm not stupid." I'd put her on a pedestal because I'd wanted to know someone who wasn't capable of this kind of deceit. It had been nothing more than a pipe dream. "You're lucky Simon doesn't know. You don't realize what he'd do to you if he found out. Or to me. He's like a father to me, and I'm lying to him. For you."

Her eyes filled with tears. "You don't... It's not what you think."

"I don't care. Do you understand?"

She turned her back on me.

I wanted to press my lips to her hair, her neck, her skin, everywhere.

I wanted to forget she ever existed.

"I don't care about you at all," I said. I almost believed the lie. "Don't give me a reason to pay attention to you again."

The door to the gym swung open. Alfonso stopped when he saw us, his eyes widening.

I stepped around Maggie. "What do you need?"

He tilted his head to the street. "Come."

Simon's Lexus idled near the curb. My blood froze. "He's out?" Either that, or Alfonso had stolen his car. Which would get him just as dead as Alonso.

"He needs you," Alfonso said.

I'd had a breather while Simon had been laid up, but now it was gone. Did he already want me to start recruiting Aguda's boys? It didn't matter. He called, I went. And I had to keep going for now because it was the only way to get something on him to take to Hopkins.

Maggie hadn't moved. Maybe she was afraid of Alfonso, or more likely Simon. "You need to leave so I can lock up," I said, shrugging on a hoodie.

She lifted her chin.

Alfonso moved in front of the door. "Her too."

She faltered. "Me?" Her eyes flicked to mine.

"Both of you." Alfonso gave me a look he didn't have to bother with. It said, *bring her or else.* He went outside. This was bad. Simon should have no reason to want Maggie unless he was using her to threaten me, or if he'd found out about Fred.

"I'm not going with him."

I moved in front of her, blocking her from the outside. "He won't hurt you."

She searched my face. "What about you?"

I scowled. "You should know better."

"It's your job, isn't it?"

"I may not be interested in you anymore, but that doesn't mean I'll hurt you."

For a long moment, her eyes never left mine. Then she took a breath and nodded.

I opened the door and cocked my head. Maggie hesitated, then went to the car. She climbed into the back seat and I went in after her.

Maggie faced forward, ignoring Simon, even though she was sitting right beside him. Alfonso got into the driver's seat.

She shifted closer to me, pressing her thigh into mine. She trusted me more than him. It felt like a win.

"Margaret Hale," Simon said. She looked at him, but leaned her shoulder into me as if she didn't want her face too close to his.

Simon smiled. He was still pale, but otherwise looked healthy. I hadn't expected him out of the hospital this soon. "I appreciate the expediency with which you handled Nico's loan. It's always satisfying to close an account."

"Great," she said. It didn't sound like she meant it.

"How did you come by the money?" he asked. "I'm curious. I wouldn't think your job at that diner would pay you enough."

Her body tensed. "It didn't."

He knew. Somehow, he knew Fred and her were connected. My legs twitched. The air in the car was stuffy. Alfonso was watching from the front, his eyes on the rearview mirror.

Simon tapped his finger against the front seat and Alfonso pulled onto the road. I was surprised he was letting someone else drive his Lexus, but that didn't matter right now. Simon's hands were covered in black leather gloves. As much as another murder would help my case, that wasn't the kind of evidence I wanted to gather.

"A girl like you probably has good credit," he said.

Maggie folded her hands in her lap. I desperately wanted to

take one in my own, to comfort her, not that she would've wanted me to.

"I assumed that's what you would do. But you didn't take out a bank loan recently. Or ever, for that matter."

Simon had done his research. I'd been hoping he'd never look into where she got the money once it was paid up, but that hope was dead now. He had to know. But why waste time with this charade?

"Then I thought, maybe you have parents with means. It's not uncommon for children to try to make their own way in the world, then run to Mommy and Daddy for help." He leaned toward Maggie. "But that's not the case with you, is it?"

Simon opened a briefcase and pulled out some papers. "Richard and Maria Hale. A preacher and his lovely wife." He held the papers out to Maggie but she didn't take them. I glanced at the top sheet, a picture of an older couple stepping off the porch of their house, their mouths open in conversation. They were both bundled up, snow nestled at their feet. This wasn't a picture he'd gotten off the internet. This was a picture he'd sent someone to take, and recently.

Maggie stared at her hands. The tips of her fingers had gone red from squeezing. I slid my hand between my leg and hers, curling my fingers so my knuckles were digging into her thigh. It was reminder that I was there, that she wasn't alone.

Simon shuffled the papers, pulling a new one on top of the other. "Hank Markham, your high school beau."

I stiffened, glancing at a photo of a goofy looking guy wearing a cowboy hat and an earnest smile. Maggie had dated *that* guy? Between him and Fred, she had terrible taste in men.

"His family runs a successful ranch. Did you borrow the money from him?"

She looked up and swallowed.

"He looks like a nice boy." Simon held the picture of Hank beside his own face like some weird comparison. It hit me then, why Maggie never gave me a chance. To her, I was more like Simon than I was this Hank. No wonder she had no interest in me.

"He *is* nice," she said quietly.

Simon's eyes narrowed. "The kind of boy who would do anything for his girl?"

She lifted her chin. "I'm not his girl anymore."

"No? Then where, may I ask, did you come up with thirteen thousand dollars? See, things just don't add up. And I like things to add up."

Maggie started to tremble. I wanted to pull her out of this car and away from Simon. Away from everything but me.

Alfonso pulled up in front of Maggie's apartment without anyone telling him where to go.

Maggie glanced at her apartment, at me, then back at Simon. "Does it matter where I got the money?" Her voice rose, fear replaced with anger. *There's my girl,* I thought, before I remembered she had never been mine. "I've paid off the debt. It's done. If I've borrowed from someone else, that's my problem with them and has nothing to do with you."

I nudged Maggie's leg, trying to tell her to shut up. She'd said too much. Simon's face went blank.

"I see." His eyes moved to me and I kept my face neutral. No doubt he was going through all the other Vegas loan sharks he knew, wondering which one she'd borrowed from. He'd look into it, or ask me to, and when nothing came up, would he put Maggie and Fred together?

My fist pressed against her leg. I couldn't let him hurt her, and yet I hated her for putting me in this mess. If Maggie Hale had never come into my life, I probably could have been free of Simon by now and doing what *I* wanted. But hadn't I learned early in life that I didn't get what I wanted?

"I don't think we need to know anything else," I said. "We can let the girl go."

Simon ignored me. "We'll talk later, Margaret."

I opened the door and climbed out before Simon could change his mind. Maggie got out after me. She looked into my eyes and I looked into hers. For a moment, I felt like we could've been other people, with simple problems, together.

And then I remembered how she had rejected me. How she thought she was better than me. How she had landed herself in trouble and now expected me to bail her out.

My eyebrows lowered into a scowl. I turned away. When I got back in the car, Simon didn't say anything until Alfonso had driven off.

"I had a lot of time to think in the hospital about where Margaret could have gotten that money," Simon said. "It's too much of a coincidence that Fred Madsen borrows fifty and then Margaret Hale pays off Nico's debt a few days later."

I didn't answer.

"They know each other. They have to." Simon put the papers back in the briefcase. "To be honest, I never would've thought that girl had it in her. Especially after digging into her family. Preacher's daughter, good student, no trouble with the law. You never can tell with some people."

"We'll need proof," I said, hoping to stall him from doing something rash. "You've got your rep to worry about if you want Aguda's boys on your side. Can't afford a mistake." My gut roiled. For once, I didn't want to punch something. I wanted to run, and take Maggie with me.

"Of course," Simon replied. "I'll call the other lenders first, just to be sure."

"You want me to handle it?"

"Have you found Fred?" Simon knew the answer from my lack of response. "Find him. Plus, I've arranged a meeting for you with Andrew Arthur. He owes me one but I want you to feel him out, see if he'll join the business."

Andrew Arthur, the worst of Aguda's boys. Convicted of multiple counts of rape and assault. Simon had gotten him off on a minor charge a while back. My body went cold. I could tell Hopkins about Arthur, but we needed something on Simon, and he wouldn't even be at the meeting. He'd be too busy looking into Maggie.

He wouldn't go after her until he had proof she screwed him.

It was only a matter of time.

CHAPTER 47

MAGGIE

THE LEXUS DROVE AWAY, but the threat didn't leave with Simon Ting's car.

I'd wanted to run away when Alfonso had told me to get in the car. Like I would go easily. Might as well beg to be shot and dumped in some river, my bloated body washing up months later. I was pretty sure I'd seen that exact scenario in a movie before.

But refusing would've gotten me nowhere, nor trying to outrun Jay. I'd seen those long, muscled legs at work at the gym. And he'd promised me. He'd promised me I wouldn't get hurt...

...and for some reason, I'd believed him.

I hadn't been hurt, but Officer Ting's threats still chilled me to the bone. He had files on my parents and Hank. Recent pictures. He didn't know about Frasier yet, but if he kept digging, he would. And Jay would no longer be able to keep that promise to me. I didn't have to guess who he would choose if it came down to his boss, or me.

His words from earlier echoed in my head.

Get off your high horse and stop judging me.

You manipulated and lied...

I don't care about you at all.

His words tore at me, broke me apart when they should have meant nothing. Jay didn't know the truth. He didn't know about Fraze or how I had nothing to do with him borrowing from Ting. I'd planned on getting the money the right way. It wasn't my fault I'd paid Ting with his own money before realizing it. But I couldn't tell Jay without getting Fraze in more trouble. Not that Jay would've listened. Or believed me.

I'd made it to my apartment without remembering walking there. For once I didn't notice the emptiness. Frustration and anger tore through me. I should've fought back, told Jay—not the truth—but something. Defended myself. Anything instead of crying like I was guilty. Like I was exactly who he thought I was.

His words stung, because there was some truth in them. I had thought myself better than him, better than Officer Ting, and Nico, even Bronwyn. Did I have the right to look down on others because they lived their lives differently? When they were just trying to get by, in the only way they knew how, like I was?

Part of me felt justified. I wasn't perfect, but I was nothing like them. I wouldn't borrow from a loan shark, I didn't condone violence, I would never date someone who was toxic like Nico had been for Bronwyn.

But I wasn't better. Just different. Hillstone was nothing like Vegas. My world was nothing like Jay's, or Nico's, or even Frasier's. It had been friends and Hank, church and school. It had been simple.

I didn't know what my world was now, or what I wanted it to be.

I got in the shower, hot water scalding my skin. My tears had dried up, my anger had dissipated. Now I felt scared, confused, and a little sad, though I didn't know why.

I don't care about you at all.

To: Frasier Hale, frazedaze@mymail.com

From: Margaret Hale, maggie-hale@mymail.com

**First of all, thanks for the Christmas present. I have no clue
how you got my exact size! Now the girls at dance class
can't make fun of my homemade pair.**

**So, this is hard, and I'd rather call you, but I don't have a
number or any clue where you are. I'm pretty sure you're
not at some job with a record producer. Even if you were,
you never said where, so I couldn't call anyway. I know
why you wouldn't tell me. I know... I just know. Someone's
been asking about you. He saw us saying goodbye, but he
doesn't know you're my brother. He hasn't said anything to
his boss and I don't think he will.**

I paused, my fingers hovering over my phone keys. Why was
Jay keeping quiet? All this time he could have told Simon what
he knew or suspected. He didn't owe me anything. He didn't even
like me, not anymore—he'd made that clear. And Ting was like a
father to him, he'd said so himself. So why lie for me?

I shook my head, then went back to my email.

**This isn't what I'm emailing you about though. It's about
Bronwyn.**

**She passed away. A drive-by shooting. I'm really sorry to
tell you like this, but I didn't want you to find out some**

other way, from some random person who heard from a person who heard from someone else.

I'm still living at her apartment, at least for now. The lease is up in the summer so I'll have to go somewhere else since I can't really afford this place (that extra money you gave me was a godsend, despite where it came from). Sometimes I don't want to be here, though. Everything about it reminds me of her because it's all hers.

Her family had a funeral for her in South Carolina. I couldn't go. I'm sorry both of us missed it. I'm sorry it happened. I'm sorry. To who, I don't know. Just a general sorry, out into the void.

Anyway, I better go. I have a new job and I still have an audition to prepare for. Hope everything is good with you and that you're safe and happy wherever you are. Don't worry about me, and *do not* come back here.

M y new job at Maquitte was everything I wanted it to be. Lacey Benwick, my boss, was like the big sister I never had with her clothing advice, asking about my day, and giving me hugs every time I walked into the store. The other worker there—Galen—was a skinny guy with light hair and porcelain skin, like he'd never seen the sun before. He was the one to train me, and it took me a few days to get used to his dry sense of humor. Once I caught on, we got along famously. I even had a bit of a crush on him, though I knew it would go nowhere (I wasn't his type). But he was fun to talk to, a nice change from Nico and Jay—the only other people I knew in the city.

Mostly, I loved the job because it felt like stepping into another world, the world I wanted to live in. A world without Officer Ting or worrying how long it would take him to find out the truth about Fraze.

When he did, would he send Jay after me? Or come himself? I thought about leaving Vegas, but where would I go? I didn't know how to disappear like Fraze did, and besides, Ting had photos of Hank and my parents. What if he went after them to get to me?

I stared at the display table, the decorations I'd placed on top blurring together.

"Have you turned into a mannequin?"

I glanced at Galen.

"Ah, back to a human girl. Just like that movie, *Spaceballs*."

I snorted. "Does this look okay?" I motioned to the coffee table covered in a silver dish full of different sized colored balls, a vase of fake hydrangeas, and a stack of magazines.

He stood beside me, his hand on his chin like he was appraising expensive art.

"If Martha Stewart barfed, this is what would come out."

I grimaced. "That bad?"

He patted my shoulder. "Predictable."

He tossed the magazines into a nearby purse, added a couple of candles and a weird wooden bird, and then rearranged it all until it looked artfully random. I huffed.

"Baby steps, Margaret," he said, patting my shoulder again, which I dodged. "Baby steps."

"The bird is ugly."

Galen went back to the hats. He put a newsboy cap on top of the mannequin, parking it at a jaunty angle. "Everything is ugly." He exchanged the cap for a vintage looking cloche hat. He stepped back. The mannequin had on skinny moto jeans, a silk blouse covered by a menswear looking tweed vest, and long dangling gold chains. He sighed, a happy sigh. "Mix the right kind of ugly and it becomes beautiful."

"Did you just make that up?"

"No, I have it embroidered on a pillow."

I rolled my eyes.

Galen had an eye for this stuff and I was learning how much I really didn't. I could appreciate a piece of clothing or an accessory, but could never make it work like he did. And he was right about one thing. He could take the ugliest of items and make them look just right, like that wooden bird watching me with its fake-jeweled beady eyes.

Lacey came onto the floor from the back, some newly steamed dresses over one arm. She glanced at the table. "Nice work, Maggie."

Galen gave me the side-eye, but he didn't need to. "Galen did it," I said with a sigh.

"Nice work, Galen," Lacey said, but she winked at me. "Maggie, find a place for these."

I took the dresses carefully, not wanting to wrinkle them. They were silky and floral and looked like they'd just slipped off a girl from the forties. I started to hang them with some other dresses but stopped when Galen gave a loud, exaggerated cough. It took three more tries—and two more coughs—to finally find the right spot for the dresses, next to some Victorian looking silk blouses.

At the till, Lacey was fiddling with some small glass dishes full of sterling silver rings.

"Are you sure you don't regret hiring me?" This wasn't the kind of question I could've asked Craig at *Holy Diner!* or my boss in Hillstone. But Lacey was more than a boss, she was becoming a friend.

"Of course not," she said. "You're a hard worker."

"But I suck at this."

"Everyone's tastes are different." Lacey leaned her elbows on the desk. "I don't expect you to be like Galen, or me." Her mouth quirked. "Even my tastes have changed in the last few years."

"They have?"

"Sure. I used to be very over-the-top. I might as well have been walking around with a neon sign saying 'Look at me! Look at me!'"

"So how did you figure all this out?"

"I hit my head, went into a coma, woke up, and got married." She laughed at my face. "It's a long story. I'm sure my tastes will change again as I get older, or if I have kids. That's how it works. All you need to focus on is putting your own touch to the pieces here."

I nodded. The bell at the front door tinkled. Galen scooped up the new customers in a flash.

"Why did you hire me, anyway?" Not that I wanted to be fired. But I wanted to know who referred me.

"My husband heard you needed a job. You came highly recommended." She shrugged, like it was no big deal, and headed to the back of the store.

I followed her, determined. "From who?"

She threw me a confused look over her shoulder. "From Jay."

"Jay Thornton?" How did he know Lacey? No, the better question was, *why* would he refer me in the first place? He didn't even know I'd been fired.

But I had told Jay. In the gym, the same night he told me he didn't care about me at all, the night Simon had shown me pictures of my family. But I'd already gotten the job at Maquitte by then.

Lacey was in her small office at the back of the store. I hovered in the doorway. My eyes went to some framed photos on her desk. She saw me looking, picked one up and handed it to me.

"My wedding day."

Lacey was radiant in a simple lace gown and long veil, the smile on her face one of pure joy. The man beside her was gazing at her, his eyes a little wide as if he was surprised she was there next to him.

"That's my Sam," she said.

"You both look beautiful."

"Here's another." She handed me a longer photo, this one of

her and Sam with their wedding party. One of the men looked familiar and I brought the picture closer to my face. I'd seen that face on TV before. A singer.

"Wait, is that—?"

"Eric Wentworth? Yeah."

"You know him?" My mom had been the one to introduce me to The Eric Wentworth Band a few years ago, and I'd been a fan ever since.

"Sam was in his band for a while."

"No way!"

"Not anymore. The last tour was rough on both of us, so we decided to settle. Sam's a high school band instructor now."

"Wow." It was weird, seeing this other side to Lacey. It made her more real to me, or maybe a little less real.

She replaced the photo on her desk. "Did you need something?"

"No, sorry." I started to walk away, then turned back. "Yes. Jay. He..." I didn't know what I was asking. All the talk of Eric Wentworth had made me forget. "What did he say?"

"Jay told me you were great with people, and a hard worker. Besides, Sam owed him a favor, and I trust his judgment. Jay was a good friend to Sam when he was in a tough spot."

I couldn't wrap my head around it. Jay had gotten me this job. *Jay.*

"Maggie?" She was grinning. "I know that look."

My face heated. "What look?"

"Trust me," Lacey said, "you're not the first girl to fall for Jay. Have you seen his abs?"

"Oh my gosh." I had *not* fallen for Jay. There was no way. "I don't like Jay." He was not a nice guy. He worked for a loan shark. He'd beaten up Nico, and who knows how many others. And did the guy ever smile? There was nothing to like about him.

Except...he was lying for me, covering for me, he'd never once hurt me, had helped get me this job and never said a word about it…

I squared my shoulders. "Trust me, I haven't fallen for Jay Thornton." It would never happen.

"You keep telling yourself that," she said.

CHAPTER 48

JAY

I'd LIED to a lot of people in my life, but I didn't like lying to Maggie. I'd lied about not caring about her, but only to make myself feel better. To cover the fact that I wasn't the man I wanted to be. It was no wonder she didn't like me.

I hated weakness—addicts, marks who begged, people who couldn't get their lives together or always blamed someone else when things went wrong. But it turned out I was just as bad. I thought I was strong, but I was still under Simon's thumb. I always obeyed, never stood up to him, never said no.

But I was done. Setting up a meeting for me with Andrew Arthur had been the last straw. I had no desire to play nice with that guy, or worse, grovel. So I didn't go.

When he found out, Simon summoned me to his sprawling mansion outside the city. I entered the passcode in the gate and drove through, parking my truck in front of his triple-car garage. The house was Spanish-style with pale stucco and arched windows. The inside was like a museum, with priceless art Simon had bought on the black market and an uneven tile floor that I used to stub my toe on as a teenager.

I'd lived here for four years, back when Simon took me off the streets until he got me my own apartment. When I wasn't learning how to fight, I spent most of my time here alone, taking care of the house and grounds and working my butt off to get my high school diploma. My room here was probably the same, still bare of anything but a bed and a dresser.

Simon was in the kitchen at the breakfast bar, drinking a coffee and reading the newspaper. I poured myself a cup and sat at the kitchen table, waiting until he was ready to acknowledge my presence. Tension made the air heavy.

"You better have a good reason for not meeting with Andrew Arthur," he said at last, folding the newspaper and setting it on the counter.

I set the coffee cup down. "I was busy."

His mouth tightened. He didn't say anything for a long time and neither did I. It was a showdown, waiting to see who would crack first. It wouldn't be me. I hadn't done what Simon asked, but had no excuse he would like.

"What about Fred Madsen, or whoever he really is?"

"He disappeared without a trace."

His fist slammed onto the table. "There's *always* a trace. You're not looking hard enough."

I rose from the chair. Simon had long ago taught me about the balance of power, and sitting lower than him wouldn't help my case.

"I'm going to buy the gym."

He frowned. "I beg your pardon?"

"Eastside Boxing. I'm going to buy it. McCrary wants to sell it to me, and I have enough set aside to put a down payment on it."

"No."

It was my turn to frown. "I'm not asking permission."

Simon stood, but his short frame would never come close to mine. "You won't have time to work for me and run a gym at the same time."

I crossed my arms. "I can't work for you anymore."

Simon was still for a moment, and then he sat back down. His lips curled up at the corners. "I must have heard you wrong. Because I *know* you're not that stupid."

My jaw tensed.

"I will take everything from you. Do you understand me? Your apartment, your salary, your truck."

My hands tightened into fists. I'd expected as much. "Fine."

"Margaret."

I feigned indifference. "What are you talking about?"

"I know how you feel about her. It was obvious in the car the other day." He adjusted his tie. "I also know her and Fred are connected. She didn't borrow from another lender. So, if you don't work for me, who will stop me from forcing the truth out of her? Who will protect you when the police find out about all the evidence you planted or made disappear?"

Adrenaline pumped through my body, my vision blurred.

"And then there's the charges your foster sister leveled against you."

"I'm an adult now, they can't—"

"You were accused of abuse. *I* made those charges disappear. I can make them reappear."

I struggled to keep my breathing even. "I didn't do it."

"Of course not." He smiled but there was no warmth to it. "But I doubt any parent would want you anywhere near their children if they knew the accusation. Doubt that will help your new business."

My body went cold. If the story got out, I would never get students. No parent would risk their children with someone who had that on their record, even as a child, especially someone who then ran away from home, from the system.

For two years I'd lived on the streets of Vegas, begging on the strip and avoiding the cops, hiding out in abandoned warehouses, making friends with the other bums, learning to use my fists to get what I needed, to keep the dealers and perverts away. And then Simon had found me.

He was staring at me now, hands clasped over his stomach, waiting. Knowing there was nothing I could do to get free of him.

I dropped into the chair.

Simon stood and leaned over me. "Look at you, all grown up and trying to leave the nest. Don't think I'm unsympathetic, son. Tell you what. Find Fred Madsen for me, meet with Arthur, and we'll discuss it. Maybe I can lighten your workload. I'm sure you could make time for both me and the gym."

It would never end. "I want something of my own. Something I can build up that's just mine. Can't you understand that?"

"I do, Jason. It's the American Dream. But you're indispensable to me. I'm sure *you* understand that."

Jason. Whenever he used my proper name, it was a reminder of who I'd been when he found me. A reminder of what he'd saved me from. I'd shed Jason from myself long ago, I was no longer that boy, but that's all Simon saw. Someone who could be used because he needed to be saved.

Simon put his hand on my shoulder. "Get me Fred Madsen. I'll set up another meeting with Arthur. Then we'll talk."

I drove away from Simon's with my stomach a tight ball of anger. Deep down I knew it would go this way, but I'd still hoped for something else. Hoped that my years of loyalty might have meant something to him.

This second meeting with Andrew Arthur was unavoidable, but maybe I could convince Simon to come with me. Then I'd tip off Hopkins. He could get pictures, or fit me with a wire. I was ready to do anything to get away from Simon for good.

CHAPTER 49

MAGGIE

AFTER WORK, I headed to Eastside Boxing to get in some dance time. I hoped to avoid Jay. I had no desire to see him, not after what Lacey had said. Falling for him? The very idea was laughable. Jay was not my type at all. I didn't like him, and he didn't like me. But I couldn't face him right then. Not with the thought still in my head, not when the memory of our kiss kept invading my thoughts, and those thoughts taking it further and further, until he was shirtless and my hands were discovering every hard and soft spot of his body and...

No, just no.

Determined not to think about Jay Thornton's abs, I leaned against the bus stop post and waited. A black sports car screeched up beside me, almost hitting the sidewalk, and I jumped back. A man got out. It was Alfonso—the big Mexican who'd treated my bullet graze and my sprained ankle.

"Simon wants to see you," he said, jerking his head toward the car door.

Fear tightened my throat. I backed away. "No, thanks."

He grabbed me and pulled me toward the car. "Sorry. It's not a request."

"Let me go!" I shrieked. A couple down the street paused. It was dark out, but between the streetlights and my scream, they would know I was in trouble. Wouldn't they?

I opened my mouth to scream again and something pressed into my side.

"I don't want to hurt you. Do not make me."

I swallowed but didn't budge. He touched the point into my side and I gasped. A knife, just barely piercing my skin. I flinched, but he had me in such a tight grip that I couldn't go anywhere.

"Cut me and I will scream," I said, but it didn't sound fierce or threatening.

He walked me to the car, the knife never leaving my side. The group down the street wasn't even looking our way anymore. I choked out a sob.

Alfonso opened the driver's side door and pushed me in. The sports car was only a two-seater, but he climbed right in after me, pushing me into the passenger seat. He tied my hands with a plastic zip tie, so tight that I cried out.

He gunned the engine and sped away, leaving the only witnesses to my abduction clueless and far behind. He drove fast, weaving in and out of traffic, not stopping for lights. "You try and jump, it will hurt worse than this." He motioned to the knife resting on his thigh.

My whole body shuddered. I wanted out of there. If Ting wanted to see me, why hadn't Jay come? Why send this guy with his knife?

While he drove, I inched my fingers toward my bag. It was mashed against my side, under the seatbelt. Not that it would do any good. My purse was zipped shut, I would never be able to unzip it or get my bound hands inside unnoticed, let alone grab my phone and dial. I tried anyway.

"I'm Alfonso," the big Mexican said. "We met. You remember?"

Was he crazy? Of course I remembered, but that didn't mean

I'd be all buddy-buddy with a guy who had kidnapped me at knife point.

When I didn't answer he looked over. "Stop it." The knife was pressed flat against my knuckles in an instant. Alfonso still had one hand on the steering wheel, his driving hadn't slowed. "No tricks."

If I could've grabbed the knife, I would have—Alfonso wasn't even looking at it, his eyes were on the road. But I was shaking. My breaths were loud. I was on the brink of tears. Ting had come to get me before, and it had turned out okay, but Jay had been there. I needed Jay.

I swallowed and choked on my own breath. He was pressing the flat of the knife into my skin, as if to remind me it was still there.

"Please." I started to cry.

Alfonso groaned. "No crying. I can't stand crying." He turned on the radio to an oldies station. He began to sing along to a Beach Boys song, loudly and badly, and I was so surprised, I stopped crying. Had he done that to shut me up, or was he trying to make me feel better? He didn't even look at me, he just kept driving and singing.

When the car left the city limits, my panic came back full force. Maybe he wasn't taking me to Ting at all. Maybe he was going to kill me out in the desert and dump my body. Would Officer Ting order him to do that? Maybe not. But Simon Ting totally would.

We pulled up to a gated mansion. Alfonso keyed in a code and the gate swung open. As soon as we stopped, I would try to run, but I had a sinking feeling that I wouldn't get very far. Even if I did, where could I go?

Alfonso stopped. He lifted the knife from my skin but pointed at me. "Stay put." While he turned off the car, I undid my seatbelt. Alfonso grabbed the keys and got out.

I fumbled with the door handle, yanking it open. The seatbelt caught on my purse. I almost fell out of the car. I wriggled free and lurched forward, running.

He grabbed me around the waist from behind. I struggled, but he'd gotten me in a bear hug.

"You cause too many problems," he said, squeezing tight. His grip loosened, but only for a moment. Then the knife was out and resting against my neck. "Easy. You cooperate, everything will be okay. Understand?"

I swallowed, the cold steel moving with me. Alfonso walked me up the steps to the front door. My mind whirled while I tried to stay grounded in reality. Maybe this wouldn't be as bad as I feared. Maybe Ting just wanted to talk, like last time, and then he would let me go. Maybe Jay would be there and he'd—

Who was I kidding? Even if Jay was there, he'd pick Ting over me—his boss, the man who was a father to him. He'd been lying for me, sure, but he wouldn't cross that line.

Alfonso herded me through the front door, still holding me awkwardly from behind. We walked through a big front entrance, past a kitchen, and into a living room. It was an open space with glass walls looking out into the vast backyard. A pool glistened out there, an inviting escape from the regular Vegas heat. Inside, three couches sat in a U-shape, one of them facing a giant flat screen TV against the wall. Alfonso pushed me forward. I didn't want to sit, but he put both hands on my shoulders and shoved me down. He sat on the couch next to me.

My eyes darted around the room, catching on a phone resting on a corner desk. On the hallway leading to who knew where, on the door leading to freedom. My body was tense, ready to run.

"I'll tie your feet too if I have to," Alfonso said, as if he knew exactly what I was thinking.

I waited. Beside me, Alfonso spun his knife, the blade a blur in his hands. If he was trying to scare me, it was working. The only way I'd get away from him was if he stabbed himself. Or fell asleep.

Minutes ticked by but I never relaxed. I couldn't. "Can we watch TV or something while we're waiting?" I asked, hoping something would distract the big man next to me. He shook his head.

When the door slammed, my heart leapt into my throat. Ting was here, and I was screwed.

"Sorry I took so long, I had a helicopter parent at the gym who was worried about…"

It was Jay, not Ting. He stopped talking. I looked at him, my heart filling with irrational hope.

"What's going on?" he asked.

"Simon told me to bring her," Alfonso said. "He's on his way."

Jay's shoulders tensed. "What for?"

"He figured out that Fred guy." Alfonso nodded at the desk. "Take a look."

No. If that was true, then I was beyond screwed. Not even Jay would save me now.

Jay glanced at me, a frown pulling at his eyebrows. He went to the desk and opened a laptop.

I couldn't read his expression. What was he looking at? What had Simon found out about Fraze?

"What is it? Can I see?" I asked.

"Show her," Alfonso said.

Jay brought the laptop over, setting it on my knee.

The screen was open to a Facebook page. Bronwyn's. Right in the middle was one of Fraze and Bronwyn amidst a group of people outside in the snow. Fraze was holding a red cup, his hair covered by a beanie, Bronwyn's was longer, in thin dreads past her shoulders. The status read, "What happens at the annual Williams party, stays at the annual Williams party, right, Fraze?"

Even though the picture was old, Fraze looked almost the same as he did now. A little less chubby, a little more like a man now, but he had the same smile, the same twinkle in his eyes.

"Who's Fraze?" Jay asked, his voice near my ear. He'd gone to stand behind the couch but he was leaning close so he could see the screen.

"That's Fred." Alfonso clicked another tab and another picture popped up. "Surveillance photo. From Pearl of China. Same night Alonso made the loan. Don't you recognize him?"

The photo was grainy, but it was obviously Frasier, sitting inside a Chinese restaurant. "What does this prove?" I asked. Only that Bronwyn knew him, not who he actually was.

"It led Simon to this." Alfonso clicked on a third tab. It was Frasier's freshman yearbook photo. Fraze hadn't sat for school photos after that. He'd been going against "the man" as he liked to say back then. Doing everything opposite of the way most people did things. His name rested below the photo in big, block letters.

"Frasier Hale," Jay said behind me.

Alfonso took the laptop, closed it, then leaned back against the couch. He caressed the handle of his knife. "Maggie's brother."

CHAPTER 50

JAY

HE WAS HER BROTHER. The guy she'd hugged on the street that day, who she'd been covering for all this time, was her *brother*. I went around the couch to look at Maggie, whose face had gone pale.

Alfonso was playing with his knife. Maggie's eyes kept darting to it, then away. "Simon's going to question her when he gets here. Wants to know where 'Fred' went."

Maggie stared straight ahead, her lips pressed together. It was no wonder she had never said anything to me, never given up his whereabouts. He was family. I thought back to how surprised she'd been when I'd accused her of screwing over Simon in the gym that day. Maybe she really hadn't known. Maybe it hadn't been her idea in the first place, but once she found out, once I'd told her what he'd done, she couldn't say anything without giving him away.

"Do you really think she knows?" I asked.

Alfonso put his hand on the back of Maggie's neck. "We can find out."

I froze, while inside my whole body raged.

"Tell us where he is," Alfonso said. "Maybe Simon will go easy on you."

Maggie looked Alfonso square in the face. "I don't know where he is."

"No point lying."

"I'm not."

"You don't tell me, you'll tell Simon later."

I tensed.

Alfonso began to stroke the back of her neck like he was soothing a wild animal. Maggie looked at me, the question plain on her face. But she didn't need to ask.

I lunged at Alfonso.

I didn't catch him as off guard as I had hoped. He slashed at me with his knife, but I knew he would. I dodged. Too slow. His knife cut into my side.

"No!" Maggie shouted. "Stop!" She struggled to get her hands free, but I couldn't focus on her. Not now.

Alfonso came at me again. He was off the couch, which was what I wanted. I taught self-defense classes that were all about people like him. He swung the knife. I moved aside and knocked his arm away. I lashed out with a kick, catching him in the jaw. He stumbled back, the knife dropping from his fingers.

He spotted his knife but before he could reach it, I kicked him in the leg. He folded like a chair, dropping to one knee. He swung wildly at me. I blocked, and punched him in the face. Then throat. He fell back, hitting the couch. His hands clutched his throat as he gasped for breath.

I leaned over him. "Sorry about this." I wasn't sorry. I knocked him out.

I picked up the knife, then turned to Maggie.

CHAPTER 51

MAGGIE

J AY STOOD in front of me, panting, the knife clutched in his hand.

"You're bleeding." His shirt was torn where Alfonso had cut him; blood had already soaked through the material.

He ignored me. "Here." He knelt in front of me and grabbed my wrists. He was so close. I wanted him to look at me, but he wouldn't. He sliced through the zip tie with the knife.

I rubbed my wrists. "Thank you."

His eyes finally met mine. There was so much to be said, so much that I wanted to know. He'd lied for me, and now he was saving me from Ting. No 'thank you' could be enough.

"We need to go," he said. "Before Simon gets here."

He helped me stand. My legs were shaky and I grabbed onto his forearms. He smelled of blood, sweat, and vanilla soap. "Jay—" I didn't know what I wanted to say.

He turned away. "Later. Let's go."

My eyes snagged on the phone. "We should call the cops." I hurried toward it but Jay grabbed my arm, stopping me.

"Are you nuts? Simon *is* a cop." Jay hissed. He pressed his hand against the cut in his side.

"He had me kidnapped! You know he's not going to stop looking for me. Or my brother."

Jay froze. His eyes went unfocused. "Hopkins."

"What?"

"Hopkins. He's Internal Affairs. He's been watching Simon. Your testimony… But Simon was never here. I don't know if it's enough."

"Give me his number. I'll call him while you bandage yourself up."

Jay quickly pulled out his wallet then handed me a card. I dialed. A woman answered. "Las Vegas Metropolitan—"

"I need to talk to Hopkins."

"I'm sorry, but Lieutenant Hopkins isn't in right now."

"Does he have another number? A cell? I need to talk to him right away!"

"Ma'am, could you calm down please?" I hated being called ma'am.

Jay looked up from pressing a towel against his side. "Tell them it's Jay Thornton and it's urgent."

"It's Jay Thornton. I mean, I'm not Jay Thornton but he's standing right next to me. Hopkins wants to talk to him."

"Can you put this Jay—"

"We were kidnapped! I was kidnapped! There's a man with a knife. He's knocked out but Ting is coming—"

A movement caught my eye.

I screamed. Jay tackled me to the ground, just as a knife whizzed over our heads. I dropped the phone.

Alfonso was on his feet.

"Stay down," Jay hissed. He jumped up, pivoting as he did, and slammed into Alfonso.

Grunts and the sounds of fists hitting flesh filled my ears, but somewhere, in the background, a woman's voice called out. I opened my eyes and searched for the phone. It was across the tile floor. I scrambled on my hands and knees toward it.

"Hello?" I said. Another smash echoed behind me. Jay and Alfonso were wrestling, hurtling away from a broken wine cart. Liquor pooled on the floor, surrounded by broken glass.

"Are you there?" the woman said. "Tell me where you are. What's happening? Is anyone hurt?"

I backed up. "I don't know where we are. Somewhere outside Vegas. A mansion, Spanish-style, with a gate. Probably belongs to Simon Ting."

"Stay on the line, we'll find you."

"You need to get Hopkins."

There was a loud grunt, and I turned, keeping the phone clutched to my ear.

"I've alerted Hopkins and I've dispatched a unit. They'll be there as soon as possible," the woman said, "but don't hang up."

That unit better not include Officer Ting or I would scream.

Alfonso crashed to the floor. Jay loomed over him, one hand still clenched on Alfonso's shirt, his fist raised. Alfonso moaned but didn't move.

"Can you tell me what's happening?" the woman asked.

Jay let Alfonso go and looked at me. I got shakily to my feet.

"Put the phone down."

We both turned to the voice.

Ting was here. He had his uniform on and his gun out, the barrel pointed at me. The phone slipped from my fingers.

Ting smiled. Slowly, he swung the barrel away from me, toward Jay.

A shot rang out.

CHAPTER 52

JAY

SIMON WOULDN'T HESITATE to shoot me. I could see it in his face. He wouldn't wait for an explanation. I'd betrayed him. He pulled the trigger, the shot whizzing over my head as I dove.

The crack of another shot. Pain surged from the back of my thigh. Grunting, I fell.

"Jay?" Maggie choked out, rushing toward me.

Simon walked toward me, his feet crunching over broken glass. He was taking his time now that he knew I wasn't going anywhere. Maggie bent over me, as if to shield me from Simon. Her hands cupped my face. Simon kicked her aside. I looked up as his foot connected with my stomach.

I fell back, groaning. I pressed one hand to the back of my leg where blood was soaking my jeans.

He knelt beside me, one knee pinning down my arm, the gun against my chest.

"Such a disappointment." He squeezed the back of my thigh. I hissed. "After *everything* I've done for you. Maybe I'll get Andrew Arthur to take your place. He knows how to get a job done. He doesn't let *feelings* get in the way."

"Stop," Maggie pleaded. "You're here for me. There's no point hurting Jay."

He looked over at her. "There's always a point. You took his loyalty from me, just like that. You have more power than you realize. Or maybe you knew it. Maybe you were counting on it. Charm my boy into coming to your rescue?"

She shook her head. "I didn't do anything."

"Oh, no?"

With my free hand, I struggled to sit up but Simon pressed his gun against my temple. He didn't take his eyes off Maggie.

"Timing is everything, isn't it? Fred Madsen borrows fifty grand, then disappears. You pay back Nico's loan, in full, within the same week. Hell of a coincidence."

Alfonso was coming to. I couldn't get up. The pain in my thigh was intense, the cut in my side still bleeding. I pushed my palm over the wound. I had to block it out. Everything. It was the only way to save Maggie.

"I did some digging and found out about your brother, Frasier," Simon continued. "I put two and two together. So now you're going to tell me. Where is he?"

"You don't need to do this," I said, my voice a croak. "She doesn't know anything."

He let out a chuckle, as if this was a game. "He's her brother. Of course she knows. And I think you should be the one to make her talk. Consider it penance for past sins."

"No."

Maggie gasped.

Simon pressed the gun harder into my temple. "Excuse me?"

I wouldn't do this, not anymore. I'd been done with it for so long but kept on anyway, because I didn't care what people thought, didn't care who I'd been hurting. Maggie had made me care. Not just because I hadn't wanted to hurt a woman, not just because she was Maggie and I wanted to be better for her, but because she was a person, just like anyone else.

I'd always justified myself by saying I only did bad things to bad people, but at the end of the day, all I really did was make things worse. People who only wanted a way out fell deeper and deeper into the hole because of guys like Simon. Guys like me. People turning their lives around was bad for business.

I was done. Nothing Simon said or did would make me lay a finger on Maggie. On anyone. Never again.

Simon's face loomed into mine. "You think your little crush will save her? You think it's so easy?"

Nothing was easy. Simon had saved me from the streets, given me purpose, and I'd taken that to mean he loved me like family. Maybe he did, in his own twisted way. But I wouldn't work another day for him.

"You are in my debt, Jason. You think you can move on with your life but *this is your life*. Son, it's high time you understood how the world really works, and why loyalty is more important than anything else."

I looked him in the eyes. "I know."

"Jay," Maggie said.

Simon frowned, as if he didn't understand me. Since that day in the warehouse when he'd told me I was smart, I'd believed him. But he'd never seen someone smart. He'd only seen someone he could use.

Not anymore.

I grabbed Simon's hand over the gun, pushing it away. He pulled the trigger. The bullet hit the floor. I followed through and elbowed Simon in the face. Rolled over him and smashed his head into the floor. His eyes didn't open.

Maggie screamed. I looked up.

Alfonso had grabbed her. She was struggling to get free.

I lurched to my feet.

Maggie's knee came up, right into his groin. He hunched and grabbed himself. She balled her hand into a fist and punched him in the face.

"For the love!" Maggie cursed, shaking her hand like she'd hit a rock.

Her punch wasn't enough to stop Alfonso. I went for him. He was angry, sloppy. I sidestepped him, grabbing his arm as he passed and hurled him into a wall head first. He went down. Hopefully for good this time.

Panting, I looked at Maggie.

Her mouth hung open. She was cradling her hand. She stumbled toward me then stopped. Close, but not close enough.

"Are you okay?"

She made a noise somewhere between a snort and a sob. "Are you?"

My side burned, my leg throbbed with pain. It was a miracle I was still standing. "I'll live." I reached for the gun, hissing at the pain shooting down my thigh.

Maggie was there, her hand on my back and her face full of concern. The desire to pull her into my arms and kiss her was intense. Stronger than the pain.

"Hopefully Hopkins will be here soon." I put the safety on then pocketed the gun. "But we should tie them up, just in case. There's zip ties in the pantry."

"Why are there zip ties in the…never mind." She shook her head as she walked to the kitchen. I grabbed the towel I'd used on my side earlier and pressed it against my leg.

Maggie came back with the zip ties. She stood over Simon and grimaced like she didn't want to touch him. I started to hop toward them, but Maggie bent down and pulled Simon's wrists together. "He won't wake up, will he?"

"Not yet. Put his arms behind his back. Tougher to get free that way."

Maggie made a face at me and then rolled Simon over. "He better not wake up," she muttered.

I couldn't stop from smiling as Maggie used the zip tie, pulling it tight until Simon's skin bulged around it.

She did Alfonso next, then stood with a shudder. "Well, that was a first." Her eyes met mine. "And hopefully a last."

My heart stopped. That sounded final. "How's your hand?"

"Hurts like all-get-out, but I'll live."

I motioned my head, telling her to come closer. She didn't hesitate.

Letting go of the towel, I took her hand gently in mine. My thumb brushed over her knuckles. Her hand was bruised, but nothing was broken.

"Who exactly is Hopkins?" she asked, shaking a little under my touch. "He's not dirty too, is he?"

"No." My eyes moved to her lips.

Maggie swallowed. "He's sure taking his sweet time." She looked down. "Your leg."

Blood was still soaking through my jeans.

She knelt, perching on the balls of her feet. She dabbed the towel against the wound. "This isn't working. You need to go to the hospital." She steadied herself with one hand on my other leg. I inhaled, and not from the pain.

I grabbed the hem of my shirt and started to pull it off.

She looked up at me. "What are you doing?"

I smirked. "It's either yours or mine."

She held her hand out and I gave it to her. She wrapped the shirt around my thigh, tying it off tight.

When she stood, her dark eyes moved up my body, lingering over my chest, then my lips, finally holding my gaze.

I knew that look. I hoped to hell I was right about that look. With Maggie, I could never be sure, but I risked it. I moved into her, rested my hands on her hips.

Her lips trembled. The look was gone, but she wasn't angry. "I'm sorry."

"Hey," I whispered.

Her eyes darted to the blood on my shirt, to Simon, to Alfonso. "You're hurt, and it's all my fault."

"Maggie, look at me."

She lowered her head but she grabbed my arms, holding on.

My fingers dug into her hips. "Look at me."

She did.

"Everything is going to be okay," I said.

I didn't believe it, and she didn't either. Nothing could be that simple. Would her testimony be enough to put Simon away? Could he wriggle out of it, based on his reputation, the cops he had in his pocket? And what about me? I wasn't innocent in all this, Simon would make sure everyone knew. If he wasn't put away for something, he'd be gunning for both me and Maggie.

I cupped her face. "I will make it okay," I said, my eyes boring into hers. "I promise you."

CHAPTER 53

MAGGIE

JAY HELD my face in his hands. I'd always seen him as dangerous, seen those hands as weapons. And they were—but he'd used them to save me. The world wasn't as black and white as I'd imagined it. I didn't want to fight it anymore.

"I will make it okay," he said. "I promise you."

He couldn't make that promise, no one could, but I loved him for it anyway.

I loved him.

Or I was starting to. There was so much I didn't know about him, about his childhood, his family, what had led him to Simon, what he liked to do when he wasn't fighting or teaching. But I *wanted* to know those things, all of them. The simple things, the normal things, the extraordinary things. I wanted badly to know everything about him.

I stared at Jay Thornton. His eyes were lighter up close, but no less intense.

He let go of my face. I grabbed his hand, entwining mine with his, like they were meant to be that way, only I hadn't seen it. I lifted his hand to my lips, pressed my mouth against his cracked knuckles.

His lips parted and so did mine. This time, when our mouths met, it wasn't unwelcome. It was real.

His lips were as soft and sure as I remembered. He tasted of blood and I probably tasted of tears, but that didn't stop us from coming together. It didn't break us apart. I felt sure nothing would.

The door slammed open and we wrenched apart.

"Police!" someone shouted. "Put your hands where we can see them."

Jay and I looked at each other.

"*Now* they come," he said.

I t was Lieutenant Hopkins. He'd known Officer Ting was dirty and Jay had been working with him to find enough evidence to put him away. My statement was a good start, enough to get him arrested. Alfonso too, when he came around. Alfonso pitched a fit, ratting out Jay, telling the police he was involved, that he worked for Ting. Hopkins had to take him in too after we both got fixed up at the hospital.

Ting said nothing. I'd watched enough *Law & Order* to know he'd lawyer up and be out of jail in no time. And then I'd be back to where I started.

Except it didn't happen that way. Officer Ting was dirty, they all knew it now. The kidnapping and illegal money-lending was just the beginning. The police had recorded my call, and even though I'd dropped the phone when Simon appeared, the dispatcher had still been on the line, and recorded everything.

To lighten his own sentence, Alfonso told the cops he'd witnessed Alonso's murder, and where the body was buried, out in the Nevada desert. Jay told me Hopkins and the other police would be uncovering Ting's shady dealings for months, but the murder charge alone would hold him.

Jay was charged with illegal money-lending and grievous

bodily harm and went to jail. It took a week but Hopkins finally came through and got the charges on Jay dropped.

I waited outside the station with my hands in my pockets. The weather had turned warm lately, too warm for March, but a light breeze blew the ends of my hair into my face.

The door swung open and there he was. He still walked with a slight limp. His face was still peppered with bruises. I had bruises too, but I'd been marked in other ways.

Jay paused when he saw me. I hadn't visited him in jail. I needed time to work through what happened. To sort out my feelings and make sure they were real. But I'd left him a note telling him I'd be there when he got out.

We closed the distance between each other, stopping at arm's length.

"Hi," I said. I wanted to grab onto him and not let go. I wanted *him* to hold me. He'd always been so confident around me, as if he knew just what to do to get under my skin. Right then, he didn't seem so sure.

"You came."

"I said I would."

"I wouldn't have blamed you if you packed it all in and went back home."

"I'm sorry," I blurted. An apology that was long overdue.

Jay stepped closer. So close. His mouth gave the barest of smiles. "For what?"

"For being such a jerk. I never gave you a chance. I didn't even try to get to know who you really are."

He grabbed my hips and pulled me in until my body was pressed against his. Heat enveloped us, from inside and out. I braced my hands on his arms.

"I'm the one who's sorry. For Simon, for letting it all get that far." He bowed his head. "For taking so long to take a stand."

"That wasn't your fault."

"But it was. I should've seen what Simon had become. I

should've stopped him the moment he got you involved. But I didn't."

"Life's never that simple," I said. "We just like to believe it is. You taught me that."

"So, where does that leave us?" Jay asked.

"I don't know. But I know where I'd like it to go."

"Where's that?"

"Where we should have started in the first place. Getting to know each other."

"You're giving me a chance?"

I slid my hands up his arms. Relished in the feeling of him. "As long as you're giving me one, too."

His fingers curled around the waist of my jeans. "You're not a chance, Maggie. You're a sure thing. The only sure thing in Vegas."

My lips, my heart, everything I was opened to him.

CHAPTER 54

MAGGIE

I LOVED Lacey and Galen and my job at Maquitte. I loved Jay Thornton. I went to Eastside Boxing every night after work, or before, depending on my shift.

I could have practiced elsewhere, Robbie had offered use of the studio at Fluidity after hours, but I wanted to see Jay, to discover all the stuff I wanted to know about him. Sometimes Jay was a distraction, watching me while I danced, his eyes so intense I went crazy and had to take a break.

He told me about his foster family, his time as a runaway, about Simon. And I told him about Hillstone and Fraze and my parents. We talked about silly things too, inconsequential things, but they meant everything.

Despite the distractions, my audition piece got better and better. I had a new perspective to bring to my "Song of the Caged Bird." I'd been a caged bird, one of my own making, and then one of Ting's, but now I was free.

April arrived and I nailed the audition. I couldn't believe it, but I was in, the newest member of Essence Dance Theater. What had seemed impossible so recently was now a reality.

My dream had come true, and so had Jay's.

Jay had enough money saved to put a down payment on East-side Boxing. McCrary was willing to do the deal without getting a bank involved. He knew Jay's word was good. But Jay needed a partner, someone to run the business side so he could teach. I suggested Nico. He knew about managing a business. He also had a little put aside. They became partners, and, as unlikely as it was for me to be dating Jay, Nico and Jay became friends.

I walked down the street toward Essence, Jay's hand in mine. It was June, the weather was already unbearably hot. My first performance was coming up, and my parents were coming to see it. Even though I was only in the corps, I was still nervous.

Jay tugged my hand, pulling me against the brick of a building next to Essence. He braced his hands on either side of me. I ran my fingers down his chest, along those muscles that used to be so intimidating, so wrong to me. Now everything about Jay felt right.

"Kill it in there," he said, trailing kisses down my neck.

"I always do." I tugged on his shirt, pulling him close, but never close enough. I always wanted more. The brick was scorching against my back, but the heat from Jay was even more intense.

"I know." He kissed me again, then pulled away. "That's why I love you."

He loved me because of my strength—strength of character, strength of will—and I loved him for the same reason. Even though we'd come from two different worlds, we were the same. And where we were different? It only made us stronger.

With me, he was better. With him, I was free.

THANK YOU FOR READING!

I hope you enjoyed Maggie and Jay's journey! If you have a moment, leave a review. Reviews are so vital for authors and every single one helps.

Also, stop by on social media and say hi! I'd love to hear from you. I'm on:

Facebook:
https://www.facebook.com/MelanieStanfordauthor/
Twitter:
https://twitter.com/MelMStanford
Instagram:
https://www.instagram.com/melanie_stanford/
Website:
http://melaniestanfordbooks.com/

ACKNOWLEDGMENTS

First, to the people who help my books go from messy drafts to real things. My critique partners: Emily Stanford, Michelle Merrill, and RuthAnne Oakey-Frost. They've been with me for a while now and I'm ever so grateful they haven't gotten sick of me yet (you haven't, right? Please say you haven't). To my editor, Noah Chinn, who is brilliant, easy to work with, and a total boss (in a good way). To Laura Brown for beta reading, to Kimberly Dawn for her fabulous proof reading skills, Shari Ryan at MadHat Books for formatting so I don't have to, and Gabrielle Prendergast for outdoing herself yet again on my cover. It's perfection.

Thanks need to go to the different writing groups who've helped me on this crazy writing journey: VioletTendencies, LDStorymakers, and Querying Authors. Thank you as well to Niki and Caleb Lenz for answering police related questions, and to Coralie MacKay for answering medical questions. Any mistakes are my own. Also a big thank you to Christina Boyd, who was my editor for my short stories *Becoming Fanny* and *The Beast of Pemberley*. At one point I became "needy, insecure writer" and she was there to pull me through it. I will always appreciate her unwavering support.

I have to thank Elizabeth Gaskell for creating a story I never thought I'd like. Shows what I know. And to Richard Armitage, Daniela Denby-Ashe, and everyone who made the BBC television serial. As soon as I watched it I knew I wanted to do a retelling. This book is the result.

Finally, thanks to my incredible family. My husband Jeff, who has supported me from the start. My children: Jade, Logan, Kori, and Avery, who amaze me every day. My parents, Noel and Rita Burt, who never crushed my dream of becoming a writer. And my siblings: Darren, Malcolm, Steven, Marlon, Coralie, and Natalie, who all helped instill in me a great love of reading.

CHAPTER 1

I never thought I'd say this, but I love my job. I bring smiles to people's faces. I make them laugh, dance, weep. Their dreams come true thanks to me. I'm like a frickin' fairy godmother.

No, a fairy godmother is always old, fat, or both. I'm a dream come true.

"The party is amazing," June said to me, her eyes surveying the room. "Better than I ever could have hoped." She took one of my hands in hers. "You've saved my life, Elizabeth Elliot."

That's me—the party-planning angel, saving lives one center-piece at a time. That should've been my brand line. Too late to change my logo?

My gaze caught on a vase that was off-center. "Excuse me, June," I said, pulling my hand from her leathery grip. I never wanted to get old. Wrinkles were gross. "I have a disaster to avert. Enjoy your party. And don't worry about a thing."

Her gratitude echoed over the string quartet, but I didn't stay to listen. I searched the ballroom for Juliet. If she didn't get her tiny behind in gear, she'd be *so* fired. Which I told her once I found her by the bar, working out a problem with the ice. Honestly, who has problems with ice?

"I'm so sorry," Juliet said about the vase, "I'll get on it right away."

She scurried away, her jet-black hair in a perfect bun, not one strand out of place. Her gray skirt and jacket were both wrinkle free, and she didn't wobble one bit on those stilettos. Honestly, I would never fire Juliet—she was the best assistant I'd ever had. Just contemplating interviews with another string of idiots set my teeth on edge—but she didn't need to know that. I'd learned, in the few short weeks she'd worked for me, that Juliet functioned much better under pressure.

"Stop shoving them in my face!" a voice said nearby. "I don't want another tacky crudité."

Tacky? TACKY? I spun toward the voice. Two men stood by the bar, one holding a plate piled high with canapés, NOT crudités. He was happily munching while the other was sipping champagne, his nose wrinkling as if his glass of Moët & Chandon smelled bad.

"These are delicious," the first man said. He was probably forty-ish, blond, and slightly chubby. There was a smear of something white on his cheek.

The other man was tall and slim, his blue suit perfectly cut across the shoulders. "I'll take your word for it," he said. His voice had a slight accent, but I couldn't place it.

The chubby one waved a canapé around. "You have to taste it."

"Stig, if you put that thing in my face again, I will shove it up your nose."

My hands went to my hips. Oh no, there would be no fights at one of my parties.

"What is your problem, Tony?" Stig asked.

"My problem is that I was dragged to yet another showy and tasteless display of wealth, with nothing to make it the slightest bit amusing or worthwhile."

Anger lit my entire body on fire.

"The pretentious string quartet, décor that looks like it came from my grandmother's living room, food that's hardly edible, and the same old people talking about the same old things."

"I think you've had enough to drink for one evening." Stig reached for Tony's champagne.

Tony knocked it back before his friend could take it, then whistled loudly for a waiter.

I marched over. He would calm down or get out.

He saw me approaching, his expression of annoyance didn't budge. He held out the glass for me to take, as if I was some kind of servant.

"Do I look like a waiter to you?" I demanded.

His eyes swept me from top to bottom. "Not interested."

My eyes narrowed. "Excuse me?"

"Whatever it is you want, I am not interested. I don't want to talk, I don't want to flirt, I don't want to date. If you're not going to get me another drink, then you can go away."

His friend, Stig, choked on his drink.

He went to move past me but I stepped in his way. "Tony, is it?" I didn't wait for him to respond. "Believe me, I don't want to date you either."

He pressed his hand to his chest in mock hurt.

"You need to step outside and take a breather."

He leaned in and I caught a whiff of alcohol mixed with cologne. He was tall, but so was I, especially when I raised my chin to meet his gaze. "Who the hell are you to tell me what to do?"

My eyes flashed. "This is my party, which makes me God, and you the mere mortal who has to obey my wishes."

He leaned back. "So you are the help."

"I am not—"

"I need a drink." He slid past me, grabbing another from the nearest tray.

No one was allowed to interrupt me. I scanned the party, making sure our interaction hadn't caused a disturbance. He'd rattled me, but I would not be unprofessional.

I followed him, lightly grabbing his elbow.

He stopped, tilting his head at me. "You again."

I gave him my nicest, most polite, smile. "If you cause a scene," I said, my voice low, "I will have you ejected from this party." I patted his arm. To anyone watching, it probably did look like we were flirting.

He guzzled another glass of champagne then smiled at me. "It would be fun to call your bluff. Liven up this fiesta."

"How do you know June?"

He blinked at my change in subject. "Her husband, Harold, is a client of mine."

"And how do you think Harold would feel if you ruined his wife's party? I can't imagine he'd be pleased."

Tony shifted his feet and avoided my eyes.

"I don't know what you do," I said, "but I've never met a businessman who likes losing a client."

"And you're an expert?" He took a shot. A couple more of those and he'd be getting into a fistfight with someone.

I placed my hands on his cheeks, forcing him to look at me. Anyone watching would've thought I was just being friendly. Hopefully. "I think you've had enough for one night. This is your last warning."

His jaw clenched. "Out of all the women I have ever met, I think I hate you most of all."

My smile was tight-lipped. "The feeling is mutual."

He stalked away, and I immediately went in search of Juliet.

"Watch that one," I said, pointing to Tony in the crowd. He was sitting at a table with his friend Stig. "Let me know if he gets out of hand."

"Will do," Juliet replied.

A few hours later, the awful Tony had left—luckily without causing a scene—and the party started to wind down. It had been a smashing success. Obviously.

June thanked me a zillion times for making the evening more than she imagined. The new caterer I'd decided to take a chance on had been sublime—proving once again my intuition was spot-on. And Juliet hadn't let me down once.

Other than the blip that was Tony, it was a stellar night.

SWAY

READ ABOUT AVA AND ERIC IN SWAY

THE FIRST NOVEL IN THE *ROMANCE REVISITED* SERIES

She'd be happy to forget...if the past would just stop hitting "replay".

Ava Elliot never thought she'd become a couch surfer. But with a freshly minted—and worthless—degree from Julliard, and her dad squandering the family fortune, what choice does she have?

Living with her old high school friends, though, has its own drawbacks. Especially when her ex-fiancé Eric Wentworth drops back into her life. Eight years ago, she was too young, too scared of being poor, and too scared of her dad's disapproval. Dumping him was a big mistake.

In the most ironic of role reversals, Eric is rolling in musical success, and Ava's starting at the bottom to build her career.

Worse, every song Eric sings is an arrow aimed straight for her regrets.

One encounter, one song too many, and Ava can't go on like this. It's time to tell Eric the truth, and make a choice. Finally let go of the past, or risk her heart for a second chance with her first love. If he can forgive her...and she can forgive herself.

Warning: Contains an actor whose kisses taste like chocolate, a pianist with scores of regret, and a sexy crooner who just wants his ex to cry him a river.

Find it everywhere ebooks are sold!

ABOUT THE AUTHOR

Melanie Stanford reads too much, plays music too loud, is sometimes dancing, and always daydreaming. She would also like her
very own TARDIS, but only to travel to the past. She lives outside
Calgary, Alberta, Canada with her husband, four kids, and ridiculous amounts of snow.

For More Information:
melaniestanfordbooks.com
Facebook: /MelanieStanfordauthor
Twitter: @MelMStanford

For More Information:
melaniestanfordbooks.com

www.ingramcontent.com/pod-product-compliance
Lightning Source LLC
Chambersburg PA
CBHW020948120726
47905CB00008B/2723